P9-EAJ-879

WITHDRAWN

TOM RYAN

I HOPE YOU'RE LISTENING

ALBERT WHITMAN & COMPANY
Chicago, Illinois

Library of Congress Cataloging-in-Publication data
is on file with the publisher.

Text copyright © 2020 by Tom Ryan
First published in the United States of America
in 2020 by Albert Whitman & Company
ISBN 978-0-8075-3508-0 (hardcover)
ISBN 978-0-8075-3509-7 (ebook)

All rights reserved. No part of this book may be reproduced
or transmitted in any form or by any means, electronic or
mechanical, including photocopying, recording, or by any
information storage and retrieval system, without permission
in writing from the publisher.

Printed in the United States of America
10   9   8   7   6   5   4   3   2   LSC 24 23 22 21 20

Jacket art copyright © 2020 by Albert Whitman & Company
Jacket art and book design by Aphelandra Messer

For more information about Albert Whitman & Company,
visit our website at www.albertwhitman.com.

FOR MY PARENTS,
WITH LOVE

1.

Transcript of **RADIO SILENT**
Episode 41

A seventeen-year-old vanishes into thin air. His family and friends have no idea where he might have gone. He leaves behind no trace, no clues.

Or does he?

Almost a million people are reported missing across North America every year. If we pay attention, if we work together, maybe we can bring some of them home.

I am the Seeker, and this is *Radio Silent*.

2.

TEN YEARS AGO

Dee feels like she's been waiting outside Sibby's house forever. She doesn't want to knock on the door, because then she'll have to talk to Sibby's mom and explain what they're doing, and she'll make them take Sibby's little sister, Greta, along with them. Greta is cute, but she can be kind of annoying, always asking questions and being slow. Besides, Dee and Sibby almost never get to play together anymore, just the two of them, and it won't be the same if they have a little kid tagging along.

Dee isn't too worried because she knows that Sibby will have a plan. Sibby *always* has a plan. While she waits, Dee sits on the edge of the porch and swings her legs back and forth, admiring her new boots. They look like her dad's boots, just a lot smaller. They're brown leather, the color of chocolate, with bright red laces that catch onto little hooks, instead of threading through holes. They're warm, but not too warm—perfect for adventures.

The front door creaks open, and Sibby's head pokes out. She grins and holds a finger to her lips. *Shhhh.* She disappears back inside, and Dee sits and waits, trying to be completely silent. A few seconds later, the door opens again, and Sibby tiptoes out. Her boots are on, and she's got one arm inside her coat.

She struggles into the other arm, then leans back inside the house and yells, "I'm going outside to play with Dee!" She stays there, waiting, and then Dee hears Mrs. Carmichael's voice, distant and muffled. Annoyed? Dee can't tell.

"We won't be long!" Sibby replies, and then she reaches in and pulls the door firmly closed, careful not to slam it.

"Let's go quick," she says, and Dee can tell from the way she says it that there's no time to waste. She hops down from the edge of the porch onto the ground. It's only a couple of feet up, but she knows that the boots help her. She can feel them grip the ground when she lands.

Giggling, the girls run to the sidewalk and turn down the street. When they make it to the maple tree at the end of the block, they both know they're out of view of Sibby's house.

"I think we're okay," says Sibby, laughing, catching her breath. "Greta made a big mess at lunchtime, and Mom had to clean her up. It was a good time to escape."

She grins at Dee, and Dee grins back. Sibby always knows how to make things work out. "So what are we going to do?" Dee asks.

"We're going to the fort," says Sibby, as if Dee is nuts for even asking.

"Without Burke and everyone else?" Dee asks. She knew that Sibby would want to go to the fort, but she feels a bit uneasy. The woods are fun when there are a bunch of them playing there. But they're also dark and a bit scary.

"Just because Burke's uncle built the fort, that doesn't mean Burke owns it," Sibby says, as if Dee should know this. "Besides, the woods belong to everyone, and it will be fun to play there by ourselves without everybody else taking up space. Burke's sisters are annoying. They're so bossy."

Dee thinks it's funny that Sibby would call someone else bossy, but she knows better than to point that out. She also doesn't bother mentioning that Mara and Alicia have only come to the fort once, right after their uncle Terry built it, and that time it was just to see it. They're older and not into playing outside the way they used to. Anyway, it's true that there are usually a bunch of people at the fort, but today Greta is out of the picture, Burke and his sisters are in the city to watch a movie, and the twins—Dee's brothers—are at hockey practice.

Sibby's right. Today they'll have the fort to themselves, and who knows when that will happen again?

"Okay," says Dee. "Let's go."

They cross the street to Dee's house, then walk two doors down to Mrs. Rose's house, because the easiest way to get into the woods is through her backyard. Mrs. Rose doesn't mind. She likes all the kids on their street. She's like a grandma, even though Dee knows she doesn't have any grandchildren of her own.

It's the end of March and still chilly enough for a coat and mittens, but there's a bit of warmth in the breeze, and as

Dee follows Sibby through Mrs. Rose's backyard, she notices little points of crocuses poking from the ground and tiny green buds on the shrubs and trees, and she knows that spring is almost here.

At the back of Mrs. Rose's garden is a hedge that backs almost all the way up onto the forest. There's a gap they can step through, and soon they're in the narrow strip of grass that separates the neighborhood from the trees.

A cloud passes over the sun just as a breeze picks up, and Dee feels a chill run down her spine.

"Let's go!" says Sibby, several steps ahead of Dee.

Under the shadow of the cloud, the woods look cold and dark and ominous. Dee wants to tell Sibby that they should just go over to Dee's house and watch a movie or play a game. But she knows it's no use; Sibby has made up her mind.

Besides, it will be fun. Sibby's ideas always end up being fun.

Sibby turns and walks into the trees. A moment later, Dee follows.

3.

What happened to Sibby Carmichael that afternoon in the woods?

If anyone should remember, it's me. I was there, after all. But ten years and a million sleepless nights later, nothing new comes to me. No sudden revelations, no deeply buried memories emerging from a haze. Just the same few fragments, still crisp and clear in my mind, still as useless as they've always been.

It's the middle of the night, and I lie in my bed, awake in a sleeping world, a broken record skipping inside of me. The same lines skimming past again and again and again.

You could have tried to stop it.

Forget that I was only seven. Forget that nobody, not even Sibby's parents, blamed me—a terrified little girl—not for a moment. None of that matters when the record starts skipping.

You could have paid attention, noticed something useful, helped them find her.

Over the years, I've heard lots of stories about incredible kids, kids who beat the odds. A girl who survived on a raft for days after her whole family was murdered on a sailboat far out at sea. A boy who protected his younger siblings from a cougar by fending it off with a stick. Three small children who climbed into a tree and waited out a tsunami, somehow managing to hang on while the only world they'd ever known rushed by, a chaos of water and destruction.

Why couldn't I have been one of those kids? Why couldn't I have dug deep, found strength, risen to the occasion?

You could have saved Sibby.

You could have saved Sibby.

You could have saved Sibby.

Enough. I force myself to sit up. My shoulders slide out from underneath the pile of blankets, and the shock of crisp, cool air is good. It clears my vision and braces me enough to stand and get out of bed.

I slide into my slippers and grab a blanket from the pile, pulling it up around my shoulders. Our house is old, big, and drafty. It costs a fortune to heat, as my parents never fail to remind me, so the thermostat is always down low. Because my room is up at the very top, hidden under the eaves in the attic, it's the coldest room of all, but that's a small price to pay for the privacy, not to mention the view.

My desk sits in the gable at the front of the house, facing a large half-moon window that looks down over the town. I drop into the desk chair, yawning and pulling the blanket tight around me.

Far in the distance, I see lights skimming past us on the

highway, a rushing river of cars and trucks and buses that could easily sweep someone away, in any direction, in the blink of an eye. On just this side of the highway is the forest, a huge stretch of spruce and pine, some bare hardwoods clustered together, thin patches in the blanket of green.

The woods butt up against a subdivision much younger than this neighborhood, full of split-levels and bungalows from the seventies. My old street runs parallel to the line of trees, and my old house still sits there, tucked in for the night like every other house in town.

From here, my childhood home looks tiny, vulnerable, just a small brick bungalow crouched in the shadow of the massive spread of forest behind it. It looks like the woods are about to swallow it up, drag it away, never to be seen again.

I like the house we live in now, in the middle of town, far from the woods. I like my room, the way it floats up here, high above the world.

I like that it would take someone a lot of effort to get up here. To find me.

I glance behind me at the door that opens to steps that lead down to a hallway lined with more doors: my parents' room, my brothers' room, the bathroom, the study. Then more stairs, almost every step harboring a telltale creak, alarms woven into the house's very sinews.

At the bottom of the stairs is a foyer, where an interior door—paned with stained glass, locked and bolted—leads out to a porch and a heavy exterior door, solid as lead, also locked.

There are neighbors to either side of us, more neighbors

across the street. All around us are windows and eyeballs. Security.

A noise catches my attention, and I turn back to my window, leaning forward across the desk so I can see right down to the street. The cute little yellow house directly across from us has been empty for over a year, since old Mrs. Dunlop passed away. I've grown used to the FOR SALE sign stuck into the lawn, but now I see that a U-Haul has pulled up outside.

The truck is still running, exhaust billowing from the tail-pipe, taillights glowing red in the night, but as I watch, it shuts off, shuddering for a moment before slumping to sleep. The driver's side door opens, and a man steps out, stretching his arms above his head and yawning. A moment later, a woman steps around from the passenger side of the truck and joins him on the sidewalk.

They stand looking at the Dunlop house, and then turn together to watch as a cool old car pulls up and comes to a stop behind the U-Haul. It's pale blue, with wide tires and two wide silver stripes running the length of the hood. The door opens, and a girl steps out. She doesn't close the door, but stands behind it instead, leaning forward to rest her elbows on its upper edge and stare across at the house, like she's standing behind a shield.

The man and woman walk over to talk to the girl. They're clearly her parents, and as they talk, they gesture toward the U-Haul. They seem to agree on something, and the man and woman move back to the truck and start digging into the cab, pulling out bags.

When I shift my gaze back to the girl she's staring right up at me.

I jerk back from the window, startled, before I remember with a wave of relief that I'm standing in a dark room. She can't see me.

I keep to the edge of the window and watch her head move as she runs her gaze around our house. I realize that she's checking out the veranda, the gingerbread trim, the turret. Shabby, drafty, and unfinished as it might be, ours is the most dramatic house on the street, and she's looking at it, not me.

But I'm looking at her. I can't help it. She's slight—not much shorter than me, but more compact. Her black hair is cut into an irregular bob, and her glasses have thick, dark frames. She's wearing jeans, leather boots, and a dark olive-green winter coat with a wide white band across the chest. It's obviously vintage and looks to be from the same era as the car.

She reaches inside her car and grabs a backpack, then slams the door shut and joins her parents, who are standing on the sidewalk with their own bags, waiting for her. Her father puts an arm over her shoulder, and together, the three of them walk up the narrow path and into the house.

I glance at the clock. It's just past 3:00 a.m.

I drop into my desk chair, pulling the blanket around me, then I open my laptop.

Except for the late arrivals across the street, everyone is asleep. My family. My neighbors. The town around me.

I open my bottom desk drawer and pull out a small USB

microphone on a stand. I plug it into the side of the laptop, then reach across the desk for my headphones and pull them on.

Somewhere, right now, somebody is disappearing.

I click on the icon for my audio recording program, and once it's loaded, I tap on the mic with my finger.

I press *[record]*.

It's time to get to work.

4.

Transcript of **RADIO SILENT**
Episode 41 — January 4

HOST: I'm happy to report that we have a development in the case of Nathan Chestnut. Listeners will remember that on the afternoon of December 27, Nathan walked four blocks to hang out at a friend's house. When he didn't return home for dinner, his mother attempted to text and then phone him, and when she received no response, she called the friend, who reported that Nathan had left almost three hours earlier. Within an hour, Nathan's parents had reached out to his other friends but came up empty-handed. By the end of the night, they'd called the police, and by the time twenty-four hours had passed, he was officially declared a missing person.

I stop recording, make a few quick edits, then apply my custom voice filter to the clip. I give it a listen, and when I'm satisfied that it sounds okay, not at all like me, I continue recording.

HOST: Nathan's older sister, Cassandra, is a fan of *Radio Silent*, and she reached out to us early the next day. I recorded and released an episode that evening and used the show's page to link to relevant details, including photographs and the official police statement.

Within an hour of the episode going live, we had several tips from the LDA, including two separate sightings from listeners in the small town of Maple Mills, a two-hour drive from Hamilton, who had spotted Nathan at the local grocery store.

We forwarded this information to the family and the proper authorities. Nathan's sister fills us in on what happened next.

I stop and slice the track, add in a few seconds of white noise to give a nice pregnant pause, then record my next chunk of text, working from the notes I've jotted down in my notebook as I record. I'm starting to get into a rhythm. I open the folder containing supplementary information and select and insert the iPhone voice recording Nathan's sister sent me this afternoon.

CASSANDRA CHESTNUT: It was bizarre and totally out of character for Nathan to just disappear like that.

We were looking for him everywhere, from local hos-
pitals to homeless shelters to abandoned buildings.
The police had told us to start preparing for the
worst. None of us had even considered that Nathan
would have left town. He gets along with everyone in the family, has good grades and plenty of
friends. There was no reason for him to run away.

Then we got the tips about Maple Mills, and
everything came into focus...

I work quickly, and as I lay out the details of the case, the
basics of this disappearance, things start to fall into place, and
a completed episode emerges in front of me.

The idea for the podcast arrived about a year ago, on a
night like tonight. I was lying awake in bed, wallowing in
helplessness, when all of a sudden, something shifted. I'd had
enough. There had to be *something* I could do. Somehow, I
found myself at my desk, waking up my laptop, opening
my browser.

I've always been kind of afraid of the internet, wary of
the endless storm of terrible stories. Terrorist attacks, mass
shootings, awful politicians saying hateful things—terrible
garbage news that fills the online space so quickly that a major
event begins to feel like last year's news in just a few short
hours. The only thing that doesn't change is that nothing ever
gets better.

But on that night, instead of pulling back from the internet,
I leaned into it. In the tiny search window, cursor blinking on
and off, my fingers hesitated above the keyboard. Then I typed

missing people, and the screen came to life. Pages and pages of news sites, small-town papers, blogs, social media pages, and many, many, many stories. Stories just like mine.

Like Sibby's.

Before long, I'd fallen down a rabbit hole of missing persons cases from all over the country, even the world. I skimmed message board after message board, and I began to notice something interesting. People were actually trying to *solve* these cases.

There were a lot of stupid theories, of course, but there were also many smart, serious people sharing clues and trying to dig into the cases in a real way. "Armchair detectives," most people would call them, although I started to think of them as "laptop detectives."

I wasn't interested in being a laptop detective. I didn't want to get too involved; it was just too close for comfort, and besides, I've already proven I'm a shitty detective. But I knew what it was like to be on the other side of one of these stories, wishing someone, somewhere, would come up with a solution. The laptop detectives needed an outlet, somewhere to bring their ideas and find some attention.

So I started a podcast. *How hard can it be?* I wondered. I bought a microphone online, downloaded some basic free recording software, and gave it a shot.

Turned out it was plenty hard. For the first few episodes, I tried to do a roundup of cases that I'd read about, but that landed flat. I decided I needed a focus.

So on my fourth episode, I picked one case. It was a brother and sister who'd been taken from their home after school, before their parents had come home from work. The day I uploaded it, an anonymous tip landed in my inbox, a tip I forwarded to the police, and that led to the kids being found in the home of a disgruntled former babysitter. They were returned safe and sound, and afterward, the police thanked the podcast for the information.

After that, *Radio Silent* fell into a groove. I would find a case, research it as much as I could, turn it into a story, and let the listeners take it from there. As first, I discovered the cases myself by searching around online, but it wasn't long before I started getting emails from listeners, drawing my attention to cases that would make a good fit for the podcast.

Radio Silent breaks a lot of podcasting rules; I keep myself anonymous, there's not a lot of consistency to the stories I choose, and I don't even stick to a regular schedule—I post when it makes sense—but somehow, it struck a chord. Gradually, listener numbers started to grow, and I learned that the laptop detectives really were willing to help. In almost no time, they'd surpassed my wildest expectations, bringing me clues and tips and self-organizing into an online community, the LDA, short for the Laptop Detective Agency. I compile the research, sift through the clues and leads, choose the cases to focus on, and record, edit, and upload the podcast, but the real work happens thanks to the LDA. And it's real work. Working together, we've *found* people.

A fifteen-year-old runaway who was found alive and safe in Seattle after she'd run away to find an old boyfriend. An elderly man who disappeared from a nursing home and was discovered a hundred miles away in his childhood hometown.

And then there was Danny Lurlee, an asshole who faked his own abduction. Thanks to the LDA, he was tracked down trying to cross the border into Mexico.

I'll be honest, that one seriously pissed me off. I wasted three episodes on that jerk.

Obviously, not all of our cases end well. Murder. Suicide. Tragic accidents. There's no way to avoid this because not every story has a happy ending. But take it from me, even a sad ending is better than no ending at all, and that's always been my goal: to deliver an ending to as many unfinished stories as possible.

I don't do much. I just bring together the facts. Listen to people when they tell me they have information. Tell my listeners about a missing person.

They do the real work. I just tell stories.

I hope that telling them might make up for the story I wasn't able to tell properly all those years ago.

The story that never had an ending.

HOST: Just over a year ago, Nathan and Cassandra's grandfather, Walter, died. Nathan took the death really hard. The two had always been especially close, and over the years, they had spent a lot of time together at Grandpa Walt's hunting camp, which just so happens to sit in the woods outside of Maple Mills.

CASSANDRA CHESTNUT: Over the holidays, my dad and his sisters had decided to sell the camp. None of us ever use it, and it takes time and money to keep it up, so they figured they'd unload it and split up the cash.

Nobody thought to ask Nathan if he had an opinion...

HOST: Upon receiving the listener tips that I passed on, Cassandra and her parents notified police of their suspicion and immediately drove to Maple Mills. As they approached the darkened hunting camp, they saw smoke coming from the chimney.

NATHAN CHESTNUT: So it was definitely the dumbest thing I've ever done, but I was pissed off, okay? Nobody even thought about asking me about Grandpa Walt's cabin, and I was the only one in the family who actually cared about the place. Anyway, I had almost a week before school started up again, so I packed some things and caught the bus to Maple Mills, so I could spend a few final nights hanging out there. I knew that my folks would say no if I asked to go, so I planned to text them when I got there, tell them I was safe and I'd be back in a couple of days. But my phone died, and I didn't count on the power being shut off... Anyway, I convinced myself that they'd know where I'd gone and wouldn't worry, which was fu—um, really stupid of me. Obviously.

CASSANDRA CHESTNUT: *(laughing)* Oh man, he is in such deep shit. The cops were pretty good about it, since it was ultimately a misunderstanding, and they're not going to press charges or anything. But my parents are a different story. He's going to be grounded until he's thirty.

HOST: So all's well that ends well with Nathan Chestnut, but as we all know, not every story has such a positive result. The world is full of missing people, and the sad truth is that many of them will never come home. But I believe there's a story behind every missing person, and maybe, just maybe, if we begin to dig up the details together, we can find our way to some more happy endings.

Is there something *you* can do to help?

Listen up.

Let's try.

* * *

Recording takes me about two hours, editing in real time, to complete the finished take. When I'm finished, I glance at the alarm clock on the corner of the desk. It's almost five in the morning, which means I should be able to grab a couple more hours of sleep before Mom is banging at the foot of the stairs telling me to get up for school.

"I'm doing my best, Sibby," I whisper.

I click *upload.* An instant later, the episode is live.

I take a minute to send a quick email to my mailing list, informing subscribers that there's a new episode. Then I post the same to my various social media accounts and several of the more popular true crime forums on Reddit.

I stretch my arms over my head, then glance past my laptop at the window. Across the street, the old Dunlop house is dark except for a single upstairs window, which glows orange from behind a curtain. I wonder if it's that girl, if she's still awake, talking to friends back wherever she came from.

There's one last thing to take care of. I erase my browser history.

Because here's the thing: I keep my shit locked down tight. I have impossible passwords. I only use private browser windows, and even so I erase my history every time I use my computer. I don't use my real name. I use audio filters to disguise my voice.

I never slip up.

I created and host one of the most popular true crime podcasts in the world, and nobody—not my parents, not my teachers, not my neighbors—knows.

5.

I wake to my alarm, completely exhausted, but with a lingering tingle of exhilaration from my late-night work session. I crawl out of bed, yawn and stretch, and grab my phone. My screen is full, announcing the thousands of notifications I received overnight, everybody with something to say about the latest episode.

I resist the urge to check out the notifications and new emails, the endlessly growing threads and subthreads on my message board. That can wait until later. It's important to keep a wall between what happens in the podcast and what happens in my real life. Otherwise, I'd go nuts.

I make my way down to the bathroom I share with the twins. After a quick shower, I rush to dry myself off, shivering against the draft that creeps in through the ancient leaded-glass window that sits somewhere on Dad's endless list of things to fix or replace. I change into a pair of faded jeans and my *Nevertheless, She Persisted* T-shirt and head downstairs.

Our house is huge. Half the rooms on the second floor are empty, closed off, with stuffed socks running along the bottoms to keep out the drafts. The ceilings are high, with elaborate plaster moldings running along the edges, big ragged chunks missing in several spots. Dad's fixed a lot of the moldings on the main floor, but he hasn't made his way upstairs yet, which also explains the peeling wallpaper and worn floorboards.

My mother complains about this house every single day, but I know she loves it. Most of all, she loves how much my dad loves it.

We moved from our old neighborhood when I was seven, after everything that happened with Sibby. Almost ten years later, this house has been hacked apart and changed in a million different ways, but it still feels like it will never be done.

I don't mind. I love its quirks and charming details. I love the elaborate original light fixtures and the intricate brass doorknobs. Most of all, I love the staircase, the wide steps that make two ninety-degree turns, the oak paneling that follows its progress, the grand, hand-carved wooden banister that took Dad years to refinish. I stop on the upper landing, like I do every morning, and glance through the bubbles of old stained glass in the gothic window that looks out onto the driveway. In the afternoon, when sunlight hits the window just right, colored light streams through and fills the staircase with a magical glow.

At the bottom of the stairs, I carefully step around the empty cans of paint stripper and pieces of cardboard covered with tools and tape and brushes. Dad's been working on the wood paneling in the main hallway for months, a bit at a time, stripping layer upon layer of old paint down to the raw wood beneath. He swears that it's going to be beautiful when it's done, but it's hard to imagine him ever finishing it at this rate.

I follow the sound of voices toward the kitchen, giving a wide berth to the twins' bulky hockey bags that have been tossed down in the hallway, a dank waft of hockey stink floating around them like mist.

"Morning," I say as I enter the kitchen, which sits in a sunny, windowed addition at the back of the house.

"Delia, please talk to your mother," says my father, standing at the sink, an apron over a paint-spattered T-shirt and raggedy work jeans. "Tell her that I'm perfectly capable of repairing the chimney myself."

I turn to my mother, who's standing at the island, dressed for work in a classy business suit, her hair pulled back into a tight bun, a thin gold chain around her neck. My parents do not look like a couple you'd expect to be married to one another.

Dad stays at home, keeping house, which involves everything from cooking and cleaning to the never-ending renovations. He's a remnant of the '90s and he dresses like it: torn jeans, faded grunge band T-shirts under plaid button-ups, scruffy hair. Mom, on the other hand, is the chief administrator at our local hospital and the kind of woman who likes to dress for success—tailored suits, manicures, classy makeup. Despite the differences in appearance, they are head over heels for each other. They both have the same weird sense of humor; they're both into good food and good wine; and judging from their constant, sickly sweet public displays of affection, they have definitely not lost the hots for each other.

"Mom, Dad is perfectly capable of repairing the chimney himself."

Mom looks up from her laptop, a bemused look on her face.

"Delia, please tell your father that he has plenty of jobs to keep him busy without climbing up onto a steep-pitched roof in January."

"Dad, you have plenty of jobs to keep you busy without—"

He raises a hand, cutting me off. "Okay, fine. I'll call around for some quotes." He comes around the island and encircles her waist with his arms. "I love it when you set firm limits." She smiles up at him, and in front of my eyes, they've turned into gooey mushballs, nuzzling noses and batting eyelashes.

The twins, Kurt and Eddie, are sitting in the breakfast nook in the large bay window at the back of the house. They groan in tandem, without even looking up from their phones.

"Jesus Christ," says Kurt. "Get a room."

"Seriously," says Eddie. "You guys are gross."

"Hey," says Dad. "You guys should just pray that you find someone who still finds you ferociously sexy when you're in your forties."

"Well, I'm out," says Kurt to Eddie. "Let's go."

The twins are up from the table and stomping toward the front door before anyone has time to react.

"Will you be home for dinner?" my mother calls after them.

"Hockey," says Eddie before the door opens and slams behind them. When it comes to the twins, hockey is a noun, a verb, an adjective, and a perpetual one-word explanation.

My father hands me a plate of eggs and toast, and I slide into one of the chairs in the breakfast nook.

"Who's moved into the old Dunlop place?" I ask. "Someone showed up with a moving van last night."

"Were you up all night again?" my mother asks suspiciously.

"No," I lie. "The truck woke me up."

"I totally forgot to mention," says Dad. "Georgina Walsh filled me in at the grocery store the other day. Some distant relative of Mrs. Dunlop's is going to take the place over."

Dad is a dedicated member of the community gossip hotline. It's not unusual to find him on his laptop in the kitchen, participating in the neighborhood group chat, his mouth hanging open as he absorbs some particularly juicy tidbit.

"A family?" asks Mom.

"A couple around our age," says Dad. "I think they have a daughter. They're from somewhere on the West Coast."

"We should go over soon and welcome them," says Mom. She stands from the island and shoves her laptop into her bag. "Anyway, I'm off. I have a consult in half an hour. You'll figure out dinner?"

"I always do," says Dad, coming around to give her a kiss full on the lips.

I studiously turn away.

"Bye, sweetie," says Mom, coming over to kiss me on the cheek. "Have a good day."

"You too," I say.

She disappears down the hallway, and Dad removes his apron before bringing a plate of his own over to the table.

"So what's on the go at school for the new semester?" he asks, sliding in across from me.

"At school?" I ask, surprised. "Same shit, different pile, I guess."

He smiles but doesn't drop it. "Come on, really? There's nothing exciting planned? Dissecting frogs? Digging into a really good short story?"

He sounds so desperate for me to tell him something interesting that for a split second, staring at his bright, needy face, I consider telling him about the podcast, letting him in on the biggest secret I've ever kept. But no. Not a chance.

"Um, I think we're supposed to be building doghouses in shop class?"

"Cool," he says. He seems kind of disappointed.

"What about you?" I ask, trying to make up for it. "What's up for today?"

He shrugs. "Probably going to get some work done on the wainscoting. Might stop at the café to see what the guys are doing."

"You want to walk with me?" I ask.

"Yes!" he says. "Just let me change."

He looks genuinely excited, like a little kid who's been offered a trip to buy ice cream. He bounds up the stairs, two at a time, and I pull on my coat and boots and wait outside on the veranda for him.

Across the street, the Dunlop house is quiet. Curtains

drawn, no activity outside. No wonder, considering how late those people arrived.

The door opens behind me, and my father steps out, bundled up in his best aging-hipster winter gear.

"Oh, hey, look at that," he says, pointing across at the blue car. "A '77 Chevy Nova. Man, when I was a kid I would have killed for one of those. My aunt dated a guy who used to fix up old cars."

"Oh yeah?" I say. "That's a fascinating story."

He grins. "Always nice to start the day hearing how boring I am."

"What? I said it was fascinating."

At a crosswalk, we pass a young man holding a little girl's hand as they cross the street. The little girl is chattering cheerfully at her father, and he's beaming down at her, gamely answering her questions. It's pretty cute.

The guy looks up at us briefly, smiling, and he and Dad share a brief head tilt and a mutual "hey man." An eye-rollingly masculine acknowledgment that they know each other.

"You know that guy?" I ask.

"Yeah," he says. "Aras." His voice is wistful, and when I glance at him, he's twisted his head around to glance back at them. "I miss that age," he says.

"What, thirty?" I ask.

"No," he says. "Well, yeah, obviously, but I mean I miss when *you* were that age. You always wanted to hold my hand. You were a very touchy-feely child."

"I was not," I say, shocked. If I were any less touchy-feely, I'd be a porcupine.

"You were," he insists. "After, you know, everything…you just needed your distance more, is all."

I consider this. "Are you saying you want to hold my hand now?" I ask, wondering what I'll do if he says yes.

He laughs. "Don't worry," he says. "I'll spare you."

We've arrived at Fresh Brews, the local kid-friendly café, and he leans in to give me a quick kiss on the cheek. "Have a good day, my sweetie."

"You too, Dad," I say.

He bounces up the steps like he's on his way to a playdate. As the door jingles open to announce his arrival, I catch a glimpse of his group of friends, Jaron and Pickle and a couple of other guys I don't recognize. They're at their regular table and raise their hands in greeting as Dad enters. Over the past couple of years, Dad has found himself a small group of young, stay-at-home dads to hang out with. He says that he likes hanging with them because they're living the life he wished he'd had when he was a young father. Stay-at-home dads are a lot more common these days.

As I walk to school, I can't help but think about what Dad said about me needing more distance. I wonder: How different am I now than I was then? What if things hadn't happened the way they did? Would I be a completely different person if Sibby had stayed? If I'd been taken instead of her?

6.

I stop across the street from the school, watching the throngs of students returning. I have at least ten minutes before the first bell rings, and I'm in no rush to join the fray, so I grab a seat on the stone wall that runs along the sidewalk and pull out my phone. My *Radio Silent* notifications are as busy as I expected. Loads of retweets and mentions and threads, which I've come to expect the day after a case has been cracked.

"Yo, Dee!"

I look up and see Burke approaching, his bag slung over his shoulder, sunglasses perched uselessly on the end of his nose as he peers over them at me. The impression is of a cheerful but slightly confused puppy, which isn't a bad way to describe Burke. He and I have been friends since we were babies. He grew up next door to me, and Sibby grew up across the street. The three of us were inseparable. Until one of us was separated.

"Yo," I say, shooting him an ironic finger gun.

He stretches out his arms and takes a deep, satisfied breath. "Wonderful day to reenter the social assimilation facility, wouldn't you say?"

I slide my phone back into my pocket and stand. "Not much choice about it either way."

"Good Christmas?" he asks as we cross the street to the school.

"It was okay. Turkey and presents. Not as good as yours, I bet." Burke's family spent the holidays with his grandmother in Florida, and he spent two weeks posting pictures from the beach on his Instagram.

"Yeah, it was pretty awesome," he says. "Sun and surf." We weave through the crowd of loiterers and push through the front door into the school foyer. "Any intriguing new cases?"

"Burke," I say, shoving him, exasperated. "What the hell?" I glance around to see if anyone heard anything, but it's too noisy, and frankly, nobody gives a shit about us *or* our conversation.

"Sorry," he says. "Just curious."

"I thought you didn't even listen," I say.

He shrugs. "It's the sign of a good friend to pretend to care about dumb hobbies."

When I say that nobody knows that *Radio Silent* is my podcast, there is one exception: Burke. The short version is that Burke is really great with computers, and I'm not. I mean, I'm good at the creative stuff—writing and organizing, using the sound editing software and setting up social media and stuff, but when it comes to security and encryption and firewalls, I'm useless, so I asked Burke for his help.

Most of the time, I forget he even knows at all, because he doesn't really give a shit about it. I mean, he's happy that the podcast is doing well, and he's always trying to convince me to monetize it, but it just isn't his thing.

"Don't look now," Burke mutters. "It's the fourth horse-woman of the apocalypse."

I turn to see Brianna Jax-Covington walking toward us. As they always do when Brianna appears, my eyeballs roll involuntarily.

Brianna and I used to be friends, back when we were little. She didn't live in our neighborhood, but her mom and Sibby's mom were friends, so we were always at each other's birth-day parties, and we even had semiregular sleepovers. That all changed when Sibby disappeared. Brianna and I didn't really hang out much after that.

That's not why I have a problem with Brianna, however. Little kid friends grow apart all the time, and the truth is we were only friends because of Sibby. My problem with Brianna is that she has a problem with me. There's a whiff of dis-approval that floats about her like perfume, a cloying, flowery scent that you know is supposed to be expensive and desirable, but is really just a warning sign: here comes a real asshole.

She nods briefly at Burke, then turns to me and smiles broadly. "Hello, Delia," she says comfortably, as if we always have friendly grown-up-lady chats. "How was your Christmas?"

"It was all right," I say. "How was yours?" I'm not sure why she's talking to me. Brianna and I don't run in the same circles. Her circle is the "who's who" of high school; my circle is Burke.

"Oh, it was lovely," she says. "We flew to Aspen and went skiing with my brother and his wife. Amazing conditions. We went heli-skiing. You have to go sometime. You'd love it."

"Oh, for sure," I say. "I'll have to dust off my skis."

"I'll dust off my helicopter," says Burke. "Teamwork."

"Listen," says Brianna, ignoring our sarcasm. "I'm wondering if I can count on you to help out with the upcoming Winter Carnival preparations. As you know, the eleventh graders are responsible for decorating, selling tickets, organizing refreshments—you know, that kind of thing. I'm the committee chair this year, and it's going to be the best Winter Carnival yet. The theme is La La Land."

"Wooooooooowwwwww!" says Burke in the voice of a dazzled, slightly stunned little kid.

She rolls her eyes at him, then turns back to me. "Anyway, I was hoping you'd be willing to volunteer."

"Volunteer?" I ask. I realize too late that I sound horrified. Burke snickers next to me, and Brianna's smile disappears.

"Yes, volunteer," she says. "You know, like, offer your skills and talents for the good of the community."

"Yeah," I say. "Sorry. I know what you mean. I just, I don't think I have any skills or talents that will be helpful to you."

"I need someone to sell raffle tickets at the RedBoy," she says. "It's not rocket science."

The thought of sitting at a table, facing throngs of townspeople at one of the biggest events of the year—the annual charity hockey game between the Redfields Cardinals and their biggest rivals, the Boyseton Thunder, commonly known as the RedBoy—literally makes me queasy. I have a hard enough time facing the bored, uninterested crowds of people at my school, let alone a couple hundred well-meaning grown-ups, all of whom know me as the girl who was in the woods with Sibby Carmichael when she was abducted. The girl who wasn't taken.

"Oh man, Brianna," I say. "I'm sorry, but I really don't think I can do that."

"Why not?" she snaps. She's obviously not used to people turning her down.

I don't really know what to say. "I wasn't even planning on going to the game," I say.

"That's irrelevant, but whatever," she says. "You know, I thought if anyone would recognize the importance of community, it would be you, after everything this town has done for you and your family."

"Wait, what?" I ask. I'm uncomfortably aware of people stopping conversations to listen to us.

"I thought maybe this would be good for you," she says, "an opportunity to interact with your classmates and the world a bit."

My mouth drops open, and my sense of embarrassment disappears, replaced by anger. "You're doing it for me?" I say. "Like it's any of your business how I choose to spend my time?"

"Well, everyone knows you're a bit messed up, and who can blame you?" she asks.

More people are listening, and I want to melt into the floor. Fortunately, Burke decides it's time to step into the situation.

"I've been meaning to ask you, Brianna. How's your chlamydia doing, anyway?" he asks loud enough to get snickers from anyone within earshot.

"Screw you, Burke," says Brianna.

He makes a face of mock horror and backs away. "Not until you get that taken care of."

She rolls her eyes, then turns her glare back to me. "It's fine, Delia," she says. "I'm sure I'll find somebody to do it, but it would be nice if you could find it in yourself to help someone else for once in your life." At that she turns on a heel before storming away down the hallway, just as the bell rings for first class. The crowd disperses, distracted by the official arrival of a fresh new semester.

"You shouldn't do that," I say to Burke as we walk toward the classroom. "It's slut shaming."

"Are you kidding me?" he says. "She was being a total jackass. Besides, I wasn't slut shaming, I was asshole shaming. Besides, why are you defending her? She just crapped all over you."

I just shake my head, dropping it. It doesn't work that way, but I don't feel like explaining it to Burke at the moment. It's not my job to educate him on gender dynamics, as much as he clearly needs it.

Our first class of the day is math. We're only a few minutes into the class when there's a knock on the door. Mr. Langley pauses in his run-through of the semester's syllabus and steps outside for a few seconds.

A moment later, Mr. Langley steps back into the room. Standing slightly behind him, hands in her pockets and a piece of black hair hanging in front of one of her eyes, is the girl from the Dunlop house.

"Class," says Mr. Langley. "This is Sarah Cash. She's new to town, so be sure to take a moment to introduce yourselves at some point."

In an easy, casual gesture, Sarah Cash reaches up and runs her hand back through her hair, opening up her face to the room. One corner of her mouth turns up, and she does a slow scan of the room as if she's taking stock of us, and not the other way around. There's a split second, a fraction of a moment, when her eyes land on me and my muscles freeze, my blood stops moving in my veins, and I worry that she'll recognize me. Could she have seen me watching her from the window last night after all? But her eyes move right past me and Langley directs her to an empty seat, directly next to Brianna. She settles and he continues with his lesson.

I catch Burke's eye, and unexpectedly, he winks. Surprising myself, I blush in reaction and turn away before he notices. I deliberately avoid looking at Sarah Cash for the rest of the class.

When the bell rings, I notice Brianna immediately accosting the new girl. I can tell that she's making some kind of pitch, but when Sarah casually shakes her head and turns away without an explanation, I can tell by the look on Brianna's face that she's been turned down for the second time today.

Maybe Sarah Cash and I have more in common than just a neighborhood.

7.

After school, as Burke and I walk out the side entrance, we notice that a small crowd has gathered near the parking lot. At the bottom of the steps, we stop and watch as Sarah Cash walks nonchalantly across the parking lot to her Nova. I notice Brianna standing off to the side with her friends, watching with narrowed eyes. As Sarah opens the back door and tosses her backpack in, Brianna—her eyes still on Sarah—leans in and whispers something to her clique. They all turn and stare, unimpressed, as Sarah jumps into the front seat and slams her door.

Brianna's clique might not be impressed, but plenty of other people are, Burke included. As she pulls out of her spot, one guy gives her an exaggerated holler of approval. The car stops, and a moment later, the driver's side window opens and her hand appears, a middle finger snapping to attention before the whole arm disappears back into the car and she squeals out of the parking lot and drives away down the street.

I reach over and tap Burke's lower jaw closed with my finger. "You're drooling."

"Oh, and you're not?" he asks. "I saw you looking back there in class."

"You did not," I say, turning around and starting to walk away before he notices me blush.

He catches up but knows me well enough to drop the subject. "Hey, can I come over for a while?"

"Sure, I guess."

"Terry is back in town," he explains.

I understand what he means immediately. "Good old Terrance," I say. Burke's uncle Terry is a classic deadbeat. No fixed address, no stable job, and a tendency to drop in on Burke's family every couple of years. He always pretends he's just visiting, but he usually needs a place to crash and ends up sticking around for weeks, or even months.

"He's staying in the basement," Burke says. "Just lying around on the couch all day, watching TV and drinking beer and farting. He's so gross."

I laugh. When Burke's sister, Alicia, moved out last year, on her way to college out of state, Burke inherited the bedroom in the basement. It's nothing fancy, just a boxed-in room in the corner, but it's private. There's a toilet and shower in the laundry room, and the rec room has some battered old couches set up around a giant old TV. It's like a personal lounge, except now that Terry is sleeping on the couch, Burke's oasis has been invaded.

We leave the school and move away down the sidewalk. "The worst part," says Burke, "is that he's talking about staying this time. He says he's 'looking for work' and as soon as he finds something he'll get his own place, but that's bullshit. He'll be around for months."

"Why don't your folks kick him out?" I ask.

"If it were up to my mom, they would, but my dad would never consider it," says Burke. "Terry's his little brother. He's a screwup, but he's family."

Instead of walking back to my house through town, we take a shortcut, heading down the alley next to the old abandoned bowling alley and skimming through the hole in the fence to get to the path that runs along the train tracks. Once we're out of sight from the street, Burke drops his backpack onto a crusty, pebble-encrusted snowbank and unzips, rummaging around inside for an old Altoids tin. He takes out a small glass pipe and packs it with some broken-up weed. He sparks up as I stand shivering, waiting for him to finish.

"You want?" he asks through clenched teeth, holding the pipe to me.

"No thanks," I say. Burke knows it's not my thing, but he never fails to offer, which I find equally irritating and endearing.

He breathes out the smoke, a thin blue cloud twisting into the air like a ribbon. I like the smell, even if I don't smoke, sweet and sour like the decay of fall. Burke shoves his little Altoids container back into his backpack and we start walking again.

"So what'd you really think about the new girl?" he asks.

"Well, she lives across the street from me," I say. It's a nonanswer, but it gets his attention.

"No shit? In that house that's been for sale forever?"

I nod.

"Why didn't we ask her to give us a drive home?" He takes another haul on the pipe.

"What, and miss out on our precious quality time?" I ask him. "Come on, man, I haven't even spoken to her. I just noticed them moving in yesterday."

"The girl next door," he says. I can hear the grin in his voice even through his clenched teeth. He exhales a cloud of smoke.

I ignore him. As always, Burke shuts up for a few minutes after he smokes, so we walk along in silence. It's fine with me, since I have some stuff to think about anyway.

We reach the path that takes me back to our house, and I climb up after him, digging the toes of my boots into the sides, where the snow hasn't been packed down into an icy slide.

At the top, I turn toward my street, but Burke stops me.

"Hang on," he says. "I want to grab some chips." He grins and rubs his hands together. "Got the munchies."

I roll my eyes, he's such a cliché, but I follow him across the street and around the corner to the gas station on Livingstone Street.

I follow him into the store and stand around near the cash register, looking at my phone while Burke slowly mulls over the snack options on display. He turns into a sloth when he's stoned, carefully picking up every bag of chips and analyzing the packaging. The guy behind the counter barely looks up from his phone. He's used to this routine.

The door jingles, and I glance up as a tall woman I don't recognize enters. She's very attractive, with long, super dark hair and a sharp, fine-featured face. She's wearing high leather boots over tight jeans, a dark green wool peacoat and a nice scarf, and huge dark sunglasses that she sweeps back onto the top of her head as she walks out of the bright sunshine of the winter afternoon. Her gaze sweeps casually around the store, passing over me. To my surprise, her eyes land on Burke and she smiles and approaches him.

"Hi, Burke," she says.

He turns, startled, and then his dumb, stoned face breaks into a grin, and I can tell that he's shifting into his patented "speaking politely to adults while stoned" mode.

"Oh, hi there, Mrs. Gerrard," he says. "What brings you here to the, uh, Fuel-Up?"

She laughs. "Just needed to pick up a couple of things."

His eyes widen as if he's had an epiphany, and he turns to me and beckons me over. "Hey, Dee," he says. "Come here for a minute."

Reluctantly, I slide my phone into my pocket and walk over to them, trying to look friendly while doing my best to send Burke "I hate you" vibes. I don't enjoy talking to adults the way Burke does.

"Mrs. Gerrard, this is my friend Dee," he says. "Delia. She used to live in your house!"

I realize too late that my mouth has dropped open in shock and scramble to slap a normal look back onto my face.

She also looks surprised, while Burke seems oblivious to the impact his bomb has had.

"Oh, no way," I manage to say. "Really?"

"Yeah," he says. "The Gerrards moved into your old place

just a couple of months ago. They've got a cool little girl named Layla."

Mrs. Gerrard is still looking at me as if she's trying to figure something out. "Are you a Price?" she asks.

"Uh, no," I say. "Skinner. The Prices bought the house from us."

"I see," she says. I can see the wheels spinning as she realizes who I am, and I brace myself for the inevitable questions, but instead she just purses her lips into a somewhat unconvincing smile. "Well, I have to grab some milk," she says. "Nice meeting you. See you later, Burke."

Burke pays for his chips and I follow him outside.

"Hey, look," he says. "There's Layla over there." He points to a car parked by one of the gas tanks, and sure enough, there's a girl sitting in the backseat, waving at him.

Before I can ask him not to, he's striding to the car.

"Hey, Layla!" he says. She rolls her window down and smiles at him. She's a small girl, tiny in fact, with a serious look on her face.

"Hi, Burke," she says.

"This is my friend Dee," he says, pointing at me. "Guess what? She used to live in your house. I think your bedroom used to be her bedroom. Pretty cool, hey?"

She regards me curiously. "You lived in my house? When you were my age?"

"That depends," I say. "How old are you?"

"I'm eleven."

"I was a bit younger than you, then," I say. "We moved out when I was eight."

"Why?" she asks.

Her question throws me. It's not like I feel that it's actually a secret or anything, but I've never put it in words for anyone before.

"My dad and mom wanted a bigger house," I say. "We still live in town."

"My mom doesn't like our new house," says Layla, matter-of-factly. "She says it isn't our forever house. She says we'll move somewhere nicer someday. When we can afford it."

"What about your dad?" asks Burke.

"He likes it, I think?" the little girl says, and then she twists her face into a knot, thinking about the question seriously. "Actually, I don't know if he likes it. He didn't say. I guess I should ask him."

"Cute kid," I say to Burke, as we're walking away.

"Yeah," he says. "My mom babysits her sometimes. She's real smart."

We reach the corner and I turn to glance back at the car. From the window, Layla Gerrard is still staring at us. When she sees me looking back at her, she raises a hand in a calm, simple wave.

As I wave back, I register with some surprise that I feel vaguely unsettled. It's been ten years since Sibby disappeared, but the memories of that day keep finding new ways to haunt me.

8.

My house is really loud when we get home. Music is blasting through the main hallway, screeching guitar and pounding discordant drums.

"What the hell is your dad listening to?" asks Burke as we kick off our boots.

"I don't know," I say, pushing through the glass porch door into the hallway. A song comes to an abrupt, screeching halt, and I yell into the house. "Hello?"

"I'm in here!" my father calls back.

Burke follows me down the hallway, munching from his giant bag of chips. I walk into the kitchen, Burke hanging back in the doorway, as another song kicks into high gear.

My father is dancing around the island, furiously chopping something. He's wearing a track suit, royal blue with stripes up the sides of the legs.

"Hey!" he calls over the music.

"What the hell are you listening to?" I yell.

"It's Soundgarden!" he calls back. "Amazing, hey?"

I walk to the stereo and turn down the volume. "What is going on?" I ask. "What are you wearing?"

He looks down at himself, then looks back up, laughing.

"Oh yeah," he says. "I almost forgot. I was telling Jaron and Pickle about the time my buddies and I drove all night to see them in concert, then back again so we could make it for an exam. Made me dig out my old CDs from the attic, and I found this tracksuit. Man I miss the '90s."

"Jaron and Pickle?" asks Burke.

"They're Dad's midlife crisis friends," I explain.

"Oh, hey, Burke!" says my dad excitedly. "I didn't notice you there!" He comes around the counter and gives Burke a friendly man hug from the side. If an adult did that to me, I'd spontaneously combust, but Burke takes it in stride.

"How's it going, Mr. Skinner?" he asks.

"Doing great, my man," says Dad. He looks down at Burke's open bag of chips. "Can I have some of those?"

"Uh, sure," says Burke, holding out the bag. Dad takes a big handful and shoves them into his mouth, then turns to look at me, a goofy smile on his face. "She's funny," he says through a mouthful of chips, pointing at me. "It can't be a midlife crisis if I'm not middle-aged."

"You're forty-seven," I say. "Average life expectancy for males is about 77, which means you're well over the hump. If that's not middle-aged, I don't know what is."

He stops chewing and stares at me with wide eyes.

"Oh my god," he says, through a mouthful of chips, "you're right."

I lean in closer and stare at his face. He shifts his gaze, but not before I notice that his eyes are glazed over, slightly bloodshot.

"Are you stoned?" I ask incredulously.

There's a long, awkward pause. Dad swallows loudly. "Please don't tell your mother," he whispers.

"Something's burning," says Burke.

We turn to see a plume of smoke rising from a pot on the stove, just as the fire alarm goes off. Dad rushes across the kitchen and grabs the pot, throwing it in the sink and turning on the water. I hurry to open the windows, and Burke stands in the middle of the chaos, taking it all in and methodically working through his chips.

"Amazing," he says.

"It just kind of happened," my dad tries to explain as he drags a stepladder against the wall and climbs up to pull the battery out of the alarm. "Pickle's brother gave him some homegrown stuff, so after coffee, we went out behind the alley and smoked. It was just a little bit!"

"Did they have their kids there?" I ask, horrified.

"No!" he says. "They were all at some playgroup thing or something."

I look at the pile of chopped potatoes on the counter, and he follows my gaze.

"I wanted poutine," he says sheepishly.

"Amazing," says Burke again.

"You are ridiculous," I tell Dad. I turn to Burke. "Come on. Let's go upstairs."

"But I want poutine," says Burke.

I narrow my eyes at him and he follows me out of the kitchen. When we get to my room, Burke collapses onto my bed in a fit of laughter. "I can't believe your dad is totally baked!" he chokes out as he pulls out his phone.

I turn on my computer, ignoring him and wondering what I did to deserve this insanity.

I open the *Radio Silent* email account and begin scrolling. A lot of messages are reactions to last night's episode, but a few of the subject lines read MISSING, which is how I tell people to get my attention if they want to suggest a case.

I begin skimming through them, but nothing I read seems like a good fit for the podcast. One guy clearly needs to accept that his wife wants a divorce, considering she packed a bag, told him she was leaving, and now won't answer his texts or calls. Another lady wants help tracking down her mother's kid sister, who ran away from home back in the '60s. I work through several others, but none of them *feels* right.

I'm about to give up and call it a day when another email catches my attention. I squint at the sender's address: QEllacott@BNN.com. The subject line reads "Interview?"

"What the…" I mutter as I open the message.

Dear Radio Silent—

My name is Quinlee Ellacott, and I am the chief crime corre-spondent for BNN, an online news outlet that seeks to "send the truth wherever you are." I have followed your podcast with great interest and would be very interested in securing an interview with "the Seeker" as you cryptically refer to yourself.

I think the role that the Seeker has played in shedding light on missing persons cases is fascinating and important, and I'd love your take on it. I'd also like to discuss your place in the investigative landscape in more depth. Our audience wants to know: Who is the Seeker?

You refer to the amateur sleuths who help you as "laptop detectives," and in several cases, it seems as if this digital investigative work has paid off. This raises the question: Is it reasonable for *Radio Silent* to step in where traditional law enforcement has failed? If so, doesn't the public deserve to know more?

We think it's a bit ironic, and an exciting slant to the story, that the host of the most popular podcast devoted to uncovering people wants to remain anonymous. I'm sure you'll understand when we attempt to find you in that very same spirit. You've laid out a very exciting challenge for us!

You might find it easier to just cooperate with us from the beginning. Please reach out to me at your convenience, and we can discuss terms of a possible interview.

Regards,
Quinlee J. Ellacott

For a moment, I almost forget to breathe. Quinlee Ellacott is the aggressive, take-no-prisoners chief crime correspondent for Breaking News Network. BNN doesn't broadcast traditionally; they're a completely online outfit, with an agenda to "tell the truth, even when it isn't pretty." They're also huge, with an enormous following online, and Quinlee Ellacott is their most well-known reporter. Her specialty is scandalous crimes with lots of dramatic twists and turns, and she never misses an opportunity to insert herself in the story.

In other words, she's everything I try not to be.

I read the email one more time. *I think the role that the Seeker has played in shedding light on missing person's cases is fascinating and important...* What does this mean? Are people starting to pay attention? Not just to the podcast, but to me?

"No way," I say, pushing the laptop away from me.

"What's up?" asks Burke, paying attention for real this time.

"Quinlee Ellacott wants to talk to me."

"You mean that reporter chick from the internet?"

I nod. "BNN. She wants to figure out who I am. Or who the Seeker is, anyway."

I twist the laptop so he can lean in to read it. He skims through it, then waves his hand dismissively. "Same old, same old," he says. "She won't figure out shit."

"Are you kidding me?" I ask, starting to panic. "She said she's been following the podcast with interest. She said the public deserves to know more! What if she starts digging around?"

He lifts his chin toward the laptop. "May I?"

I slide my seat out of the way. "Be my guest."

He sits down and starts opening up browser tabs. Using jargon that I only barely understand, he rapidly explains what it is that makes my system so secure.

"Basically," he concludes, "nobody is going to find you unless you want them to find you. Someone would have to be outside your bedroom window, actually watching you record, for you to be found out. So unless you're worried about Spider-Man climbing up the side of your house and spilling the beans on *Radio Silent*, you're cool. I promise."

"Okay," I say, breathing a sigh of relief. "Thank you. I'm sorry I keep asking you this. I know it must be annoying."

He waves me off. "Your secret identity is between you, me, and the walls." He stands up from the chair. "Anyway, I'd better get home. My mom wants us all home for dinner. Maybe I'll see if your dad wants to grab a toke with me on the back deck before I head out."

"Not funny, Burke," I say, forgetting about the email for a second to spin around in my chair and glare at him.

"I kid, I kid," he says, showing me his palms. "Another secret that's safe with me. I'll catch you tomorrow."

He disappears down the steps, and I sink back into my chair. Burke has managed to calm me down, but a seed of worry has been planted in my mind, and I know it's not going to just disappear that easily.

I didn't start *Radio Silent* to bring myself attention. I started it for the opposite reason, to bring attention to cases and people who deserved it. To draw my own obsessive attention away from the mystery that's haunted me for more than half my life.

It's never been about me. It's about the people who need finding.

9.

After Burke leaves, I turn back to my laptop and delete the email from Quinlee Ellacott, then set a block so her future emails will be deleted automatically. I'm about to shut my laptop and head back downstairs to give my father a hard time when a new email, subject line MISSING, appears in my inbox. I open it.

Dear Seeker,

I am writing from Houston. My friend Vanessa Rodriguez has been missing for almost a week. She didn't show up for work six days ago, which is extremely unusual for her. Because of an unusual series of events, nobody—not her boyfriend, her family, or any of her friends—realized she was missing for almost two days. We have reported her disappearance to the police, but although they tell us they are looking into her whereabouts, we are worried that they aren't taking Vanessa's disappearance seriously. My sister is a big fan of your podcast and suggested that I reach out to you. Since we have no idea what else to do, here I am.

We are very worried about Vanessa and hope you will consider featuring her on your podcast. Maybe someone out there knows something.

Thank you,
Carla Garcia

I reread the email, and a feeling I've come to recognize builds inside me: this is a case worth exploring. I quickly respond, asking if I can ask her a few follow-up questions. She replies almost right away, and we move to an online chat to continue our discussion. We go back and forth for almost an hour as she fills me in on the details of Vanessa's disappearance. I'm soon convinced that this is a good case to cover on the podcast, and she's agreed to do some legwork to help me, such as recording some quick interviews to include on the show and getting me a copy of the police report.

By the time we sign off, I'm charged with the electric thrill that always comes from deciding on a new case. I'm ready to tell this story, and if I do a good enough job, maybe the LDA will kick into overdrive and we'll find Vanessa, or at least some closure for her loved ones. I know what it's like to be in their shoes, and as long as this trail is still hot, I'm determined to do my best to help them follow it.

Once again, *Radio Silent* calms my anxiety and helps me focus on what's important—what I can *do*—and as long as I'm hidden from Quinlee Ellacott by voice filters and firewalls, I don't have to worry about becoming the story myself.

* * *

Unfortunately, it isn't long before a wrench is tossed in my plans. When I wake up and reach for my phone first thing the next morning, it's literally hot, thanks to a twitter feed that is completely on fire with so many mentions I can barely get a handle on them. It's normal for a successfully solved case to churn up a bunch of fresh activity on my accounts, but this is beyond anything I've experienced.

I get to school a bit early and head straight to my first period classroom so I can have a few quiet minutes to dig around on my feeds.

There's no way that @RadioSilentPodcast isn't being bank-rolled by some big enterprise, says one tweet. *I think we should channel the LDA and figure out where we can find them?* says another. There are dozens and dozens of cryptic tweets like this, and the clincher: *If anyone can figure out who she is, @QuinleeEllacott can.*

My blood goes cold, and I click through to @Quinlee-Ellacott's feed. Sure enough, pinned at the top is a brand-new message.

Do you know who is behind @RadioSilentPodcast? Help me and the @BNN team figure it out. Time to start our own online investigation!

"Oh for the love of—"

"What's happening?" asks Burke, sliding into the desk next to me.

I show him my phone. He reads it and, to my immense irritation, laughs.

"She sure is stone cold," he says.

I grab my phone back and stare at him like he has two heads. "This is a disaster. People want to know who I am, and now Quinlee Ellacott is trying to weasel her way into my business."

"Dee," says Burke reassuringly, "you have nothing to worry about. This isn't the first time that you've been asked for more information."

"Yeah, but it's the first time an investigative journalist has been on the case too. What if she starts digging? What if she makes a connection between me and Sibby?"

"How would she?" he asks. "Besides, what's the big deal if she does?"

I just shake my head. It's easy for Burke to say. He isn't trying to keep himself a secret.

He goes on. "I really don't get it, Dee. I mean, you have a successful podcast. Your ratings are big and getting bigger. Maybe I don't know what I'm talking about, but isn't it a good thing that you're starting to get attention?"

"No," I say louder than I intend, bringing a few glances from the people in the hallway. I drop my voice and lean closer. "I wanted to stay anonymous. I did this because I thought, stupidly, it was a way to give back."

"You are giving back," he says. "And I think you're crazy not to let yourself get acknowledged for it. But don't worry,

Dee. I give you my honest, most sincere promise." He stops and puts his hand on his heart. "You are one hundred percent incognito. Your voice is disguised, your upload location is secure and encrypted, and nobody, not even Quinlee Ellacott and her crackerjack investigative team, is going to figure out who you are."

I smile, realizing that I'm being kind of ridiculous. "Okay," I say. "Thanks."

"Besides," he says. "Didn't you say BNN is based in Vegas? That might as well be a million miles away. She'd have to do some crazy digging to figure out that the most popular true crime podcast—"

"Eleventh most popular," I correct.

"Sorry, *eleventh* most popular true crime podcast is being recorded in the attic bedroom of some grunge-era stoner's daughter."

I groan. "Don't remind me."

"You're a needle in a haystack, Dee. You're an interesting needle, with a helluva backstory, but it's one big-ass haystack."

The first bell rings, and Sarah Cash saunters into the room, pulling earbuds off and shoving her phone into her bag. She runs her hand absently through her hair before she sits, and the way it falls back down into place, loose and slightly out of place, sends a tightness up my back. I realize I've been watching her and quickly drop my eyes to my desk, sinking back into my seat.

When I reach down into my backpack to grab my book, I notice Brianna across the room, her zipper case of colored pens and her hot pink Leuchtturm open on the desk in front of her. She's making a big show out of picking out the perfect color pen, but when I look her way, she glances up at me with a smug, knowing smirk on her face. It's obvious that she's noticed me watching Sarah and has opinions about it. I want to grab her stupid perfect bullet journal and throw it out the window. Organize that, jerk.

I turn back to my phone, trying to ignore her.

Class has only just begun when there's a rap on the door. Mr. Calderone lifts a finger, telling us to hold the thought, and walks over to answer it. He steps outside, and a moment later, he comes back into the room and points at Burke.

"Mr. O'Donnell," he says. "Your presence is requested in the office."

I turn to look at Burke, surprised, and he shrugs at me as he stands from his chair and walks past me on his way out of the room. A buzz makes its way through the room, but Mr. Calderone shuts it down, and soon we're back to talking about the Russian Revolution.

Burke is gone until halfway through our next class, civics. He hands a note from the office to the teacher and returns to his seat beside me. I glance at him and he gives me a wide-eyed stare and mouths *holy shit* before pulling his textbook from his bag.

I'm not the kind of person to get interested in school gossip, but I'm dying to know what's going on. I assume that if he was in trouble, he wouldn't be back in class already.

When the teacher steps into the hallway to take a call, I turn quickly to Burke.

"What's going on?" I whisper.

"You remember those people we met at the gas station yesterday?" he says, one eye on the doorway. "The ones who live in your old house?"

A shiver runs down my spine. A few seats over, I notice Brianna stiffen slightly, and although she's staring intently at her textbook, running a finger down the page, I know she's listening carefully.

"Yeah," I say. "The Gerrards right?"

He nods. "The police wanted to talk to me because I'm a neighbor."

"Why?" I ask, although my spidey senses are tingling: this can't be good.

"It's Layla," he says. "Their little girl. She's missing."

10.

TEN YEARS EARLIER

The forest is darker than normal, a hundred thousand layered shadows sliding over and under and into one another, and as Dee follows Sibby into the woods, she feels like they've lost hours and hours just by stepping through the tree line.

The fort is pretty deep into the woods. Burke's uncle Terry started building it for them a couple of months ago, when he moved into the basement in Burke's house. All the kids in the neighborhood helped out, on and off, but mostly it was Terry and Burke and Delia and Sibby, with some visits from Terry's girlfriend, Sandy. Dee's dad even came out to help and brought lumber that he had left over from the deck he'd been building, but he was pretty busy with work, so it was just a couple of times.

Since then, all the kids from the street play there every afternoon: Dee and Sibby and Greta, Dee's little brothers—

although they've been at hockey practice a lot lately—Burke, and even his sisters, every once in a while.

"It's about time we had the fort to ourselves," says Sibby. "There's never enough room when everybody shows up."

As always, Dee is happy to hang out with Sibby one-on-one, but she's not sure she agrees about the fort being better when it's just the two of them.

But most of all, the woods are scary without a big gang.

Ahead of them, the treehouse comes into view, a ghostly structure of weathered wood, just barely visible through the trees, suspended in the air.

"Last one there is a rotten egg!" yells Sibby gleefully, and without waiting for Dee to catch on, she begins to run.

Dee stands where she is, frozen in place. She doesn't want to hurry to the treehouse. In fact, she wants to turn and run back the way they came, out into the clear air, the houses of their neighborhood in full view, and eyeballs looking through a dozen windows, watching them.

But as Sibby crashes away from her through the underbrush, branches snapping and dead leaves crunching underfoot, Dee realizes that she's going to be left behind, all alone, if she doesn't follow in Sibby's wake.

Her boots, when she does start to run, are solid and thick. They aren't the best for a footrace, but they'll keep her feet warm. They'll keep her tightly gripped to the ground.

11.

It's snowing heavily by the time I arrive home from school. In the front entryway, I stomp to knock the snow off my boots, then I step through to the foyer. There's a low murmur of voices coming from the living room. It sounds like my parents, which is odd since my mother usually doesn't get home from work until a lot later than this, and there's another voice in the mix too. A man's voice.

"Dee?" my mother's voice calls out from the living room. "Is that you?"

"Yeah," I call back. I glance at the twins, and they raise their eyebrows. I wonder if they've heard about Layla Gerrard.

"Can you come in here, honey?" It's my father this time.

An uneasy feeling rises from my stomach, and I let my backpack slide off my shoulder and drop it next to the stairs, then head down the hallway and into the living room.

My parents turn to me from their perch on the couch as I enter. Their mouths are smiling, but it's their eyes—wide and anxious—that express how they're really feeling.

Across the room from them, sitting in one of the beat-up leather wing chairs that flank the fireplace, is a face I haven't seen in ten years. I remember it well, though. The face of the man who was charged with finding out what I knew after Sibby disappeared.

Detective Reginald Avery stands to greet me, stepping forward to give me his hand.

"Hello, Delia," he says, shaking firmly.

"Hi," I say, looking back and forth between him and my parents.

"It's been a while," he says, and all I can do in response is nod.

"Delia, honey," says my mother, "come sit with us."

My mother insists on calling me "honey," even though I'm about as far from a "honey" as you're likely to find. She'd do better to call me "champ" or "buster."

I squeeze onto the couch between them, the three of us staring across at the detective. Both of my parents are turned slightly toward me in a subtly protective gesture. The effect is of an awkward family photo, but as much as I wish they'd give me a bit of breathing room, I'm comforted by their concern.

"You've grown up," he says, smiling. I hate it when adults say this kind of shit. How am I supposed to respond? *You're looking older yourself?*

The truth is, he does look older now. I know that's obvious, but when I was a kid, he seemed really old, although he couldn't have been much more than forty at the time. That was at a point in my life when every adult was one of two kinds of old: parent and teacher old, and grandparent old.

Now I realize that this man was pretty young when he interviewed me, and he's since moved well into middle age. His face is the same, but he's aged. Lines on his face, gray in his hair, a slight paunch where there used to be a fit, trim figure.

What interests me most, though, are the changes I can't see. The hidden thoughts and considerations that sit behind his eyes.

Maybe he was trying to be a savior back then. Maybe he thought he could fix things, make things right, find Sibby and bring the kidnappers to justice. Back then he was the man who was trying to solve the case.

Now, ten years later, he's the man who didn't.

It's funny to think about, but I realize suddenly that Avery and I have come to the same place from two different directions. We're both haunted by the girl we let down.

He smiles at us, then drops his gaze to his hands, clasped as if in prayer in his lap.

"You might have heard some rumors at school today," he says.

"About the missing girl," I say. Next to me, I feel both of my parents tense, like dogs who've spotted a squirrel.

Avery lifts his gaze to mine and nods. "Yes. What have you heard?"

"Just that a girl is missing," I say. When none of them say anything, I go on. "She lives in our old neighborhood. Burke and a few other kids from the area were pulled out and asked questions."

"That's everything you've heard?" Detective Avery asks.

"Yeah. What else *would* I have heard?" I sit up in my seat, suddenly alert, my spidey senses beginning to tingle. "Why are you here? What's going on?"

My mother reaches out and gives my shoulder a squeeze. "Take a breath, Dee," she says. "Everything's fine."

"Obviously," I say, forcing myself to keep my voice calm and steady, "you're here for a reason. Something is going on that involves me."

"Not exactly," he says. "Not directly, at least."

"Delia," says my mother. "The girl who went missing lives in our old house."

"I know that," I say. I glance at my father, who looks shocked, and hasten to explain. "Burke told me about it. It's Layla, right?"

"You know her?" asks my mother, surprised.

"Not really. I mean, I met her. The other day when I was out with Burke, he said hey to her. She was in a car, with her mom."

"When was this?" asks Avery. He's fumbling for his notebook.

"It wasn't a big deal," I say. "It was a few days ago. We stopped at the gas station on Livingstone because Burke wanted to buy some chips. We met her mom in the store, and Burke introduced me. When we came out of the store, Burke dragged me over to the car to meet Layla for some reason. That was it."

"How did she seem?" asks Avery.

"Who?" I ask. "Layla or her mother?"

"Both," he says.

I shrug. "They seemed normal. Like, the mom was nice, you could tell she likes Burke. I mean adults always like Burke, so no surprise there."

He nods, takes a couple of quick notes. "And the girl?"

"She seemed normal," I say. "Like a little girl. She seemed smart, I guess. Mature."

He keeps taking notes. "Nothing else?"

"Not really," I say. "I literally just met them and then forgot about them. There were no kidnappers lurking in the bushes or anything."

Avery finishes writing and tucks his notepad into his belt.

"I understand," he says. "But you never know when someone might have relevant information and not even realize it. That's not why I'm here though."

My stomach seems to collapse in on itself, and I bite on my lower lip to calm myself down.

"There's more to this story," Avery continues. "I wanted to come see you all because of something that was discovered at the scene."

He reaches into a leather bag sitting propped up next to his chair and pulls out a simple file folder. It's purple, and the scratched out and rewritten labels tell me that it's obviously been recycled many times. He places it on the coffee table between us and leans forward, placing one hand on the folder.

"There was a…a note," he says.

"A note?" my father asks, pushing forward and looking at him with some urgency.

Avery looks at me and hesitates.

"You can tell me," I say impatiently. "You can't screw me up more than I already am."

"Dee," says my mother, calmly reassuring. She puts her hand on my knee and squeezes, worried, I know, that I'll have some kind of attack.

"I'm fine," I say. I turn back to Avery. "Please just tell us."

He takes his hand off the folder and pushes it across the table toward us, then sits back and waits.

I slowly open the folder. Inside is one simple piece of paper, a color copy of what I assume was the original. It looks like a stereotypical ransom note from an old TV show, letters cut out of magazines and glued to a plain background. It would be almost ridiculous, a childish cliché, if it wasn't for the message it spelled out.

YOU KNEW YOU WERE PLAYING WITH FIRE
WHEN YOU MOVED INTO THIS HOUSE.

"What does this mean?" I ask, my heart thumping.

Avery shakes his head. "We really don't know," he says. "It's cryptic to say the least."

"Were there any other clues?" asks my father.

"Nothing that I can talk about," says Avery. "We're still examining the scene of the crime. I can tell you that this is the only thing we found that implies a connection to...to the events of the past."

"It doesn't make any sense," says my father. "Why would they target our old house and not the Carmichaels' old house? Isn't there a family with kids living there?"

"The Tufts," says Avery. "They've lived there since the original...event."

"You can call it an abduction," I snap. "I was there, remember?"

"Delia," says my mother, rubbing my back. I pull away.

"It's okay," says Avery. "You're right, Dee. I'm still trying to figure out how to approach this. The Tufts have a couple of boys, but they're both off at college. They were teens when the Tufts bought the house. To answer your question, we don't know why anyone would have targeted your old house."

"It's been almost ten years," I say.

"You're right," he says. "It's been a long time, and we probably wouldn't even be making a connection if it wasn't for the note. To be honest, we'd still be exploring other possibilities—that the girl ran away or was at a friend's house—if it wasn't for the note."

"No," I say. "I mean it's been ten years almost exactly, since Sibby went missing. Maybe someone is obsessed with the case, like a copycat."

Nobody says anything for a long stretch.

"Right," says Avery, and I can tell that this is the first he's considered it. "Like I said, we're trying to figure things out on the fly."

"The internet is full of stuff like this," I say. "People obsess over old cases. There are copycat serial killers. Why not copycat abductions?"

"We will consider every angle," says Avery. "I can promise you that."

"Do you think there's anything to be worried about?" asks my mother.

"Do you think she's in danger?" asks my father more abruptly.

"Jesus, Jake," says Mom, shooting him a *what the hell* look.

"No, no, it's okay." The detective brushes off her concern. "I don't think there's any danger. We really don't. But we do think it's best to be extra vigilant for the time being. Basically, don't go wandering around by yourself, okay, Dee?"

"I'm not in the habit of doing that anyway," I say.

"Well, that's good," he says. "Until we've got some kind of an answer to what happened, keep it up." He stands, reaching for his bag, and I can tell he's relieved to have delivered his message and ready to get out of here.

"What happens if you don't figure it out?" I ask. "You didn't figure out what happened with Sibby."

His face blanches. "You're right," he says. "And we don't want the same thing to happen twice, obviously."

"It isn't an insult," I say. "But isn't it true that…" I hesitate, realizing it will sound kind of weird if I spout the exact percentage of unsolved missing persons cases. "A lot of cases like this go unsolved?"

He nods slowly. "We're going to do our best," he says. "I promise that. But you all know the reality here. We can only do what we can do. Beyond that, we'll have to figure it out as it develops."

Before he leaves, Detective Avery reaches inside his coat pocket and pulls out a card. He hands it to me, pressing it into my hand and folding my fingers over it.

"If anything occurs to you, or if you are suspicious of anything or anyone, even if you just want to talk, you get in touch with me," he says. "Don't hesitate. That's my cell number. Call or text me anytime."

"Okay," I say. "Thanks."

He looks at me like he wants to say something else, but then he just gives me a tight-lipped smile. "You have nothing to worry about, Delia. We are going to do everything we can to find out who did this, and we will put your mind at ease."

I snort. *At ease.* As if anything they do can put me at ease.

"What happens now, Detective?" asks my mother.

"We're having a press conference tomorrow evening," he says, "and we'll be organizing a search in the woods as soon as the weather cooperates." He turns and glances out the window at the snow. "This obviously isn't ideal, but unfortunately we're stuck with it."

Avery makes his goodbyes, and I stand with my parents in the front window, watching as he gets into his car and pulls away.

"I'm sure there's nothing to worry about," says my father. "I mean, yes about that poor girl, of course. But this has nothing to do with you, Dee."

"What were you talking about back there?" asks my mother. There's a funny tone in her voice. "All those questions about copycats and unsolved crimes. Delia, have you been obsessing over Sibby online?"

"No," I say quickly. "Not at all. I've never looked into that online."

She looks at me skeptically.

"Seriously, Mom," I say. "I have no interest in reopening that can of worms. I'm better off forgetting about it as much as I can."

I can tell by the look on her face that she believes me and is relieved.

"That's good, honey," she says. "I think that's very wise of you. You have your own life to live, and you've come so far."

She embraces me, and I let her. I feel my father come in from the side, and soon we're sharing a giant, obnoxious family hug. Part of me wants to cringe at the sitcom moment, but the rest of me can't help but lean into the comfort it gives me.

I wonder what my parents would think if they knew the whole truth. It's true that I haven't been reading about Sibby's disappearance online, but that hasn't stopped me from digging into other cases, to put it lightly.

"I think I'm going to head up to my room and do some homework," I say, pulling away from the love fest.

"You sure?" my dad asks. "I could make us all hot chocolate. Maybe we could watch a movie?"

"I'd love to, but I have an essay due for poli sci next week, and I haven't even started researching yet." They both look so frazzled and concerned that I force a smile onto my face. "You guys don't need to worry about me. I'll be fine."

I'm not fine. Back in my room, I drop into my desk chair and do some controlled breathing. I think of Layla, and a hundred different outcomes run through my mind, one after the other. It's a mystery just like the ones I've been covering on *Radio Silent*, but I didn't ask for this one, and just like the one that got its claws into my almost ten years ago, it's far too close to home.

I think back to the note Avery showed us. *Playing with fire.* It was a warning for the Gerrards, but it might as well have been directed at me.

I shake my head to remove the invasive thoughts. Desperate to shift focus, I turn to my laptop and check my email. Waiting at the top of my inbox is a message from Carla Garcia in Houston. She's sent me the information I requested about her friend Vanessa, along with a whole lot more.

This is just the kind of distraction I need at the moment.

12.

Carla's email is a podcaster's dream. Not only has she taped a video of herself and a friend walking the route between Vanessa's work and her house, and made a list of the people Vanessa interacts with on a regular basis, she's gone to the trouble of recording high-quality interviews with several of Vanessa's closest contacts, each of whom state their explicit permission for me to include their recordings on *Radio Silent*.

I sift through the information and begin to make notes, and it isn't long before I'm ready to record the first episode about the disappearance of Vanessa Rodriguez.

I've just set up my recording equipment when I hear the doorbell ring downstairs. It's an antique doorbell, an ancient contraption that my dad found on eBay and arrived a week later in two boxes. It took him weeks to put together and install, and it sounds like an off-key gong in the center of the house. The twins call it the "horror movie chime."

I hear my parents talking to someone downstairs. For a moment, I worry that I'm going to have to talk to more police, but the voices sound cheerful, if muffled, and soon they move down the hallway toward the kitchen and out of earshot. It seems weird that anyone would choose tonight to stop by for a visit, but at least it'll keep Mom and Dad from stressing out about me for a little while. I turn back to my computer and am about to turn my headphones on when there's a knock on the door at the bottom of my stairs and the door opens.

"Hello?" an unfamiliar voice calls up the stairs.

I scramble to shove my microphone back into my desk drawer as someone ascends the steps. I slam my computer closed and spin around in my chair just as, to my immense surprise, Sarah Cash appears at the top of the stairs.

"Hi," she says.

"Hi," I say. I must be unable to disguise my confusion because she laughs and takes a final step into my room.

"Sorry to just pop in on you like this, but my parents decided we should visit the neighbors. I told them it wasn't cool to just show up unannounced, but they said that's how people do things in small towns and insisted that I come along. I'm Sarah, by the way. I know we're in the same class, but we haven't really met exactly."

"Come on in," I say, somehow managing to compose myself. "I'm Dee."

She gazes around the room. "The truth is, my father has had a boner for this place since the minute we moved in. He and your dad are downstairs talking about renovations while our moms drink wine in the kitchen."

"Sounds like a match made in heaven," I say. "Dad loves to talk about this house."

"No kidding," she says. "I didn't realize houses had genders," said Sarah. "But he called it *she*. Just like a sailboat, I guess." She glances at me, amused. "Have you always lived here?"

"No. We've always lived in Redfields, but we moved into this house when I was eight."

There's no sense playing coy about it. "My room's pretty great," I admit. "I'm lucky they let me have it."

She stands for a moment longer, just looking around. "This might be the coolest bedroom I've ever seen," she says.

I feel a rush of pride at the way I have it set up. The only other person outside my family who ever comes here is Burke, and he's never even commented on it. I might make fun of my father for his renovation obsession, but I've inherited his love of interior design, and over the years, he's helped me collect a few cool things. On the worn wooden floorboards, I've laid a bunch of faded multicolored rugs that we've found at yard sales and antique shops. There's a beat-up old leather couch against one wall, and my bed sits in the gable opposite the big octagonal window. I try to keep the walls mostly bare, but there are a couple of posters neatly tacked onto the angled ceiling, an "I'm With Her" poster from when my mother and I went to a Hillary rally in the city back during the '16 election and a vintage Runaways poster that I bought on eBay.

Sarah glances up into the rafters, where I've hung tiny

white lights, then walks over to stand in the gable window, and lets out a long whistle.

"You can see the whole goddamn town from up here," she says. "It almost makes Redfields look cool."

"I wouldn't go that far," I laugh.

"Oh, hey," she says, pointing. "That's my house, like, right there."

"Yeah," I say, doing my best to stay cool. "Mrs. Dunlop's place."

"Jeez," she says. "I'd better not get changed in the window. You've got like a full view."

Do not turn red. Do not turn red.

"Does it always snow this much around here?" she asks. Beyond her, the snow continues to swirl.

"Yup," I say. "On the bright side, we probably won't have school tomorrow."

She goes over to the sofa and flops into a corner. Instead of joining her, I grab the desk chair and drop into it backward, then roll it around so I'm facing her.

"I hope that little girl isn't out there in this weather," she says. "It's pretty crazy."

"Yeah," I agree. "It's messed up."

"I wonder what happened," she goes on. "There are so many perverts out there. Hopefully she's just lost and she'll turn up safe and sound."

"Hope so." I don't mention the note that Avery showed us. It's pretty clear that it isn't public knowledge. Not yet, at least.

"Apparently there's going to be a press conference sometime tomorrow," she says.

I nod. "They're planning on a search of the woods too. As soon as the weather clears up."

"Are you going to go?" she asks.

The thought of going back into the woods for the first time in ten years sends an uncomfortable feeling into the pit of my stomach. "I'm not sure. Maybe." I search for something else to talk about, anxious to change the subject. "I really like your car. It's a Chevy Nova, right?"

She looks impressed. "Good eye! You into cars?"

"Not really," I admit. "My dad told me it was a Nova. It's really cool looking though."

"I bought this one back home," she says. "Saved up for months. Worked two part-time jobs, which my parents weren't thrilled about, although I managed to keep my grades up, so they couldn't say much about it. I knew I wanted a muscle car, and when this one came up, I couldn't turn it down. My dad says the road salt here will do a real number on it, but I don't care. Cars were made to be driven, right?"

"Yeah," I say. "It's definitely a cool-looking car."

"My parents don't like it, but there's nothing they can do about it as long as I pay for it myself. We've been fighting a lot," she says abruptly. "Me and my parents. I didn't want to move here."

"I don't blame you," I say. "Redfields isn't exactly exciting."

"It's not like I was even all that attached to the last town," she says. "But I wanted to be. That's kind of the thing. We move so much that I never have time to get attached to any place. I just want the opportunity to settle in somewhere. Now they're all over me to make friends, meet people, and I'm like, why bother?"

"Yeah," I say, suddenly very self-conscious.

She laughs and puts her hand on her face. "Oh shit, I'm such a dummy. No wonder I don't make friends easily. I'm glad you're here. You seem cool. Maybe we can hang out. You can check out my car. Maybe I'll even let you drive it."

"That'd be great," I say. I don't mention that I've never learned to drive and have no interest. I just want to be *in* her car.

"It's kind of crazy about that girl going missing, hey?" she asks. "That's like, big-city shit."

"Yeah," I say. "It's terrible."

"My mom says another girl went missing here a few years ago." She leans forward eagerly. "It's such a bizarre coincidence. Do you remember that?"

"I was just a little kid," I say, deflecting. It's only a matter of time before she learns my connection, but I don't have the energy to have that conversation right now.

"I wonder what happened to them," she says. "Here's a random question. Do you listen to podcasts?"

My heart skips. "Podcasts?" I say. "Not really. I mean, I know what they are, but they're just not really my thing."

"You should," she says, suddenly eager. "I'm obsessed with this true crime podcast. It's called *Radio Silent*, and I can't stop listening. It has this really cool host. I think they disguise their voice, because it sounds all filtered and weird, but in a cool way. They talk about missing people, like people who are missing *right now*, and then their followers kind of act like detectives and help them solve cases and shit. It's awesome."

"Oh, yeah?" My mouth is dry, and I can't figure out how to respond without sounding completely guilty or obvious. "Sounds cool."

"It's such a cool premise," she says. "I mean, they actually find people. It's crazy. It's happened like a million times."

I want badly to correct her, to tell her that it's only happened a handful of times, that most of the time it doesn't help at all. But I force myself to just smile and pretend I think this is all very interesting.

"Anyway, I've been wondering if they'll cover this case. The missing kid. Layla Gerrard. I keep thinking I would try to help, like investigate it or something."

"There are a lot of missing person's cases, aren't there?" I ask. "Don't you think it's a bit of a stretch?"

"Maybe." She shrugs. "But I feel like it's the kind of case the show would take on. It's kind of perfect, and the most important thing is that it's totally fresh. After the first forty-eight hours, cases start to go cold. We'll see what happens. Anyway, you should check it out."

"Yeah, for sure," I say.

I'm saved by the bell, or really, the knocking.

"Hello up there! Can we come up?" my father yells.

He doesn't bother to wait for my reply, just clomps up the stairs to my room, followed by a very tall man who I recognize as Sarah's father from the night they moved in.

"This is great!" he says, looking around. He looks at me and grins. "You must be Dee. Sorry to intrude on your sanctuary, but your old man said you wouldn't mind. I'm just really in love with this house."

"Old man," echoes Sarah. "You sound like a hippie," she says.

She's right, and I wonder if tall Mr. Cash is going to be tagging along with Dad before long, hanging with Jaron and

Pickle and smoking blunts behind the grocery store between errands.

"We should probably be getting going, sweet pea," he says to Sarah. "School night and all. Let's go drag your mother away from her business talk."

Sarah gets up from the couch and stretches. "Guess I'll see you at school tomorrow, hey?"

"For sure," I tell her.

Dad steps aside and lets them exit first, and I follow him down to help see our guests out.

"That was unexpected," says my mother once they've left. She drops into an armchair and yawns. "I can't say I was in the mood for company after the day we've all had, but they seem like nice people."

"Hard to blame them for being neighborly," says Dad. "They're probably the only people in town who don't know about…our background. What did you think, Dee? Sarah seems cool. Cute too!"

"Welp," I say, ignoring his comment, "I still have homework to do." I turn and escape upstairs before he has a chance to pry any further.

Back in my room, I stand in my window and look down at the house across the street. To my surprise, Sarah is standing at her window, about to close her curtains. It happens so quickly that I don't have time to duck out of the way before she spots me, so I just stand there like a deer in the headlights.

But instead of being freaked out, Sarah just grins and throws me a peace sign. I find myself grinning back and returning the gesture.

She gives me a final wave, then draws her curtain. I stay in the window for a few moments, staring through the snow at the forest in the distance. Could Layla really be out there?

I pull myself away and return to my desk, then I pull my microphone back out of the drawer and begin to record.

13.

Transcript of **RADIO SILENT**
Episode 42

HOST (intro): A woman goes missing in Houston,
after a routine shift at work. Police have asked
the public for help, but so far, there are no leads.
Does anyone out there in *Radio Silent* land have any
relevant information? Is there something we can do
to help?

Listen up. Let's try.

Almost a million people are reported missing
across North America every year. If we pay attention, if we work together, maybe we can help bring
some of them home.

I am *the Seeker*, and this is *Radio Silent*.

HOST: Earlier this week, I received an email from
Carla Garcia, a woman in Houston, asking me to

look into the disappearance of her friend Vanessa Rodriguez. Vanessa, twenty-one, was first reported missing four days ago, but friends say that she's actually been missing for longer than that. She didn't turn up for her shift at a busy diner six days ago, which her employer thought was strange, since she'd never missed a shift before. When multiple texts and calls to her cell phone went unanswered, they assumed she'd quit her job. Over the weekend, her family assumed that she was staying with her boyfriend, Johnny, but he was out of town visiting family in San Antonio.

RECORDING: *(voice of Johnny)* "I got back home around two or two thirty on Sunday. Vanessa and I had made plans for when I got back. You know, just hang out. She didn't answer any of my texts, and when I tried calling, it went straight to voice mail. Finally, I went over to her place. She didn't answer the door, so I let myself in—I have a key—and nobody was home. Nothing seemed weird or out of place, but I started to get a bad feeling. That's when I got in touch with her mom, and when *she* said she hadn't heard from Vanessa, that's when we started to get real worried."

HOST: Johnny and Vanessa's mother began reaching out to her friends and family, which is when they realized that something was wrong.

RECORDING: *(voice of Carla Garcia)* "None of us had heard from her in two days. I'd last seen her at work earlier in the week. We'd made plans to grab an after-work drink on Friday, because we were working the same shift, but then she didn't show up on Friday. It was weird because Vanessa never missed a shift at work. I texted her, but I didn't hear back. I didn't think a lot about it until I heard from Johnny on Sunday night. We went to the police and they told us we had to wait forty-eight hours to file a missing person report, even though none of us had seen her in over forty-eight hours. It was bullshit, but they said it was standard procedure. It was clear that *they* weren't concerned, but *we* were concerned.

We were a lot more than concerned.

HOST: Carla and Johnny and Vanessa's family immediately began a search of their own. Her phone was discovered underneath a mailbox a few blocks from her apartment, and when they finally gained access to her bank accounts, it turned out that they hadn't been touched.

HOST: You all know why I'm here. I know why you're all here. The world is full of missing people, and the sad truth is that many of them will never come home. But I believe there's a story behind every missing person, and maybe, just maybe, if we begin to dig up the details together, we can find our way to a happy ending.

It might be too late for Vanessa. But what if it isn't too late? What if she's still out there, waiting somewhere, hoping that someone noticed something?

Maybe it was someone you know.

Maybe it was you.

Carla Garcia has been an incredible friend to Vanessa. She's doing everything she can to help Vanessa's family, her boyfriend, and her friends bring Vanessa home. She's spearheaded a grassroots effort to turn over every stone. She reached out to me to see whether the LDA can help. She recorded the clips you heard on this episode, and she's on the ground in Houston, willing to follow up any lead we can send her way.

I've put all of this information on our show page, including several photos of Vanessa.

I want to use this platform to tell you about Vanessa. I want to give her story the space it deserves.

Is there something *you* can do to help?

Listen up.

Let's try.

14.

Sure enough, I wake up to learn that school is canceled for the day. Normally, that's a good thing, but today all I can think about is how it's holding up the search for Layla. By the time Burke picks me up for the press conference, after dinner, the snow has finally stopped and I am itching to get out of my house. He rings the bell just as my parents are in the middle of gently discouraging me from going for the hundredth time, and I dart for the entryway, pulling on my coat and boots and yelling a quick goodbye before escaping outside.

"Let's get the hell out of here," I say to Burke as I hurry past him and down the front steps.

"You fighting with your folks or something?" he asks, hustling behind me.

"Worse," I say. "They want to talk about my feelings."

Burke groans. "Gross. So they don't like this shit any more than mine do, hey?"

"They seem to think that being close to a missing person case will bring back bad memories."

He laughs. "Wait till they find out about the podcast."

I stop and turn to him, jabbing a finger in his chest. "They'll *never* find out about the podcast. Capisce?"

"Jesus, Dee. Relax. How many times do we need to have this conversation? I'm on your side, remember?"

I nod, suddenly embarrassed. "Sorry. I'm just tense. This is heavy shit."

"No kidding," he says. "My family got questioned this afternoon."

"Wow, really?"

"Yeah, they sat us down and asked a trillion questions. They're trying to come up with a detailed schedule explaining where everyone in the neighborhood was at the time of the abduction."

I nod. It makes sense. I know that the most likely suspect in a missing person case is someone who lives close to the abducted. Usually it's a family friend or relative, but sometimes it's a neighbor or someone who works in the vicinity. Someone who had knowledge and opportunity.

"Where were her parents?" I ask.

"They were out running errands," he says. "Apparently she was doing homework and they figured they wouldn't be gone for long, so they left her alone. When they got back, she was gone."

"And it's all been proven?" I ask. "I mean, did people see them?"

Burke nods. "Yep. Multiple people saw them at the grocery store and the hardware store. I know you're thinking the parents often have something to do with it, but not this time."

The parking lot outside the school auditorium is packed. As I approach, I notice several news vehicles lined up along the sidewalk, including a conspicuous baby-blue van with the BNN logo on it.

"Shit," I say, stopping on the other side of the street.

Burke follows my gaze. "Shit," he says, agreeing. "Do you think Quinlee Ellacott is here?"

"I don't know," I say uneasily. "I hope not."

"Even if she is, it's not like she'd ever pick you out of a crowd and say, 'Hey! Are you the Seeker?'"

"Maybe not," I say. "But it's still way too close for comfort."

The inside of the gym is packed tight, and it genuinely feels like everyone in town is here. At the back of the room, conspicuous in a dark suit and overcoat, among a room full of jeans and parkas, is Detective Avery. His arms are crossed, and his eyes scan the room slowly, as if he's taking notes on everyone in the gym.

Near the front of the stage, cameras are set up on tripods and reporters mill about, chatting with each other and occasionally soliciting a local resident for a quick impromptu interview. Sure enough, I catch sight of Quinlee Ellacott—not difficult, since she stands out from the crowd in her signature bright red jacket.

Although the cameras are trained on the stage, I lead us toward the back of the room, yanking my hat down low and pulling my hood as far forward as it will go. Despite my best efforts to stay inconspicuous, I notice a few people looking my way and whispering. What happened in the woods has never totally disappeared, but usually people are pretty discreet. This new development, though, seems to have the old case on people's minds. Ugh.

The energy in the gym shifts toward the stage, as a small group of people come out and sit behind the table that's been set up at the front. Flashes go off, and microphones on poles get shoved in toward the action. I recognize Mrs. Gerrard right away. She's being guided toward the table by a tall, handsome man whose hand rests protectively on her back.

I lean in to whisper to Burke. "Is that her husband?"

"Yeah," he says. "Adam. Nice guy."

Once the Gerrards are seated at the center of the table, in front of the microphone, they're followed by a man in a suit, then the mayor and chief of police.

The suited man leans forward and drags the microphone over in front of him.

"Thank you for coming," he says. "I'm representing the Gerrards, who will make a brief statement. Then I'll take questions."

He pushes the microphone back in front of his clients, who give him a nervous look. With one hand under the table, presumably holding on to his wife's, Adam Gerrard leans forward. "We appreciate very much that you've all come out here today," he says. "Bonnie and I are in a lot of shock right now, as you can imagine, but we are taking faith in the outpouring of love and assistance that's come from the community and beyond."

He looks shell-shocked, his face blank and drawn. He stares down at the microphone, composing himself, then speaks in a halting, unhappy voice.

"We have a message to whoever is responsible for the abduction of our daughter." He looks up from the microphone and straight down into the bank of cameras. "Whoever you are, wherever you are, please, stop and talk to our little girl. Tell her that her parents love her and that this is a big mistake. Then please take her somewhere safe, where you can't be seen. Leave here there, and phone the helpline that's been set up for Layla. It's anonymous and has been set up by the police so that you can't be tracked. Just send her home to us and everything will be forgiven."

"Yeah right," Burke whispers to me. "If that girl makes it home, the cops won't rest until that guy is strung up by the balls."

"Shhh," I say. This is the first actual missing person press conference I've attended, and I want to hear it.

There's a long pause onstage, and the crowd is completely hushed as Bonnie Gerrard continues.

"We have a message for Layla," she says, and her voice, quieter and softer than her husbands, cracks. "Layla, baby, we love you. We know you're waiting to get home, that you just want to hang out with BamBam and watch Planet Earth. We're here, baby, just waiting for you."

With an abrupt shudder, she jerks forward and puts her face into her hands and begins sobbing. Her husband leans forward and covers her with his body, leaning his face down onto her shoulder, and the two of them sit like that, shaking and crying.

Their lawyer reaches across and grabs the microphone away from the Gerrards' faces, but not before their combined, gasping sobs have filled the auditorium. I glance around me. Most people are exchanging horrified glances or staring awkwardly down at their shoes. It's embarrassingly intimate.

"Mr. and Mrs. Gerrard!" The voice that breaks the awkward moment is inappropriate, but it still comes as a relief. Quinlee Ellacott is pressing against the front of the stage, her red-sleeved arm holding her microphone up toward the table. "Can you say anything about the rumors that someone might have kidnapped Layla as an act of revenge or payback?"

A ripple goes through the crowd, and I turn to Burke, who shakes his head at me, wide-eyed. This is obviously the first he's heard of this theory.

The lawyer leans in toward the Gerrards and speaks to them in a hushed, urgent voice. Adam Gerrard nods and begins to stand, reaching down for his wife, but she shakes off his hand and leans forward over the table, her glare fixed on the reporter, who stares right back .

"That's ridiculous," she says. "Payback for what?"

Her husband leans in and tries to say something to her, but she shakes him off and listens to the reporter.

"There are rumors of debts," Quinlee continues, unfazed by the commotion, probably relishing it. "Gambling, defaulted mortgages. Why did you move to Redfields in the first place?"

"How dare you?" screams Bonnie, and her voice is so clear and loud and tight with anger that the entire auditorium goes still, as if her grief and rage have stopped time. Adam Gerrard's hand hovers over her shoulder, the lawyer is momentarily silenced, and for the moment, all of Bonnie Gerrard's energies are focused on Quinlee Ellacott.

"Who the hell do you think you are?" Bonnie continues. "Don't you see what has happened to our family? And you have the audacity to place blame on us?"

Quinlee doesn't back down; instead, she takes another step forward, but I think I can see a tiny tightening ripple across her shoulders as she braces herself to continue.

"I'm not placing blame on anyone," she says. "But it's important to examine all possibilities here, and when a child goes missing, the likeliest possibility is always someone close to them."

"We have alibis!" yells Bonnie.

"Yes," says Quinlee, "but alibis only remove suspicion from you. I'm exploring whether some kind of association you've made elsewhere led to Layla's abduction."

As if they've been released from a spell, the people onstage snap back into action. The lawyer leans in and whispers something to Bonnie, who seems to shake something off before getting up and pushing past everyone to get backstage.

Adam Gerrard leans forward to the microphone.

"If you're looking for some Sopranos-style heavies who are out looking for me to repay debts, you'll be looking a long time," he says before pushing away from the table so aggressively that the microphone falls sideways with a loud thump.

The lawyer ushers him away from the table and gestures to the mayor, Emma Jin, as they leave the stage. She steps forward to the microphone and leans in to address the crowd that is already beginning to chatter excitedly among themselves.

Quinlee Ellacott has turned to her camera guy, and I can see the smug look on her face from here. Everything Adam and Bonnie Gerrard said was true, but with just a couple of well-placed questions, she's prompted a dramatic reaction and created a new narrative out of thin air. This will make for much more exciting television than a straightforward press conference.

"Thank you all for coming," says Mayor Jin. "The entire town's thoughts and prayers are with the Gerrards. The weather has finally cleared up, and fortunately, tomorrow's forecast looks clear, so we'll be going ahead with a search of the woods behind Layla's house tomorrow. We ask that anyone who is interested in helping meet on Red Spruce Lane at first light so we can organize and head out. Police Chief Garber is going to say a few words about the search before we disband, but I'd like you all to think long and hard about whether you may have seen something strange in the days leading up to Layla's disappearance."

The chief steps up to the microphone.

"As Mayor Jin mentioned, we're organizing a search for tomorrow," he says. "We'll be meeting at first light, around 0800, and spreading ourselves through the woods behind the block and the highway. The circumstances are far from ideal, since so much snow has fallen since Layla was reported missing, but we're going to move ahead anyway, and we could use your help. I'll go over these details again tomorrow, but for those of you who participate, remember not to touch anything. Take your cell phones with you so we have pictures. We'll see you in the morning."

We join the crush of the crowd as it moves slowly toward the doors on the far end of the gym, until we finally escape outside. The air is crisp and light, just cold enough not to feel wet, just warm enough not to hurt your face. Reflected in the bright gleam of the parking lot, tiny crystal snowflakes drift down and melt on the sidewalk.

"Are you going to do the search tomorrow?" Burke asks.

"Yeah," I say as we move off to the side, letting the crowd move past us. "Definitely. I feel like I have to do it."

"Me too," he says. "I'm definitely going to search. Why don't you come to my house first? My mom would love to see you."

I nod. "Sounds good. I'll text you."

"Hey, check it out," he says, staring past me. I turn back toward the school and notice that Sarah is coming out of the double front doors.

"You should go see if she wants to walk home with you," he says, a small smile on his face. I blush, cursing myself that I can't control it, and the smile broadens. I swear an actual twinkle pings off his scrunched-up eye.

"You think you're adorable, don't you?" I ask.

"I'm just your friendly neighborhood Cupid," he says. Then he spins on a heel and sprints away without looking back. I look after him, grinning as he disappears around a corner, then turn in the other direction, ready to leave. I'm assuming Sarah is already gone, but then I see her across the parking lot, walking away in the direction of our neighborhood. She's close enough that I could catch up with her pretty easily, but for some reason I hesitate, and soon she's turned a corner and the opportunity has passed.

15.

The morning air is colder and a bit thicker than it was last night. It sure feels like some weather is moving in.

I arrive at Burke's house a half hour before the search is supposed to begin. Cars are already lining Red Spruce Lane and the surrounding streets, people sitting inside them with their engines on, hands cupped round their takeout coffees. I climb the steps of the O'Donnells' split-level and ring the bell. While I wait, I glance across the street at my old house. The Gerrard house now, I suppose. There are several cars in the driveway, and through the sheer curtains in the front window, I can see people moving about. Extended family, I guess. Friends from out of town. Everything I've heard about the Gerrards suggests that they didn't know many people in Redfields yet.

The door in front of me is yanked open, and Burke's mother, Marion, pushes the screen door open for me. I catch it and step inside as she puts both hands to her cheeks and shakes her head, a look of complete awe on her face, as if I've just returned from ten years at sea.

"Jesus, Mary, and Joseph, Delia," she says, reaching up to give me a big bear hug. "I can't believe how quickly you've grown up."

Her reaction is a bit over-the-top, considering I saw her at the grocery store just a few weeks ago, but it doesn't come as a surprise. Burke's mom is dependably over-the-top.

"Come on in," she says. "We're just finishing breakfast."

I kick my boots off into the giant pile beside the door and follow her across the thick carpeting of the family room into the kitchen. On the other side of the kitchen, Burke is sitting at the large, battered wooden table, engrossed in a comic book.

He glances up at me. "Hey, Dee, I'm almost done."

A small man sits in the corner, hunched over a plate of toast and looking at something on his phone.

"Delia, do you remember my brother-in-law, Terry?" asks Mrs. O'Donnell.

The man looks up at me and lifts a hand halfheartedly off the table in greeting.

"Yeah," I say. "Kind of. From when I was a kid."

"How you doing?" Terry asks. It's a brief, obligatory snippet of politeness, not a question I'm expected to answer. He returns to his phone.

"You ready to go?" I ask Burke, unwilling to get caught up in a conversation about Sibby.

Burke peels himself away from the comic and pushes his

chair back, pushing to get around from the back of the table. "Yeah," he says. "I just want to show you something in my room first."

I follow him down to the basement. His room is walled up into the back corner. Just like he said, Uncle Terry has taken over the rest of the basement. The couch is covered with blankets and pillows, and a giant, beat-up old duffel bag is sitting on top of the coffee table, ragged jeans and faded T-shirts and various mismatched socks pouring out of it onto the floor.

"It's like a tree fort," I say.

"Don't get me started," says Burke as we step into his room. To be fair, his bedroom isn't really all that different from Terry's camp on the couch, with clothes and papers strewn everywhere, but I know better than to point out the similarities.

Burke shuts the door behind him and immediately turns to me. "I listened to your show this morning," he says. "Why didn't you say anything about Layla?"

"I thought you don't listen," I say.

"I listened today," he says. "Because I wanted to hear what you'd say about it. You didn't even mention it! What the hell?"

"Come on, Burke. Do I really have to explain this to you?" I reach up and squeeze my temples, worried that this is going to turn into a headache. "It's not the right kind of case for *Radio Silent*."

"Not the right kind of case?" he repeats, and he sounds so upset that I take a step back.

"Shh," I say. "Please keep your voice down."

He rolls his eyes, points at the ceiling. "They can't hear us up there. Dee, a girl on my street is missing, a girl living in *your old house*, and you host a podcast that helps find missing people! Think about it. You'd be closer to the action than ever. You could get right into the thick of things."

"That's literally the opposite of what I want," I say. "You realize the entire reason I started the podcast was so I could stop obsessing over Sibby, right?"

"Yeah, but this isn't Sibby."

"It's close enough," I say. "*Too* close."

"You could still disguise your voice," he says. "Nobody would need to know it was you."

"That's not the point," I tell him. "My job is to tell the stories and then the internet takes over. It would be a totally different thing for me to get involved on the ground."

He scoffs. "Give me a break. You live in the same town, you used to live in her frigging house, for crying out loud. You were *there* when Sibby disappeared, and now you run a podcast devoted to exactly this kind of thing. It's almost like you were put here to solve this case."

I shake my head. "I'm not going to do it, Burke." And I realize as I'm telling him that I've made up my mind. "It's too close to home. I can't go there, and if you don't understand why, I'm not going to try to convince you."

He looks like he wants to keep arguing, but then he turns and drops into the chair at his desk. He points to another chair on the other side of the room.

"Pull up a seat," he says.

I use my elbow to push the pile of dirty laundry off the extra chair, because I'm sure some of that stuff hasn't been washed in weeks, and drag my chair over to the desk.

His computer is already open, and I can see that his browser is open to a fan-run *Radio Silent* message board.

"Why are you on here?" I ask him suspiciously.

"Because someone was abducted on my street, and I figured it made sense to check out what people were saying about it online. For one thing, a lot of people think *Radio Silent* should cover the case, not just me. For another thing, people have started picking up on the connection."

He turns and looks at me with an ominous lift of an eyebrow, and my heart begins to sink.

"Connection?" I ask, although I know already exactly what he's going to say.

He turns back to the computer and begins to read. "BeneaththeSurface17 writes: I'm kind of amazed that the media hasn't picked up on one of the craziest details about this case. A girl named Sibyl Carmichael disappeared into thin air from *the exact same street in the exact same small town* ten years ago. That can't be a coincidence."

I lean forward and put my face in my hands. "Shit. Shit, shit, shit, shit, shit."

"They haven't mentioned you anywhere. But..." He trails off, but his meaning is clear.

I lift my head and look at him. "But it's only a matter of time before every news crew in the country tracks me down."

He gives me a sympathetic look. "At least they can't use your name, right? Since you were a minor?"

"Everyone in town knows who I am," I say. "The media can hunt me down, ask for comments, make my life hell, as long as they don't print or announce my name."

Burke lifts a finger in the air and lifts his chin so he's peering down at me over the top of his glasses. "The good news is that there might be a more interesting story out there." He spins back around in his chair and scrolls down through the page. "Listen to this little tidbit, courtesy of old KarmaWillGetUsAll."

He clicks on a post and I lean in to read over his shoulder. I recognize the account name, KarmaWillGetUsAll, right away. She lives in San Diego and her real name is Penny Jenkins, a detail she included in one of her first emails. An email that she used to give me her credentials as a data analyst. She's forwarded me a few useful clues since I started *Radio Silent*.

"Mark my words," Burke reads from KarmaWillGetUsAll's post. "This is going to be cut-and-dried. Everything comes back to the father. I've found several outstanding loans in his name, along with evidence that this family had to leave their old home and move quickly to avoid being foreclosed on. My best bet is that someone was looking for repayment, made some threats, and the family tried to escape it. Now the chickens have come home to roost."

"That must be what Quinlee Ellacott was talking about last night," I say. "Remember her question about whether someone kidnapped Layla to get back at her father?"

He nods. "So if this is true," he says, "this means that there's a good chance that it wasn't some sadistic pervert who took Layla."

"Anyone who would kidnap a child is a sadistic pervert," I say.

"True, but don't you think that this sounds more promising? Like there might be an opening here to find her still alive?"

I think about this for a moment, then shake my head. Even if it's true that Layla was taken by someone who is trying to get back at her father, that doesn't mean this is going to end well.

Burke must take my silence as an opening. He turns around in his chair and leans forward, looking me right in the eye.

"Come on, Dee," he says. "Do an episode! The Laptop Detective Agency is already starting to dig around, even without your involvement. Imagine how quickly you can get this case solved if you *do* get involved! Don't you see that you're in the right place, at the right time, with a perfect opportunity to help?"

I stand up. "Burke, I am going to help." I realize that my fists are clenched so hard that my nails are digging into my palms. "I'm going to help right now, by joining this search party. Now are you coming or not?"

I leave his room without waiting for him, and after an exasperated sigh, he pushes out of his chair and follows me. In the entryway, we pull on our coats in silence. I can't tell if we're fighting, and to be honest, I don't care.

"Hang on a minute. I'm going to come with you." We turn to see Terry O'Donnell standing in the kitchen door, tucking his phone into his back pocket.

"Great," mutters Burke. His mother steps up behind Terry and shoots Burke a warning look.

"That's a great idea, Terry," she says. "I'm sure they can use all the help they can get."

"I'm just gonna grab my cigarettes," says Terry before heading down into the basement.

"This is the perfect morning for him," says Burke. "He can wander around outside and smoke and not have to listen to Mom vacuuming."

Terry thumps back up from the basement and joins us in the entryway. "You ready?" he asks.

Burke just rolls his eyes and steps out the front door in front of me onto the step. Terry is close behind us, shimmying into his boots and slamming the front door behind him. Together, we walk down the steps and toward the tent that's been set up by the cops near the road.

There are already a lot more people out than when I arrived. Every spot on the street is taken, and people are strolling together in groups from where they've parked on other blocks. I recognize a bunch of kids from school and plenty of teachers and other familiar faces too.

"Come on, gather 'round, people," booms a voice over the crowd. It's Chief Garber, standing by his cop car and speaking into a megaphone. "We're going to get started shortly. It's supposed to start snowing early this afternoon, so we don't want to waste time."

As he goes over the general plan, volunteers wander around handing out maps of the woods, divided into grids. The one we're handed has a section of the grid marked with a pink highlighter.

"Follow the volunteers who are wearing the color indicated on your map," says Garber. "That way we know that we're covering ground in equal measure. We're looking for clothes, new garbage like bottles or cigarette packages, anything that looks out of the ordinary. Signs of a struggle. Anything at all, come and find one of us in uniform and we'll try to keep track of things."

I glance around the crowd and notice for the first time how many cops there are. At least a couple of dozen, obviously here to help from other towns and counties.

"Narc central," mutters Burke, obviously reading my mind.

"What do you have to worry about?" asks Terry, giving him a jokingly suspicious look.

"Nothing that's any of your business," says Burke.

"I'm just joking around for chrissake," says Terry. "Man, you used to be such a cute kid. What the hell happened to you?"

Burke ignores him, and as the crowd begins to move into the forest, following our guides, he gestures to me to move away from his uncle. No sweat off my back. I step into line with Burke, and we're soon out of sight of Terry. We reach the tree line and stop, peering into the trees, at the figures of people moving slowly forward, like zombies.

We step into the woods.

16.

I haven't been back to these woods in almost ten years, when, a few days after Sibby's disappearance, I accompanied the police, along with my parents and a child psychologist hired by the cops, back to the site of the abduction.

The woods had always been our playground, a wild, free space where we'd been completely in charge. But on that day, our refuge was taken over by adults trampling over our pathways, crashing through our hidden dens. The air was thick with mist, and my father held me close to him as Detective Avery walked with us to the treehouse.

Until then, it had been a normal thing for us kids to push through one of the gates at the back of our yards and step into the quiet darkness of the friendly forest. We'd cut passageways through the trees and built little dens under the boughs of large evergreens, but on that morning, we headed straight for the treehouse, where I was asked to describe as much as I could about the people who took Sibby; their height and builds, the clothes they were wearing, which direction they'd come from, which direction they took her away.

I remember that trip better than the abduction itself. My parents' calm reassurances, the gently coaching questions from the psychologist, serious-faced forensic investigators methodically searching for clues.

I remember my rising panic as we approached the treehouse. My breakdown when we arrived. My screams and tears, the frantic attempts of my mother to talk me down, my father yelling at the police that he'd known this was a terrible idea. The psychologist kneeling in front of me, talking me down from my panic attack, encouraging me to breathe, to close my eyes, to listen to the memories.

But I could come up with no new description of the people who'd taken her, no details about Sibby's reaction, or where they'd come from or gone. Just a darkness around me, a dim flickering awareness of their receding footsteps. The squelch and crunch of shoes through the wet springtime leaves.

And then, as I stood there with the psychologist, a new memory appeared.

Just one: a voice. A clipped line, far enough away that I could hear it between Sibby's gasped cries. A man's voice, raspy and low.

"We've only got one chance at this. Now hurry up."

Back in the woods that day, I remembered it as clearly as if the kidnapper were leaning in from behind me, whispering directly into my ear.

You can describe a person's face, remember the details to a sketch artist, watch as they bring your memory to life on paper. But good luck trying to describe somebody's voice. You might as well try to explain someone's fingerprint.

That voice has haunted me forever. It runs through my mind at the oddest moments. In class. In the shower. When I'm out for a run. As vivid as anything else I've ever remembered and equally as useless. The cliffhanger at the end of a book, the last piece of an unfinished puzzle.

They tried their best. They asked me over and over again to think of something else that they could connect with the voice and begin to zone in on a culprit, but it was an impossible task. There's no other way to say it: I failed. But now, as we approach the ragged remains of the treehouse, I can hear that voice echoing through the trees as clearly as if it had just been said a few short terrifying moments ago.

* * *

All the snow we've had over the past few days means the search is going to be difficult. Any footprints will be obscured, and other clues will be hard to find. But the forest is still full of people eager to help.

We don't even know for sure that Layla was taken through the woods, although it's the safest bet. It would have been so easy for someone to pull over beside the highway, make their way through the forest, and take someone back the same way, without ever having to deal with the risk of eyewitnesses.

There's no indication that Layla's disappearance had

anything to do with the treehouse, but that's where I find myself walking, almost in a trance.

"Where are you going?" asks Burke as I begin to tread my way through the snow toward the huge maple tree where our house had been.

I don't answer, just gesture vaguely, not sure whether I want him to accompany me or not. He does, but I'm annoyed when I realize that Terry is also heading in the same direction, although he's hovering back far enough to not make it obvious.

This irritates Burke even more than it does me.

"I don't know what the hell he's trying to prove," he says, barely trying to stay out of Terry's earshot. "Nobody expects him to help, but if he has to, couldn't he follow someone else around the woods? It's not like I don't have to see him enough as it is."

"He's probably just as unsure of what to do as everyone is," I say. All around us, people are stepping carefully through the snow, between and around trees and tangles of bushes, stopping erratically to stare at the ground, into the crooks of branches, up and into the treetops, as if Layla might be floating above the woods, peeking down at us.

"He's unsure of how to live like a normal adult," Burke grumbles. He stops and points. "There it is."

I stop and stare ahead to where a maple tree sits in the middle of a stand of birches.

"That's not it," I say. "It's smaller than our tree."

"This is it," he insists. "You just grew faster than the tree did."

"There's no treehouse," I say.

"This is the tree." Terry has stepped up beside me and he points up into the branches. "Look."

Sure enough, there are a few rotting old boards arranged in the tree's bigger branches, what's left of the platform. I walk around to the other side of the tree and find the steps that were nailed onto it.

"This goddamn thing," says Terry, and Burke and I both turn to look at him, surprised at the anger in his voice. "You kids wouldn't have been in the woods at all if I hadn't built this stupid treehouse."

"You built it?" I ask, almost whispering, but I'm already remembering. Of course it was Terry who built the treehouse, Terry who corralled us kids together to collect old bits of lumber and put together a work party. He and his girlfriend, who I found so very glamorous.

"It was your girlfriend, wasn't it?" I ask Terry. "She had the idea to build a treehouse back here for all the kids. What was her name?"

"Sandy," says Burke. "I remember Sandy. She was at the movie with us too, wasn't she?"

"It was her idea," Terry replies. "I'm glad of it; otherwise, I would've been a suspect."

I'm shocked by this. What does he mean exactly?

He answers my question for me. "An itinerant, unemployed dirtbag like me? Who the hell else would they have pointed at?"

"Whatever happened to her?" asks Burke. "To Sandy."

Terry's face goes dark. "Didn't work out," he says. "She turned into a holy roller, got in with some religious nuts. We weren't together all that long."

"Too bad," says Burke. "She was really nice. Super pretty. I think I had a crush on her."

"Yeah, well, I'm sure it'll all be smooth sailing if you ever manage to score yourself a girlfriend," says Terry bitterly. He lights a cigarette and begins to walk around the old tree, kicking at bits of lumber that have rotted into the leaves.

I laugh. "He got you there, Burke," I say.

"Yeah, yeah, you can both screw off," says Burke. He turns around, scanning the ground. "So no signs of anything happening here, right?"

I look up at the rotten old structure. It's obvious that if Layla was in the woods, she didn't come here. Even if someone did want to climb the ladder, there's nowhere safe to sit once you get to the top. If there is a connection between her disappearance and Sibby's, the treehouse is not the common denominator.

Throughout the woods, people call to one another through the trees. Occasionally someone yells out Layla's name, as if she's playing hide-and-seek, and might just appear from behind a tree, safe and giggling.

"We should probably go out there and help with the search, hey?" asks Terry.

"Yeah," says Burke. "Why don't you go on ahead? We'll catch up with you later."

Terry gets the hint. He nods and then turns and continues on into the woods without a word.

"Let's go in the opposite direction," says Burke.

He turns as if to start walking away, but instead of following him, I reach out and put my hand on the tree's trunk. Everything around me seems to disappear, the sound of Burke speaking my name recedes into the distance, and the trunk seems to shrink and twist into the ground, or maybe it's me who is shrinking, back to that year, that spring, back to that small, shy person I was.

I close my eyes against the dizziness, lean forward to put my forehead against the tree, and try once again to remember. It feels close, so painfully close, closer than I've ever been before. But then it fades away, and once again, as always, nothing comes to me. No memories. No sudden flashes of insight. Just the awful voice I've spent more than half my life trying to forget:

We've only got one chance at this. Now hurry up.

"Dee?" Burke's voice is just behind my shoulder. "You all right?"

I drop my hand and step back from the tree. "I have to go," I say. "I can't stay here."

"Hey," he says, reaching out to put a hand on my arm. "It's okay."

I push past him and begin to run.

17.

I hear Burke yelling after me. "Dee! Are you okay? Delia!"

I turn. "I'm fine," I manage to call out. "I'll text you later!"

He hesitates, and I can tell he's considering following me, but I turn away and continue to the edge of the woods, and he must think better of it. When I glance back again a few seconds later, he's still just standing there, watching me leave.

When I finally step out of the trees, it takes me a moment to realize where I am. I'm in a backyard one door over from my old house, Layla's house. This one has obviously been neglected for a while, if the boarded windows and dilapidated back deck are any indication. I glance across at my house— Layla's house—and realize with a shock that there's a couple standing in the kitchen window, staring out through their backyard at the woods and the random collection of people wandering through the trees.

I freeze, and then the woman turns her head and looks out the side window at me. It's Layla's mother. She sees me, but her expression doesn't change; she just stares blankly at me before turning and putting her head back on her husband's shoulder.

I jerk out of my trance and hurry out of the yard and onto the street.

"Delia?" The voice comes out at me from nowhere and I jump. "Delia Skinner?" A man, probably in his late thirties, approaches me, smiling, his hand reached out to shake. I realize now that he's been standing on the sidewalk waiting for me.

"Who are you?" I ask. I don't have the time or the energy to be polite.

His smile doesn't fade, but he drops his hand. I realize that he's holding a notebook in the other one. "I'm sorry," he says. "I didn't mean to startle you. I'm Jonathan Plank with *The Brighton City Vanguard*."

"You're a reporter?"

He nods, and he looks almost sheepish. "Yeah, I'm here with the other media." He jabs a finger at his notebook, then gestures back to the cluster of news vans and well-coiffed men and women who are milling about holding microphones as if waiting to go onstage for their chance at karaoke.

"You all travel in a pack?" I ask, noticing them for the first time.

"No," he says. "We just kind of end up collecting together wherever there's a development, and right now this search is the most interesting thing happening with this story."

Story. I want to say it's not a story; it's a life, a bunch of lives, but I realize how hypocritical that would be, and so I keep my mouth shut, wondering what he wants from me. He must realize I'm not going to just start talking to him, and so he clears his throat.

"I heard someone call after you," he says. "I was just over here trying to collect my thoughts, and I heard that guy call your name."

"I'm just leaving," I say.

"You don't remember me, do you?" he asks. I don't, but he doesn't wait for my answer. "I wouldn't think so. You were so small, and it was such a crazy time."

"I don't know what you're talking about," I tell him, although I'm starting to get the idea.

"I was here," he says. "Ten years ago. I'd just started at the *Vanguard*, and they sent me in to do a series of stories on the aftermath of the disappearance. I mean, I was here when it was happening, but I came back a year later. I came to your house, your new house. You and your father were going inside from the car. I think you'd been grocery shopping."

"I didn't talk to any reporters," I say. "I was a minor. Still *am* a minor. You shouldn't know my name, let alone be talking to me."

"I know that," he says, "but your name was common knowledge among all of us back then. This is a small town. We weren't allowed to mention you by name in our stories, but we were allowed to print comments from your family if they came willingly. I tried calling, emailed both of your parents, talked to the neighbors, but nobody would give me the time of day."

"I don't have anything to say to you now either," I tell him, turning away.

"They'll find out," he says. I stop, waiting for him to finish. "Someone will make the connection between this case and the Sibby Carmichael case, and then they'll come looking for you."

"You haven't told them?" I ask. I glance past him at the news crews lined up, waiting for something sexy to film. I notice for the first time that he doesn't quite fit their image. In his rumpled clothes, gripping his grubby little notebook, he looks more like a substitute teacher than an ambitious reporter.

"No. So far nobody has made the connection, and to tell you the truth, that gives me a leg up on them. Talk to me. Just do the one interview, and we'll call it an exclusive. That'll keep the rest of the vultures from hunting you down."

My mouth drops at his audacity. "I don't have anything to do with this," I say. "And I don't want to talk to anyone. It's not my style."

He looks like he's trying to decide whether it's worth pushing me further, but then his eyes shoot past me, and I turn to see my old neighbor Mrs. Rose standing in the half-open doorway of her house, just a few feet back from us.

"Delia?" she calls out. "Is that you?"

"Yes, Mrs. Rose," I say, deeply grateful for her timing.

"Come in for some cookies, will you?"

She doesn't need to ask me twice. I move toward her porch.

"Wait," says Plank. He reaches into his pocket and pulls out a card, hands it to me. "If you decide you want to talk, call me. I'll be in town for a while."

I take his card and shove it into my pocket without looking

at it. Then I turn and walk up Mrs. Rose's steps and follow her inside without looking back.

Mrs. Rose has been living on this street since this development was first created. She and her husband bought the house when it was built, and after he died, she stayed. I never met Mr. Rose. By the time I was old enough to remember, he was dead and she was the nice old lady on our street. She liked to sit outside on her porch, drinking iced tea and watching us kids play. On Halloween, she would have special bags of treats for all of the neighborhood kids.

When I walk into the house, I'm hit with a wave of nostalgia. Her kitchen looks exactly the same as it always has: pink-and-turquoise wallpaper, checkerboard tiles on the floor, the giant Boston fern hanging in the corner between two windows. All of it brings up long-hidden memories.

Against one wall is a chrome table with a cheerful yellow top, and I have a sudden image of sitting at this table while Mrs. Rose poured tea and chatted. Was I with my mother? It couldn't have been; my mother wasn't the "hang out with old ladies and drink tea" type.

Then it hits me. I didn't visit with my mother. I visited with Sibby and *her* mother. I remember sitting in the living room with Sibby, no television, flipping through the books on the shelves, mostly romances and travel stories, playing with her little dog. Turning back to the kitchen door as Mrs. Rose entered with a plate of warm cookies, smiling.

But as I glance around the room, the vibrancy of the colors dims, and I realize that the kitchen is actually much dingier than I remember. The smell is different too. Not the warm spice of cookies and the soft powder of an old lady's bedroom, but a sour, dank smell—the scent of decay and neglect.

Mrs. Rose gestures for me to sit, then grabs a kettle from the stove and walks over to the sink to fill it. "What did that man want?" she asks. There's no attempt to catch up; she talks as if I step into her house every day, as if the last time we've spoken wasn't almost a decade ago.

"He's a reporter," I say, dropping gratefully into a chair at her small chrome and Formica table. I remember the table, too, as the fanciest I'd ever seen. The speckled, gleaming, lemon-yellow top, the shiny, grooved chrome edge and the metal maple leaves applied halfway down each leg. But now the yellow surface is stained and chipped, and the chrome around the edge is rusty. When I lean forward to put my chin in my hands, the table wobbles and I quickly pull back and sit up straight in my chair.

"Careful with the table," says Mrs. Rose, walking across to put a plate of cookies in front of me. "One of the legs is loose, so you can't put too much weight on it."

She sits across from me and waits as I pick a cookie up from the plate. It's store bought, not the warm homemade ones from my memory, but it's good, and I realize I'm hungry. I inhale the first one and reach for another, and Mrs. Rose smiles, as if this is what she's been waiting for.

"A reporter," she repeats, picking up the loose thread. "Lots of reporters around these days. Reminds me of when that little girl went missing. Carmichael girl. Did you know her?"

I stare at her, wondering if she's joking, but she doesn't look like she's joking. She just looks a bit spacey, as if she's trying to place a memory. Could she really not remember what happened?

"Yeah," I say. "We were good friends."

"She lived across the street," she says, sounding pleased that she's made the connection. "And you lived a couple of doors over from me."

"That's right," I say. "She and I visited you once, I think. With her mother maybe?"

She frowns. "I don't know, dear. My memory isn't what it used to be."

"You had a little dog?"

Her eyes brighten, and she reaches out to rap the table twice. "I did indeed. I did. Tippy. If you remember Tippy, you must be right. You must have been here after all. It's been seven years since Tippy died. My husband brought him home for me, a gift, then he up and died six months later. Not sure which one of them I miss the most."

It's a very sad thing to say, but she sounds almost cheerful about it.

"Come with me," she says, standing up, not giving me an option to refuse.

I step after her into the living room, and I see for the first time that the entire place is packed with stuff. Cardboard boxes stacked haphazardly on top of each other, piles of magazines, clear garbage bags stuffed with blankets and sheets and clothes. The only clear surface in the room is a ratty-looking old armchair that's been shoved into a corner, directly opposite a huge old TV built into a wooden cabinet. Mrs. Rose, I realize, has become a hoarder.

She doesn't seem to register my discomfort at this state of things. Instead, she continues down a hallway, and after a moment, I follow. The hallway is also full of stuff, boxes and plastic cartons and overflowing bookshelves. She pushes open a door, and we walk into a small bedroom, equally crammed. *Where does she find this stuff?* I wonder.

"Tippy," she says, and I realize that she's standing next to a small framed photograph of a tiny white dog.

"Oh yeah!" I say with forced cheerfulness, trying to hide the weirdness of the scene.

She gazes fondly at the photo for another few seconds, then her gaze shifts to the window. She pulls back the curtain and peeks out, then beckons me over with a finger, as if she's about to tell me a secret.

"Look out here," she says.

I join her at the window and realize we're looking out into the backyard I just walked through. The empty beige split-level that sits on the other side of Mrs. Rose's house from my old house. The DaQuinzios used to live there, but I think they moved out a few years after we left the neighborhood, and from the looks of it—broken glass, a sagging roof, and stained siding—it hasn't had anyone living in it for quite a while.

"It's been empty for years," she says. "The police were very interested in it."

I perk up. "They were?"

She nods. "They spent a lot of time in there after they realized that girl was missing."

I look at her, wondering if she means Layla, or if she's still stuck in the past, thinking of Sibby. She seems to know what

I'm thinking, because she says, "The new one. The family who just moved in a couple of months ago."

"The Gerrards," I say, and she nods.

"Nice family. The father saw me trying to clear off my step one day and came over to help right away. Told me to let him know if I needed help with anything, so I asked him to come back and move some things around for me. Too many boxes. Hard to get rid of things. He brought the girl with him, and I gave her some cookies. Smart little thing."

I glance back out the window at the empty house next door. "What were the police doing in the house next door?" I ask.

"Not rightly sure," she says. "I watched them from here. They were in and out of the back door. Back and forth through my backyard too."

I can see that underneath the deck that juts out from the back of the DaQuinzios' split-level, there's a small utility door. It's mostly sheltered from view, and from that door, it would only be a few steps across Mrs. Rose's driveway, into her backyard, and into my old house, where the Gerrards live.

It also doesn't escape my notice how easy it would be to then take someone back through the shrubs and bushes in Mrs. Rose's wildly overgrown yard and straight into the woods. There's no question that the empty house would have made taking Layla a lot easier.

She nods. "I pretended I wasn't listening, but I was. They think that girl was taken into that house first, then whisked away into the woods." She leans in toward me conspiratorially. "They think the kidnapper might have used my yard."

Beyond the back of the two yards, I can still see people milling through the forest. On the street, I'm sure, there are still reporters. I wonder if that man, Jonathan Plank, is still standing on the sidewalk, waiting for me to come outside.

I step away from the window and sit down on the bed, suddenly exhausted, weary at what waits for me outside. Mrs. Rose lets the curtain drop and looks at me, concerned.

"You look tired, dear," she says.

I nod. "Yeah. I am. I'm just…"

"Why don't you lie down and have a little nap?" she says. "I'm sure this has been quite a day for you."

"Oh I couldn't," I say. "I should really go home." But even as I protest, I find myself lying down, putting my head on the pillow, and it must be only seconds before I've fallen into a deep sleep.

18.

Sibby is sitting beneath the window, cross-legged, playing with the little white dog.

I sit up in bed and prop myself on my elbows, and she looks up at me, smiling.

"This dog is dead," she says. It barks at her, agreeing.

"You haven't grown up," I tell her. "You look the same as you did then."

She giggles and stands up. "Your memory is messed up," she says. "Watch. I'll show you how old I really am."

She moves toward the door.

"Wait!" I say, panicked. "Don't go!"

She smiles at me. "I'll be right back. I just need to change, so you can see how different I am now."

She steps out of the room, and the door closes with a little click. I glance at the floor and realize the dog is gone.

"Sibby?" I whisper.

I get out of bed, stepping carefully, quietly. I don't want to wake up Mrs. Rose. I don't want Sibby to know that I'm following her.

I open the door and step through, but I'm not in the hallway. I'm in my bedroom. It's dimly lit, just the light of my laptop glowing through the gloom. I sit down in front of it and put my headphones on, then pull my microphone toward me across the desk. I tap the mic, which sends a hollow echo into my ears, then press record.

"This is *Radio Silent*," I begin. "I hope you're out there, Sibby. I hope you're listening."

Something is off. I stop recording and return to the beginning of the timeline, pressing play.

The voice that speaks back at me is a child's voice. My own, seven years old. Unfiltered.

I jerk awake, slapped with panic as I take in my unfamiliar surroundings, then a long let-out breath as I remember where I am. My phone tells me I've been asleep for over two hours, and there's a text from Burke asking if I'm okay. I'll text him back later.

Mrs. Rose is in the living room, sitting in front of the television, watching some stupid game show. She looks up as I step into the room and smiles.

"Thank you," I say. "For letting me sleep."

"That's quite all right, dear. We all need a good nap now and then."

I glance past her at the picture window that looks out onto the street. The news vans are gone, as are the throngs of vehicles from earlier today.

"Is the search over?" I ask.

"Seems to be," she says, not taking her eyes from the TV. "I doubt they found anything, or it would have been on the news."

"Well," I say, "I think I should probably get home." I wonder if I'm being rude, just picking up and leaving like this when she's been so kind, but Mrs. Rose seems completely content where she is.

"It was nice to see you, Delia," she says. "Come by anytime."

As I follow the narrow path between boxes and bags and piles of stuff to get to the door, I think with a twinge of guilt that it's unlikely I'll be back. I can only imagine how crowded with crap her basement must be if there's this much stuff overflowing in the living area of the house.

It's started to snow by the time I get outside. Tiny, sparkling molecules puncturing the crisp, dry, suddenly very cold air. I remember something my mother used to say—*little flakes, big snow*—and I wonder if that means we're in for a dump.

I pull my phone out and see that I've just gotten a text from my father.

> Heading out to pick up the boys and take them to this afternoon's game. Mom working late. Lunch in the fridge.

As I walk home, I realize I feel more rested and relaxed than I have all week.

It doesn't last.

As I round the corner onto my street, I notice a news van parked outside my house. I stop in my tracks, wondering if I can turn back without being noticed, but it's too late. The passenger door opens and a flash of red swirls toward me.

"Delia Skinner?" Quinlee Ellacott, moving astonishingly fast down the icy sidewalk for someone in heels, approaches with her microphone thrust out in front of her like a sword. Behind her, a young woman gets out of the driver's seat, hoisting a camera over her shoulder and hurrying to keep up.

My skin crawls as I register the predatory look in Quinlee's eyes. Has she made the connection between me and the podcast, or is this just an awful coincidence? I put my head down and duck past her, moving toward my front door, but she and the cameraperson spin around on their heels and follow me.

"Delia!" Quinlee yells. "Dee? Do you prefer Dee? People are wondering, do you think this new case is somehow connected to the disappearance of Sibby Carmichael? Are you worried for your safety?"

I realize that Quinlee has deftly stepped around so that she's now on my other side, in the middle of the sidewalk to my front door. Her camera operator is also good at this, and together the two of them duck and weave, blocking me from my path, like a couple of sheepdogs.

"Excuse me," I mutter, trying to move past her. With practiced agility, she walks backward down the sidewalk, leaving me no room to get around.

"Delia, what do you remember about that day in the woods? Do you have any information that could help Layla Gerrard?"

"You can't use my name," I say. "I was a minor then, and I'm still a minor now."

She smiles, and the effect is of a predator honing in on prey. "Delia, darling, you know that the internet is a wild, chaotic place, right? You're absolutely right that I can't use your name in my broadcasts, but I can't help it if someone takes it on themselves to drop your name into the comments or quote tweets it out along with one of my videos. Privacy is dead, sweetheart. You're far too interesting to stay hidden."

"You're an awful person," I say. "Why won't you just leave me alone?"

"I'm just doing my job," she says, taking a half step toward me. "I'm giving people the news, and like it or not, you're part of the news. Come on, Delia. Let me interview you. We'll blur your face. We'll even alter your voice."

The thought that my voice could be altered and sent out into the world terrifies me. What if the effect is similar enough that someone connects me to the Seeker? My lower jaw starts to shake uncontrollably. I'm blank. I want to get away from here, but I don't have the will to push her out of the way.

The noise comes out of nowhere. A long bellow that seems composed of three sounds at once, a low guttural moan, an insistent holler, and a high-pitched, ear-piercing shriek. Quinlee reaches up and yanks her earpiece out, a horrified grimace on her face, her microphone dropping to the ground next to her. She scrambles to her knees to pick it up, and I notice the camerawoman glance past me and then hurrying to get out of the way.

The noise continues, and as awful as it is, I'm so grateful for it that I don't mind if it keeps going all day. I turn around and realize what I've been hearing. A distinctive blue and silver Nova is crawling down the street toward me, and Sarah Cash is behind the wheel with a determined grimace on her face, pressing insistently on the horn. She stops next to me and opens her window.

"You coming or what?" she yells over the sound of the horn.

She doesn't need to ask me twice. I hurry around the car and slide into the passenger seat.

As Quinlee hurries toward the car, her camera operator close behind, Sarah presses down on the horn again.

"Duck down," she says. "Don't give them anything they can use."

I take her advice, crouching forward and putting my head in my hands. She presses on the gas, and we lurch forward. As we pass the news van, she gives another quick blare of the horn, and then we're around the corner and off.

"You're cool," she says. "We're out of the minefield."

I sit up, intending to respond, but the words don't come to me, and it's only now that I realize that I'm trembling. She glances over at me and shakes her head.

"What an asshole," she says. "As if it wasn't crystal clear that you didn't want to talk to her. Not that it makes a whole lot of difference to the leeches. You want a smoke or something?"

I manage to shake my head. I close my eyes and take a few deep breaths. I'm glad that Sarah doesn't say anything while I collect myself. When I open my eyes again, she's cruising along Main Street, one hand thrown casually over the steering wheel, the other at her head, fingers running through her hair.

"I didn't realize you smoked," I say.

"I don't," she says. "It just seemed like the right thing to ask."

I laugh, surprised that I'm finding anything funny right

now. "Thanks," I say. "Seriously. I should have been able to just walk around her, but I froze."

"Well, at least she didn't get anything she can use," she says. She presses on the horn twice quickly, releasing two blasts of noise. "They don't make car horns obnoxious like they used to. So where are we going?"

"I don't know," I say. "What do you have in mind?"

"Let's just drive," she says, "and see where we end up."

I'm relieved that Sarah doesn't ask me about what happened, as we drive out of town. Instead, she hands me her phone and tells me to pick out whatever I want to listen to, and as I skim through her music, happy for the distraction, she talks to me. It's not like she's trying to fill up an awkward silence; instead, she's easy, smooth, and comfortable to talk to, as if there's nothing weird about what just happened. As if having a sensationalistic news reporter show up on your doorstep is something that happens to all of us every few months or so.

About ten miles out of town, she slows and pulls off at a rest stop, a gas station with a diner built into the side.

"Come on," she says. "My treat."

We navigate around the slushy puddles that have collected against the parking lot curb. My boots are frosted with white already from the buildup of salt.

Inside, the diner is warm and comforting, almost empty. Old country music is playing on the stereo, and we slide into a booth that's up against a wide window that catches the cold winter sun and turns it into a warm greenhouse of a space. When the waitress, an elderly woman who strolls over to the table in her own damn time, offers menus, Sarah looks at me.

"You hungry?"

"Not really."

She smiles at the waitress but holds out her hand to refuse the menus.

"Just a couple of coffees, please."

The waitress walks away without comment. A moment later, she walks back with a pot of coffee and reaches in to flip our mugs right-side up. With a practiced flourish, she reaches in with the pot and fills us each up, then walks away without a word.

"Delightful," says Sarah, holding the mug to her face and inhaling deeply. "Garbage coffee is my favorite."

I take a sip. It's superhot and bitter, not nearly as good as the coffee they serve at Fresh Brews, or the stuff my parents make for that matter. But Sarah is obviously enjoying hers so much that I can't help but smile.

She puts her mug back down on the table and cups her hands around it, warming them.

"So. You going to tell me what happened to you?" she asks, staring across the table at me.

I drop my head, wondering how to even begin with a question as loaded as that. I half expect her to laugh, to apologize for her phrasing, tell me she didn't mean to say it that way, but when I look up across the table at her, she's still looking at me intently, and I realize that she meant the question exactly the way she asked it.

"Do you remember when you asked me about the girl who went missing ten years ago?" I begin.

She nods, clearly curious about where I'm going with this.

"Sibby was my best friend," I say. "I was there when she went missing."

I have to stop for a moment to think about how to begin because I realize that I've never had to explain this to anyone. Everyone in this town, everyone in my whole life, has always known what happened to me.

Sarah stares at me, waiting for me to continue. I take a breath, and then for the first time in ten years, I tell *my* story.

19.

TEN YEARS EARLIER

This far into the forest, things are quiet and still. The wind moves lightly along the tops of the trees, so that the canopy high above them rustles lightly, but distant enough that the noise only serves to make it feel calmer and quieter in the treehouse.

The fort, as Dee had suspected, isn't as much fun with just the two of them. For a while, they sit up in the treehouse, which is really just a platform and two walls. When everyone else is here, they can play games like Capture the Castle and Space Station, but that isn't possible with just Dee and Sibby, and so they end up just sitting there.

"Maybe we should just go back and play at my house," says Dee.

"No!" says Sibby, panicked at the thought of leaving. "We can play something here!"

"Like what?" asks Dee, skeptical.

Sibby thinks about it for a minute. "Hide-and-seek!" she says.

"We can't play hide and seek with just two of us," says Dee. "That won't work."

"Sure it will!" insists Sibby. "One of us will stay up here and count to a hundred, and the other one will hide."

"That doesn't make any sense," says Dee. "You need a bunch of people for hide-and-seek."

"Not this kind," says Sibby. "Just trust me. You count first, and I'll go hide. Once you find me, we'll switch."

Dee thinks that sounds kind of stupid, but she knows better than to argue with Sibby when she's decided on something like this. It's a waste of energy.

"Okay," she says.

"Great," says Sibby. She gets up and goes to the edge of the platform and begins to climb down the ladder. "Don't start counting until I'm on the ground," she says before her head disappears over the edge.

"I won't," says Dee.

A moment later, she hears a light thud as Sibby jumps from the bottom of the ladder and hits the ground. "Okay!" she yells. "Start counting!"

Dee hears Sibby run away, giggling, her feet crunching on dead leaves. Even though she's backed up against one of the walls and can't see over the edge, Dee puts her face in her hands anyway, because it would feel like cheating not to.

One hundred. Ninety-nine. Ninety-eight.

The footsteps become fainter, and then slow down, as

Sibby begins to move more deliberately. Dee wonders if Sibby is trying to fake her out.

Seventy-four. Seventy-three. Seventy-two.

There's no noise at all now, just the rustling of the trees high above. Dee feels a chill as a small gust of breeze rushes through the trees and into the treehouse. She knows Sibby is out there, hiding behind one of the big old maples or underneath the boughs of a spruce, but she isn't comfortable here by herself. She begins to speed up her counting.

Fifty-oneFiftyForty-NineForty-eight...

Another noise breaks through her concentration, and Dee stops counting abruptly. Footsteps have picked up again, crunching quickly through the underlayer, heavy and determined. Not close, exactly, but loud. Much louder than Sibby's footsteps. And more of them?

Then another sound. A yelp, a short, surprised scream, like a dog that's had its paw stepped on accidentally. But it's not a dog. It's Sibby.

Dee thinks she hears voices, muffled, and she wonders if maybe Sibby's parents have come to get her.

Nothing about this feels right, and Dee stands, scared, and moves to the edge of the platform. She crouches and shifts around so she can push her way over the edge and catch the ladder. She scurries down the rungs of wood that have been nailed to the tree and hops to the ground.

The noises have stopped, but they don't feel gone. They feel paused. Is Sibby watching her from somewhere, playing a joke?

"Sibby?" Dee calls out tentatively. No response. Dee takes

a few steps away from the treehouse, moving in the direction that she's pretty sure Sibby ran in. "Sibby?" she calls again.

Dee walks faster, her heart pounding in her chest. She thinks she'll be furious if Sibby *is* playing a joke. But even as she thinks it, she knows it isn't a joke. There's nothing funny about this.

Dee stops as the sound of footsteps picks up again. They're moving toward her, branches snapping and the light between the thick stand of trees shifting and her heart pounding and then, like a monster from a horror movie, a figure steps out and stands in front of her about twenty feet away.

It's a man. Or at least Dee *thinks* it's a man. It's hard to tell for sure because whoever it is, is wearing a ski mask, a black wool cap that pulls down under the chin, with holes for the eyes and mouth. She registers a bulky gray jacket and jeans, but that's all she has time to take in because the figure suddenly lunges at her, and Dee screams and ducks out of the way as he reaches for her, and then she runs.

She knows he'll catch her. She knows it even as she picks up her speed, moving as fast as her legs will carry her, branches scratching her face and yanking her hat off her head. She focuses on her boots, imagines them carrying her away from those people, out of the woods, up her front steps, and through her front door. She imagines them taking her all the way home.

She does *not* think of Sibby. Everything is happening so quickly that all she has time to think is *must get away* and so she tries to do that, to get away, until all of a sudden she pushes into a small clearing that she recognizes right away, because even though she feels like she's been running forever, she knows that this clearing is actually really close to the tree-house, which means she's been running in circles, and then she turns around and everything else *except* Sibby leaves her mind.

Because Sibby is in front of her, just a few feet away, and her eyes are wide and pleading when she sees Dee, but her mouth is covered with duct tape, and there's another figure in a ski mask, big and tall and holding Sibby, who has been tied around the arms so that she can't move.

Dee stands, frozen for a long moment, and then the blood rushes back into her head and she begins to scream at the top of her lungs, and then a hand clamps over her mouth from behind.

Everything happens very quickly after that. Dee allows herself to go slack, the fight gone out of her, and duct tape goes over her mouth too, and the man holding Sibby digs into a duffel bag on the ground and pulls out some rope that he tosses to the man holding Dee. The next thing Dee knows, she's being taken to a tree and pushed down to sit on the ground with her back to it, and then she's being tied to the trunk.

The two figures in the ski masks don't say anything to each other, but they appear to be communicating with their eyes. Once Dee is tied tight to the tree, the man stands and walks over to where Sibby and the other man are standing.

Then the taller man is picking up Sibby and tossing her over his shoulder like a sack of potatoes, and although Sibby wriggles and tries to get away, she's so much smaller than the man, and he's so much stronger, that she gives up almost immediately.

The other man, the one who tied up Dee, picks up the duffel bag and slings it onto his back like a backpack.

The man holding Sibby turns and begins to walk, and Sibby catches Dee's eyes, and for a moment that seems burned in time, they stare at each other, and then she's being carried into the forest, away from the treehouse, away from the path back to the neighborhood, away from Dee.

There's a pause, and then the other man takes a step to follow, but he stops. He turns back to look at Dee, seems to hesitate.

The other man stops and turns back halfway.

"We've only got one chance at this. Now hurry up," he says.

The man looking at me just shakes his head, then turns to follow, and they disappear into the forest.

Dee listens to the sounds of them leaving, getting more distant with every second, until she can't hear them at all.

Until she's alone.

20.

I go quiet. That's the story. That's what happened as far as I remember it. I expect Sarah to start in with an interrogation, a thousand questions about what happened next, how hard searchers looked. How much I was able to help them out.

Instead, she just looks at me with what must be sympathy. Her calm response would be almost unsettling, if I didn't appreciate it so much.

"So," I say, because I need the silence broken, "it's pretty messed up, hey?"

She nods her head slowly. "How long were you there?"

"Almost three hours," I tell her. "It was getting dark, and when we hadn't come back home, Sibby's dad came into the woods looking for us. He found me, but by that time she was long gone."

"It must have been terrifying," Sarah says quietly.

"Afterward, it was," I say. "But while it was happening I… I know this sounds weird, but I wasn't really even scared. I mean, I must have been, but I don't remember feeling that way. Part of it was probably shock. Part of it was just…I don't know, the concept of being stolen or hurt by strangers never crossed my mind. Not even for a moment. We'd been playing that game, and I was in that headspace, and I don't know…" I trail off.

"It was like it became part of the game," she finishes.

I nod. "Yeah, pretty much."

"And now everyone's looking for you to relive it all," she says. "The reporters. The police."

"Everyone," I say. "They want me to tell them something that will help, and the truth is, I don't have anything to tell them. Usually, I don't care what people think of me. When people like Brianna Jax-Covington decide to stick their noses in where they don't belong, I don't have time for that," I say. "You think I'm stuck-up? Fuck you, I don't care."

Across the table, Sarah pulls her head back slightly and smiles at me, as if trying to figure me out.

"You think I'm surly? Fuck you, I don't care. You think I'm unpleasant? That I don't smile enough? That my best friend is a waste-of-space pothead? Fuck you, fuck you, and fuck you. I don't fucking care."

I glance at her, worried that I might be sounding a bit unhinged, but she's smiling at me as if I've just said something totally normal.

"I think I get the picture," she says. "You don't care what people think of you."

"Except for this," I say. "Except when it comes to Sibby.

That's the place where I think everyone is right. I should have done something."

"Dee," she says. She begins to lean across the table, but when I flinch, she stops and withdraws. "Nobody thinks that. Literally nobody."

"Well, they all think I have something to say," I tell her.

"Sure, of course they do," she says. "It's a good story. I mean, *I* don't think it's good; I think it's awful, but it's the kind of story that people want to talk about. Why do you think people listen to that podcast I told you about? Because they're drawn to these stories. They want to help, and maybe people want to help you." Her eyes widen, as if she's just realized something. "You should contact them, tell them about Sibby. Explain the connection to Layla. I bet you anything that this is the kind of case the Seeker would want to investigate."

The podcast, again. I want, so badly, to tell her. To talk to someone other than Burke. Someone who understands. Who cares. Who listens.

I think about the night I started the podcast, how all I wanted to do was help. I glance up and allow myself to look her in the eye for the first time since I finished telling my story. We hold each other's gaze, and I realize that I wasn't telling the truth. Maybe I do care what some people think about me. What she thinks about me.

This could be the perfect moment, and Sarah could be the perfect person to explain everything to. Someone who isn't Burke, who wasn't part of it.

Instead, I sigh and drop my eyes again. I reach for my phone to check the time and see that I have a DM from Carla Garcia.

I want to read it now, but I don't want to be rude. It can wait until I get home, which I realize is exactly where I want to be.

"Can we get out of here?" I ask. "I'm kind of exhausted. It's been an intense day."

"Of course." She nods, as if nothing weird has happened, as if I haven't just told her the most messed-up story she's heard all year. "Let's go."

We stand, pulling on our gloves and hats, shrugging into our jackets. She leaves cash on the table and then I follow her out of the truck stop into the glaring January sunshine.

I brace myself as we turn onto our street, preparing myself to face the throng of aggressive reporters, but they're gone.

"Too bad," says Sarah. "I was kind of looking forward to pissing them off with the horn again. I guess it worked the first time."

I nod vaguely, but I have an uneasy feeling it's not that simple. I'm happy that they're gone, but I'm worried about why they're gone. Has something more interesting happened to draw their attention?

"Thanks for getting me out of there," I say as I step out of her car.

She smiles at me from across the roof. "It was good to hang out with someone. I was worried I was going to have to become friends with Brianna. Do it again soon?"

"That would be great," I say. I wonder how she means it. Are we friends or something more than that? I'd be happy with either option, but I know which one I'd prefer given the choice. I hesitate. "It was really good to have someone to talk to," I say.

Sarah reaches out and puts her hand on my shoulder. "Dee," she says, and her stare is direct and sincere, "I am literally always here if you need to talk. Always."

I smile and turn to get out of the car.

When I get to my front door, I turn to glance back at her. She's looking back at me, and I blush, happy that she's far enough away that she can't see me. We wave, and I step inside.

I pull off my coat and boots, and then walk in my socked feet into the kitchen. My dad has left a sandwich in the fridge for me, and I pull it out and peel off the plastic wrap. I sit at the counter to eat, and open Carla's chat window on my phone.

hi there, wondering if we can get online to chat as soon as you have a minute? I've learned something...

I message her back, intrigued.

Definitely. I just got home and going to eat quickly. Can we do it in 10 minutes?

Carla responds almost right away.

Yep, I'll be here.

The doorbell rings, and I'm jerked away from my phone. I go to the front door and look through the window. To my surprise, Burke is on the porch, fidgeting. He's about to press the doorbell again when I open the door.

"Hey," I say, confused.

"Can I come in?"

"Sure." He follows me to the kitchen, and I push the plate with half a sandwich across to him. "You want some of this?"

He just shakes his head, impatient. "Have you heard the news?"

"No," I say. "Did something happen with Layla?"

"It's Uncle Terry," he says in a rush. "They came and took him away today, right after we got home from the search. My parents are a total mess."

"Wait, what?" I ask.

"They think he took Layla. They found some stuff in the empty house next to your old place. They think he was using it to spy on the Gerrards."

"You mean the DaQuinzios' house?" I ask. "I heard the cops were interested in it."

"Who told you that?" he asks, frantic.

"Mrs. Rose," I say.

He looks at me blankly, trying to process.

"It doesn't matter," I say. "What did they find?"

"They're calling it his den," he says. "There was an armchair in there, and some old magazines and an ashtray full of butts. Some empty liquor bottles. The bedroom had a full view of the Gerrard house. From the window, you could look directly into Layla's room." He runs his hand through his hair. "It sounds bad, Dee."

"Are they sure it was him?" I ask.

"He's denying it, but they found a notebook," he says. "His handwriting was all over it, and…and newspaper clippings."

"What kind of clippings?"

Burke's face looks even more miserable. "They were old. A bunch of stories about Sibby's disappearance, follow-up stories from months and even years later."

"What the hell?" I ask. "What does that even mean? Why would he have those?"

Burke just shakes his head. "I have no idea, but that's not even the worst of it. Apparently, they've found evidence that Layla was in the room too. It's got to be some kind of awful coincidence. I mean, I don't like Terry, but he wouldn't do something like this!"

"This is messed up," I say.

"You're telling me. I had to get out of there, Dee. I'm not even allowed in my room because there are cops in the basement, searching through Terry's shit." He rubs his hands through his hair. "I can't believe this. I mean, I can't stand Uncle Terry, he's such a loser, but I don't want him to go to jail. I know he didn't do anything to that girl. Dee, you need to do a podcast about this. You need to help find out who really did it."

"Burke, I can't," I say. "I wouldn't be any help."

"What do you mean?" he asks, obviously frustrated. "That stupid podcast has already helped find a bunch of people. Why won't you help?"

"It's too close to home!" I say, ignoring his "stupid" comment but letting my own frustration getting the better of me. "Do you know how difficult it is to live through all of that again? Quinlee Ellacott was waiting on the front steps for me when I got home this afternoon. Besides, I'm right in the middle of another case. I can't just drop that and start another one."

"You can do whatever you want!" he says. "It's your podcast!"

"It's not like that," I say.

"Fine," he says. "Don't help. Listen, I've got to go." He turns abruptly and marches back down the hallway to the front door.

I follow behind him. "Don't be like that," I say. "Please, Burke."

He angrily shoves his feet back into his beat-up, old sneakers, then turns to look at me.

"Maybe you think the cops are just doing their job," he snaps. "Just keep in mind that cops screw stuff up all the time. They blew it with Sibby, and they're going to blow it with this."

"Burke, I'm really sorry you're going through this. I'll help, I promise. I just can't use the podcast."

He scoffs and turns away from me, grabbing the door handle. "Don't worry, Dee. I won't reveal your secret identity." With that, he shoves out the door, letting it slam behind him.

I stand and stare at the door, trying to break down what just happened. I'm reeling from what I just learned—did Terry really take Layla?—but I'm also angry. I know Burke is in a bad spot, but it's not fair of him to take it out on me.

I remember that Carla is waiting for me and run upstairs to my room, guiltily relieved that I have something else to focus on that isn't happening in Redfields.

I'm back! Sorry, got caught up in something.

A message appears immediately.

Okay, so you're not going to believe this.

I wait, holding my breath, watching the dots that tell me she's typing a new message.

I learned about another missing woman today, and I think there's a really good chance that she's connected to Vanessa.

21.

HOST (intro): Imagine this: A neighborhood like many others. Families hustle to get their kids to school. People run to catch the bus or hurry to get out the door in time to walk to work. Elderly folks stop to talk to neighbors as they make their way to the local grocery store. Dogs are walked. Library books are borrowed. And in the middle of this normal, everyday activity, a woman goes missing, and it isn't until almost three days later that someone notices, the police are brought in, and a search begins.

As I told you on my last episode, that's what happened to Vanessa Rodriguez, in a neighborhood like the one I just described. Maybe it was a one-in-a-million occurrence.

But what if it wasn't? What if I told you that another woman had disappeared under very similar circumstances, in exactly the same neighborhood, about two months before Vanessa?

Almost a million people are reported missing across North America every year. If we pay attention, if we work together, maybe we can help bring some of them home. I am *the Seeker*, and this is *Radio Silent*.

RECORDING: *(voice of Danetta Bryce)* Nia Williams is my cousin. She's a fun girl, likes to have a good time. Loves music. Loves her family. She's a chartered accountant, and she works hard, but she always finds time for the people in her life. She's always got a million things on the go: hanging out with her nieces and nephews, volunteering, making spur-of-the-moment weekend road trips with some of her girlfriends. It isn't unusual to not hear from her for a while because she's just so busy.

That's probably why it was a couple of days before anyone noticed she was missing.

HOST (intro): The woman you just heard is Danetta Bryce. After learning from a friend about *Radio Silent*'s series on Vanessa Rodriguez, she contacted Carla Garcia and told her about her cousin, Nia Williams, who disappeared just over two months before Vanessa went missing. The two missing women didn't live in the same neighborhood, but they lived close enough that they frequented some of the same spots.

Notably, Nia was a semiregular at the Impact Café, which astute listeners might recognize as the very same restaurant where Vanessa Rodriguez worked full-time as a server. The same restaurant she didn't show up to on the same day that her friends, family, and presumably police believe she went missing.

Is this a coincidence? Or is there more to it than this?

So far, nothing is known about the whereabouts of either woman, and police have not publicly speculated on whether or not they believe the cases are connected, but there are a couple of notable coincidences. The first, and most obvious, is the connection both women had to the Impact Café. But it's worth noting that both women are in their mid to late twenties, both described by friends and family as attractive, personable, and outgoing.

It's also very important to mention that according to Vanessa's acquaintances and coworkers, she often chose to avoid the busy stretch of road between the café and her apartment building, preferring instead to take a slightly longer, but much quieter route of back streets, through a residential area and past a couple of small parks.

With the help of Nia's cousin Danetta, we were able to confirm that Nia's home, the second floor of an old house, fell along this very same route that Vanessa would often take on her way home from a late shift, meaning it was highly likely that both women would have taken this same unconventional and quieter route when walking to or from the Impact Café.

I'd like to highlight one more important detail.

Both women are visible minorities: Nia is black; Vanessa is Latina. This is worth noting because statistically, women of color are significantly more likely to have their disappearances underreported and underinvestigated by authorities.

These cases were different enough to not have raised too many suspicions—in fact, we don't even know if police have examined any connections between the women—but as I've pointed out, there are obvious similarities.

Is there a connection? Possibly, although as I've mentioned, the police haven't indicated as such. The reality is, it's hard to find a lot of information about any of these cases, other than the basic one- or two-paragraph stories on local news websites. Facebook groups have been set up for each of them, but the information there is light on details as well. It's more or less impossible to figure out how much has been done by police.

We need to do better. And Carla and Danetta are making an effort. They'll be hosting an LDA meetup for their local area this coming Saturday. They want people to help: putting up posters, knocking on doors, reaching out to potential witnesses through social media, you name it.

I want *Radio Silent* to help them, so please, think hard. Do you live in the area? Are you a regular at the Impact Café? Details of the meetup are on all of the *Radio Silent* social media pages, and as always, you can reach out to us through any of them or through email.

Is there something *you* can do to help?

Listen up.

Let's try.

Once I've edited and uploaded the new episode, I lean back into my chair and close my eyes. It feels like the Houston case is building toward something. Bits and pieces of information collecting and shifting and clustering together, and if I put them together just right, the story will start to come into focus.

So why don't I feel the same way about what's happening right here in Redfields?

Sibby. Layla. Burke and Terry. Quinlee Ellacott. Even Sarah. I feel as if everyone and everything is conspiring to bring me back into the center when that's literally the last place I want to be.

Am I a completely different person in real life than I am online? Is there any of Dee Skinner in the Seeker? More importantly, is there really any of the Seeker in Dee Skinner? Should I listen to Burke and let the lines blur?

I sigh and sit forward, reaching to wake up my computer. I send Carla a quick message to tell her that the new episode is live, then quickly check my feeds. Word is already spreading, and people are discussing the new developments.

Downstairs, the front door slams, and I can hear laughter and chatter as my family arrives home. I'm about to slam my laptop shut and head down to join them when a new message appears in my inbox, and my mouth goes dry as I read the subject line.

SIBBY CARMICHAEL STILL ALIVE?

Dear Radio Silent,

I just read online that connections are being drawn between Layla Gerrard, the missing girl in Redfields, and the older case of Sibby Carmichael who also went missing in Redfields ten years ago. I have held on to this information for years because I was never sure if I was right or not, but this has never left me and I can't keep it to myself anymore under the circumstances. I am almost certain that I met Sibby Carmichael about five years ago. I can't go into details because I fear for my personal safety, but I can say with almost complete certainty that it was her. I don't know the state of the investigation into Sibby's disappearance, but it is my belief that she is still out there and alive. I can't approach the police about this for personal reasons. I recently began listening to your podcast, and it occurred to me the Seeker might be able to help.

The email stops there. No specific information. No signature, just a random Gmail address: PrettyInInk_1988.

I write back, asking for more details, and then reread the email a dozen times. There's every reason to believe that this came from another crackpot, one of the hundreds of people who send me false information or useless leads every single month, but still... The message stares back at me from my screen like a beacon, a glimmer of hope that maybe, just maybe, I could be reconnected with Sibby after all.

22.

In the morning, there's a reply from PrettyInInk_1988, but the terse message is not very encouraging.

> I'm sorry to waste your time. Maybe I shouldn't have written. I do think I saw Sibyl Carmichael, but it was years ago, and I can't give you any details or help you more than this. I just needed to say that I believe she's still alive and maybe you can look into it with your podcast. Don't bother writing me back. That's really all I've got for you.

I chew my lip in frustration. There's no way to trace a Gmail address…or is there?

I texted Burke before bed to see how he's doing, but he still hasn't responded. I send him another one, asking how things are going, telling him we need to talk. I know he's mad at me, but I need his help.

When I get to school, there's no sign of him at the entrance. I wait for him until it's almost time for class, but he doesn't show, so I hurry inside to my first class.

I walk into English class just as the bell rings, and see that everyone is huddled around a laptop on Denny Pike's desk, Ms. Grisham included.

I squeeze in and see that they're looking at a livestream on the BNN homepage. Onscreen, Quinlee Ellacott is standing in front of Burke's house. I notice that the curtains are all drawn.

"Authorities have confirmed the arrest of forty-six-year-old Terrence O'Donnell in connection with the disappearance of Layla Gerrard. We've also learned that O'Donnell recently moved into this house, which belongs to his brother. According to neighbors, O'Donnell is unemployed and spends his days aimlessly and can often be seen on the porch behind me, smoking cigarettes."

An unflattering black-and-white photo of Terry appears onscreen, eliciting laughs from a couple of the guys.

"He looks like Burke," someone says.

"That's enough," says Ms. Grisham.

The camera cuts back to Quinlee.

"BNN has learned that O'Donnell was also living at this address ten years ago when seven-year-old Sibyl Carmichael was abducted from this exact same neighborhood, and was investigated at the time but had a solid alibi corroborated by several witnesses. Sources tell us, however, that police believe that O'Donnell recently gained entry into an abandoned house and was using it as a den of sorts. According to these sources, items found in the house indicated that O'Donnell had a fascination with the older case. BNN has also learned, exclusively, that DNA belonging to Layla Gerrard was also found in the house."

"They think he's a copycat." I turn, surprised that Brianna has spoken up. "He was close to the first case. It might make some kind of sick sense to him to return to this adventure and try to get involved."

"Holy shit," says Denny. "Isn't that Burke's mom?"

On the livestream, Marion O'Donnell is hurrying down the front steps to her car, her head down. The camera jostles as it pushes around other news people to get as close to the sidewalk as possible.

"Excuse me!" a voice yells, and the camera swings around to catch Quinlee as she shoves her way between other news gatherers. Her voice, as loud and clear as a bell, chimes out over the other yelling reporters, and somehow, despite the fray of people, she's managed to instinctively position herself next to the O'Donnell's mailbox in such a way that nobody can get around her, and her camera operator has a perfect shot of her yelling, with Mrs. O'Donnell in the background.

"Mrs. O'Donnell!" Quinlee yells, her shoulders back, her microphone held carefully to her mouth, her bouffant sweep of blond hair perfectly arranged to frame her face. "What can you tell us about your brother-in-law's involvement in the disappearance of Layla Gerrard?"

Marion stops in her tracks and turns to stare at Quinlee, and the other reporters go completely silent, not wanting to ruin the moment and miss a good sound bite.

Quinlee comfortably fills up the space on her own. "Do you think Terrence kidnapped that girl?" she asks loud and clear.

Just walk away, I think to myself, willing my thoughts to transport to Burke's mom telepathically. Instead, she takes a deep breath and walks over to the mailbox. Quinlee maintains a solid professional face, but her eyes glitter with triumph. *I've got her*, I imagine her thinking.

"Terry hasn't admitted to anything," says Mrs. O'Donnell forcefully. "My husband and I believe one hundred percent that he is not involved in Layla's disappearance. There's no way that he would do something like this to a poor defenseless child. Don't you think if he wanted to kidnap a child, he would have hidden his tracks better and cleaned out the bedroom first? And also, the letter could have been written by anyone!"

Oh shit.

"What letter are you referring to, Mrs. O'Donnell?" asks Quinlee, who now looks like the cat who caught the canary. She glances briefly around her shoulder at the other reporters, half to sell the point that she was the one to score this scoop and half in irritation that she has to share it.

Mrs. O'Donnell gets flustered, opening her mouth to say something, then closing it again.

Just walk away, I plead silently. *Just turn around and walk away.*

"There was a letter found in Layla's bedroom," says Mrs. O'Donnell. "It was written for De—for the other child who was with Sibby when she went missing."

Behind them, the front door of the house opens again, and I see Mr. O'Donnell stick his head out and a look of alarm crosses his face. He disappears inside again as the door slams shut, and a moment later it swings out again, and he's hurrying outside, struggling into his rubber boots even as he begins down the steps.

"Marion!" he yells. "Get away from those animals! No comment! No comment!"

Burke's mom seems to come to her senses and steps back from Quinlee, then turns and hurries to her husband, who shuffles her back up the steps and into the house. Quinlee turns back to the camera, totally unruffled, and holds her microphone back up to her face.

"One thing is for certain: police will surely be looking for answers from Terrence O'Donnell, and as this case enters its fourth day, we'll have to wait and see if the focus of this investigation shifts. For BNN, this is Quinlee Ellacott, in Redfields."

"What does that mean?" someone asks. "Wait and see if the focus of the investigation shifts?"

"It means they might not be looking for a girl anymore," says Brianna. "They'll be looking for a body."

In the uncomfortable silence that follows, Sarah catches my eye. The sympathetic look she gives me is more than I can handle right now, and I look away.

"Okay, everyone," says Ms. Grisham. "That's enough. Back to your seats."

"Dee is that true?" asks Hugo Broad as we make our way to our seats. "Did you get a letter?"

"No," I say, wishing I were anywhere else than here, the object of the entire room's attention. Ms. Grisham doesn't even shut it down; she obviously wants to hear what I have to say. "I mean, they found a letter, but it wasn't to me. It just mentioned the…the old case."

"That's crazy," says Miranda Ng. "You're like, part of the story now. Maybe you'll get to do an interview with Quinlee Ellacott."

"Yeah right," I say, trying to keep my voice light. "Not if I have anything to do with it."

To my relief, Ms. Grisham finally claps her hands and people reluctantly turn to their copies of *Great Expectations*.

I slip my phone out of my pocket and compose one final text to Burke.

> I saw your mom on TV. Sorry you guys are going through this—text me back asap—we need to talk.

Almost instantly, three dots appear, telling me that he's composing a message. I wait, keeping half an eye on Ms. Grisham, who's writing out the themes of *Great Expectations* on the giant whiteboard at the front of class, but after a moment, the dots disappear, leaving me wondering what he was going to say.

* * *

We're sent home from school before noon. The snow has started falling, and although the roads are still bare, it's clear from the chatter in the hallway that the forecast has only gotten worse.

I'm on my way through the parking lot when I hear someone call my name. I turn to see Sarah strolling across to me. She's wearing her old green parka, and she's also in a knit cap I haven't seen before, burgundy with a tassel. It hides her hair and she looks so hot it's all I can do not to stammer when I open my mouth.

"Hey," I say.

"I'm glad I caught you," she says. "I looked for you between classes, but I couldn't find you. Wanted to offer you a ride home."

"Oh, cool," I say. "Thanks."

"I got you a present," she says with a grin. She unslings her bag from over her shoulder and digs around inside, pulling out what looks kind of like a can of spray paint with a tiny red trumpet attached to the top. She takes in my confused look and laughs. "It's an air horn," she says. "In case I'm not nearby next time you need to shut down pesky reporters." She presses on the trumpet and an extremely loud, extremely obnoxious blaring noise fills the air. Everyone within earshot stops and looks.

"In your face, Anderson Cooper!" she yells before handing me the horn.

"Thanks," I say, putting it in my backpack. "Nobody's ever given me a noisemaker before."

"So, you want a ride home?" she asks. She holds a mittened hand out in front of her, and for a second I think she is going to take my hand, but then she flips it palm up and we both watch as it quickly fills with snowflakes. "My mom was pissed that I took the car in the first place. I think she was probably right, but I've got to get it home now, right?"

I hesitate. For some reason, I don't know what to say. Of course I should take a ride with her. She lives right across the street from me; it would be weird not to.

I'm hit with an urge to tell her about the podcast, about the email from last night, about everything I've tried to do to make up for what I didn't do back in the woods ten years ago.

Her face is open, smiling in a way I haven't seen yet, lacking the subtly sarcastic twist to the corner of her mouth. Open and encouraging. I feel a pang, and I know that something's happening in front of me, something I can have for myself if I just reach out and take it. Part of me wants it more than anything in the world, but for some reason, I know I can't allow myself to follow it. Not now. Not when there's so much else at stake.

"Um, I don't know," I say. "I mean, I appreciate it, but I have some thinking to do. I think I'm going to walk."

She looks taken aback. "Oh. Okay. No problem."

"Nothing serious," I say, hurrying to make up an explanation. "Just some stuff with my family."

"I'm a good listener," she says. It's something I already know, and I ache to get into the car and tell her everything.

But I can't allow myself to get distracted. I can't let myself get close, drop my guard.

The missing girl, the visit from the cop, the email telling me that Sibby might still be alive—all of it is pointing toward a new and serious realization: I can't hide from the past any longer.

And if I'm seriously going to do this, if I'm going to dive deep into Sibby's disappearance, I need to do it completely. I need to put everything else out of my mind. There were only two of us in the woods that day. One of us is missing, and one of us was left behind.

There's no room for anyone else right now.

"I think I just want to be by myself right now," I tell her, and I force myself to turn away before the look on her face causes me to change my mind.

23.

So far, I only have two flimsy emails to go on, and it's quite possible that there's nothing to them. I've received my fair share of wild claims since I started the podcast, and as much as I want this one to be true, I have to be prepared to accept that the sender may just be a delusional listener who wants to be part of something.

But still…if I'm being honest with myself, I don't think that's it. There's something about this one that rings true. It's what the sender didn't say, rather than what they did say. Instead of an elaborate, complicated theory, full of names and dates and certainty, it's just this: I think I saw her. I'm pretty sure it was her.

I really want Burke's take on this, but he's still ignoring my texts, and he still hasn't come back to school. I can't blame him for keeping a low profile, considering what's going on with his uncle, but I still need to talk to him, so I decide I'll have to go to him.

I've hung out at the dugouts with Burke before—or more like I've *gone* to the dugouts with Burke. The concrete bunkers at the old ballfields behind the school are the perfect place for stoners to hang out. They have a full view of anyone approaching and an easy exit into the woods behind the fields in case someone spots the cops.

On the few occasions I've come here with Burke, it's been a quick visit. Enough time for him to score some weed, maybe smoke with the guy he buys it from. I don't love it there, but I don't generally mind potheads. They don't cause shit. If anything, they generally want you to like them, to validate what they're doing with their time, or to laugh along with their jokes. Drinking makes people unpredictable. Weed is the opposite.

But this visit is different. Usually I'm just tagging along with Burke, and it's easy enough for me to just stick to the side and wait for him to be done, maybe shoot the shit with one of the guys who's hanging out there. This one guy who everyone calls Donkey but whose real name is Pete is pretty funny, and he always tries to make me laugh, like I'm some kind of challenge or something. Maybe I am, maybe I come across as surly. Burke tells me I have resting bitch face, but honestly it's not like that. I'm just quiet. Donkey's a funny guy though, and once he makes me laugh, it always calms me down a bit.

I know Burke is here, because I saw him out the school window during final period, walking across the field with a couple of people. As I approach across the field, I can feel their eyes on me from the dark of the dugout. It's only three thirty, but the sun is already low in the sky, and it'll be twilight within the hour.

As I step up to the edge of the dugout, I feel a wave of uncertainty, and I wish I'd waited until I could have found him alone, but he hasn't answered any of my texts, and I suspect that he'll be likelier to talk to me if he's baked.

Besides Donkey and Burke, there are three other people in the dugout: two older guys I don't recognize, and Maggie Dunne, a senior who I've known a little bit since we were kids, although we've never really been friends.

"Hey, Delia," she says when I step up to the concrete-edged space. I'm actually kind of relieved to see another familiar face, since the other guys are staring at me unnervingly. "What are you doing here?" She doesn't even attempt to hide the surprise in her voice.

"I was looking for Burke," I say.

I look directly at him for the first time. He's sitting on the bench in the corner, hunched over a battered textbook, breaking up weed for a joint. He glances up at me.

"Hey, Dee, just let me finish with this."

I feel such a rush of relief that he's talking to me normally that I want to rush across and kiss him on the head, but I hold back.

"Yeah, sure," I say.

"So, Dee," says Maggie, "what do you think is going on with that missing kid?" She leans forward and pushes her hood off her head, as if to better hear my response. "Since you're the expert and all."

I almost choke on my words. "Expert?" Does she somehow know about the podcast? What the hell is going on?

Behind her, the guys on the bench seem to sit up a bit straighter and start paying attention for the first time.

"You know," she says. "Like, because you kind of went through something like this. I mean, you know, when Sibby went missing." She looks genuinely awkward, like she realizes she should take back her words. "Sorry, Dee. I guess I kind of thought you were over it."

I force myself to relax. "What happened back then doesn't really make me an expert," I say, shrugging and trying to keep my words calm. Getting myself worked up would only serve to give them something to think about and that kind of argument would be bound to escape the confines of the bunker.

"Jesus, Maggie," says Burke, saving me from the awkwardness of the situation. "Do you really think I want to be hearing this bullshit right now?"

"Sorry, Burke," says Maggie sheepishly.

Burke finishes rolling the joint, pinching the end and slapping it against his thigh a couple of times before twisting the paper and tucking it behind his ear.

"You gonna spark it up?" asks Donkey.

"Give me a minute," says Burke. He hops down from his perch and gestures for me to follow him.

Outside the dugout the air is crisp and getting colder by the minute as the sky darkens. Across the ball field, a streetlight comes on, and the halo around it enhances the flurries that spin through the blue glow.

"What's up, Dee?" asks Burke. He doesn't sound angry, just wary, a tightness in his voice.

"I need your help," I say. I dig inside the pocket of my coat and pull out the paper I printed this morning, the email with the Gmail address at the top of it.

He reads it, then looks up at me. He's not shocked, just mildly interested. "So some wing nut thinks they know what happened to Sibby," he says.

"I don't think they're a wing nut," I tell him. "I have a feeling about it."

He nods. "A feeling. So what do you need me for?"

"They haven't responded to any of my emails," I say. "I was hoping maybe you could try and see where it came from?"

He laughs. "It's a Gmail address. I can't trace a Gmail address."

"I thought maybe there was something you could do, like look up the IP or something," I say.

"Burke!" yells Donkey from the dugout behind him. "I'm freezing my nuts off! Let's smoke this thing and get the hell out of here!"

"Yeah, hang on!" Burke yells back. He turns back to me and shakes his head. "It doesn't work like that. Sorry, Dee."

"I figured it was worth a shot," I say. For a moment, neither of us says anything. I can't tell what's going on in his face, but I can tell that he's hurting.

"Why didn't you tell me about the note?" he says suddenly. "Why didn't you tell me the cops came to see your family about a note?"

I stare at him, trying to find the right words. "Everything just kind of happened so quick," I say.

"Not that quick," he responds right away. It's obvious that he's given this a lot of thought. "You knew about the note before anything happened with Terry. You could have told me."

I throw my hands up. "What was I supposed to say, Burke? That someone was out to get me? That I was scared shitless? Because I was."

He shakes his head. "You could have told me what's up. I would have told you."

"Well, you'll never have to worry about something like this," I say. "You weren't there. You haven't spent your life wondering what would have gone down differently if you'd done something. You don't know what it's like! Everybody else gets to move on, and I'm the one left behind feeling guilty! I'm the one who feels responsible! Okay?"

His mouth drops open, and suddenly he is angry.

"Oh yeah, Dee, like you're the only person who was affected by this. Like her parents—*your* parents—didn't have to deal with a lot to get over this. Like she didn't have any other friends besides you."

He stops, his mouth still half-open, his eyes wide, as if he's said something he didn't want to say.

"I don't feel that way at all, Burke," I manage to say, but he's already got his hands up, palms out like he's warding me off.

"Do you know what, Dee? Just forget about it. There are plenty of people who do care enough to give a shit."

This is rapidly spinning out of control, and I'm aware of Donkey and Maggie and the others listening to our conversation. I step farther from the dugout and drop my voice to a harsh whisper, so he has to lean in to hear me.

"I'm sorry I didn't tell you about the note, Burke. But they told me not to say anything." I'm annoyed. What right does he have to my personal information anyway?

"Well. I thought you were supposed to be my best friend. She went missing from my street after all."

I stare at him, unable to think of anything to say. Why is he so angry?

His face drops and he closes his eyes. "I just…I don't know what to do. I feel like if I'd known something earlier, I could have helped figure something out. I mean, Layla is still missing."

"I don't know what you could have done," I say. "Honestly."

He stares at me beseechingly. "I don't want to believe he did it, Dee, but it's getting clearer by the minute. Even my mom thinks he did it. My dad doesn't, but only because it's his brother."

"I guess that's understandable," I say.

"Well, he's going to have to start facing facts soon," says Burke. "I can't stop thinking that if I'd only paid better attention, maybe I could have stopped it. Do you know they think he left that note for you as a bait and switch? His alibi for when Sibby disappeared was so tight that they think he tried to connect the two cases so he'd be off the hook. Maybe he cut up the magazines for that note right under my nose and I was too stupid to notice."

"Burke," I say, "you can't blame yourself."

He ignores me. "Here's another thing." He leans in close to me, and a waft of sticky, pungent weed breaks through the icy cold of the night. I see a clear point of desperation in the middle of his glassy eyes. "Do you know how hard it is to live across from the Gerrards? It's awful. The mom just sits in the window, glaring across at us, hating all of us."

"Burke," I say. "She doesn't hate all of you."

He ignores me. "And the dad has gone completely nuts. I've seen him go out of their house into the yard and back into the woods. He's out there at all hours, leaving the wife behind by herself. It's really sad. My mom tried to bring them some food, but she was barely even aware that there was someone else in the room with her. He even went out into the woods in the middle of that snowstorm. He's looking for that kid, Dee. And if my uncle did what they're saying he did, he might be the only person who knows where she is."

I look back at him, not sure what to say.

"I can't help you, Dee," he says. "Sibby's gone, just like Layla, and the sooner I'm able to forget about them both, the happier I'll be."

He turns and walks back to his group.

24.

I still have Jonathan Plank's business card shoved into the inside breast pocket of my parka. I'm not sure what to expect, but when I call him the next afternoon after school, he picks up his phone right away.

"Plank." His voice on the other end is professional. Brisk, like he's in a hurry.

"Hey," I say. "This is Delia Skinner."

There's a pause on the other end of the line, as he works to remember, then his voice returns, and now his voice is smoother, full of calculated recognition.

"Delia," he says. "How are you?"

"Do you have time to meet me?" I ask. "Like, kind of under the radar?"

"Yeah," he says, snapping to business. "How about half an hour in the restaurant downstairs at the Best Western?"

I didn't expect to see him almost instantly, but I was the one to call him. I can't very well turn him down now.

"That works," I say. I pause. "Don't tell anyone, okay?"

"I won't," he says immediately. I'm still not sure whether I can trust him or not, but the tone of his voice reassures me at least a little bit.

By the time I arrive at the restaurant, Jonathan Plank is already sitting in the window, nursing a coffee. He waves and half rises from his seat as I approach.

He waits until I slide into the booth, across from him, before sitting again. The waitress appears.

"You want something to eat?" Plank asks me.

"No, I'm okay," I say. "Just an iced tea," I tell the waitress.

As Plank orders his sandwich and fries, I look at him, trying to understand from his face and the friendly way he talks to the waitress what kind of person he is.

"I'm glad you got in touch," says Plank, turning back to me. "I didn't think I'd hear from you." His fingers reach out and slide a small black notebook toward him, he flips it open and pulls a pen from his breast pocket.

"I'm not here to give you an interview," I say, looking at the notebook pointedly. "None of this is on the record."

He nods slowly, then looks down at his notebook, where I see a list of questions neatly written down and numbered. He considers them for a moment, then flips the notebook upside down and shoves it to the side, sticking his pen back into his pocket.

"Sure," he says. "That's totally fine. Whatever works for you." He seems willing to hear me out, but I still feel uneasy.

"I just want to know what it was like back then," I say. "When Sibby went missing. You were here, right? What did people think had happened?"

He looks at me quizzically, and I know that he's trying to figure out what I'm working toward here. "How much do you know?" he asks.

This is the million-dollar question, the glitch in the matrix: I don't know anything. I've kept myself so isolated from the truth about Sibby's disappearance that I don't really know what it was like. I have my own few scattered memories, but I've never really spoken to anyone about it. Not my parents. Not Burke.

Only Sarah. Until yesterday, the thought of her made me soften, relax, but now the thought of her puts a sour taste in my mouth.

"I don't know much," I admit. "I haven't really wanted to rip open that wound."

"But you're here now," he says.

I shrug. "I guess I can't hide from it any longer."

"So," he says, "what exactly are you looking for?"

"I want to know what you think happened to Sibyl," I say.

He laughs, not unkindly. "Don't you think if I knew that I would have written about it by now?"

"I know you don't know exactly what happened to her," I say, "but you must have had some broad theories. I dug up some of your old stories last night. They all took the angle of the 'mysterious small town with a big secret.'"

"Because I believed it," he said. "I still do. There's no way in my mind that this could have been some random event. Two kidnappers just happened to be in the woods together at the same time and just happened to stumble across two girls playing in the woods? It doesn't make any sense. Whoever did this had to know the area, had to know that kids played in that forest, had to know that there was a perfect spot to hide a car to make a clean getaway onto the highway."

"So you think that whoever did it was from town?" I ask.

He nods slowly. "From town or closely connected to town. I've gone over it and over it, and I keep coming back to the same thing: it was too clean to be random." He leans back in his booth and holds his hands out, palms up. "But that's as far as my theory goes."

"Do you think Sibby and Layla are connected?" I ask.

He shakes his head. "Terry O'Donnell was one of the first people we looked at when we were making our list of possible suspects. He was an unemployed transient with a criminal record. But he had an airtight alibi. Several witnesses corroborated that he was at the movies with his girlfriend and his nieces and nephew on that particular afternoon."

"So you do think he took Layla," I confirm. "Just not Sibby."

Plank shrugs. "I can't think of another scenario that fits as well as that one."

I'm about to push back, maybe for Burke's sake, since what he's saying seems true to me, but his eyes shift abruptly to stare behind me, and suddenly we're interrupted by a loud, confident voice that seems to have snuck up right behind me.

"Nice trick you pulled with the car horn the other day. I never would have thought that one up myself."

I recognize the voice before she's even stopped next to our

booth: Quinlee Ellacott. She's got an unlit cigarette pinched between the fingers of one hand, and with the other, she's holding a coat in place where it's draped over her shoulders, clearly about to step outside for a smoke.

"How'd you score this interview anyway, John?" she says, half-amused, half-annoyed. "Candy? Cannabis?"

"I don't smoke weed," I say, "and since you're on your way out to suck back some nicotine, maybe you should hold back on the judgment calls."

She grins. "I'm impressed," she says. "You've got some attitude. She giving you some good dirt, Johnny boy?"

I stand from my chair.

"As a matter of fact, I haven't told him anything," I say. It's one of those truthful statements that sounds so much like a lie that I blush, cursing myself right away for it.

"Is that right?" asks Quinlee.

"Yep," I say. "I asked him to meet me because he's about the only journalist I trust in this town, and I wanted to know if he had any advice about keeping vultures like you away from me and my family."

Quinlee doesn't miss a beat. "That's all fine and good, sweetheart, but not talking to you is only a minor speed bump. I'll find loads of people to talk, don't worry. Everyone wants to be on TV."

"You're not on TV," I say, pushing back. "You're on the internet, in a tiny little window."

She makes a mock sad face. "That might just about hurt my feelings if millions of people weren't watching that little window."

"We aren't all like you, Quinlee," says Plank. "Some of us are actually interested in real journalism, not just sensationalism."

"You just keep telling yourself that," says Quinlee. She looks at me. "Listen, you might already be starting to figure this out, but these stories are linked. They might not be connected, but they're sure as shit linked. There's one hell of a spicy parallel between this missing girl and the shit you went through as a kid, and believe me, it's not going to go unnoticed. Whether you like it or not, Sibby Carmichael is about to become a household name again, and you're going to be dragged into it too. You can waste your time talking to Mr. Plank here, and get your story out into a tiny little market only to disappear in a day or so, or you can trust me to give you some serious and sympathetic exposure."

"I don't want exposure," I say. "I don't want anything from anyone except to be left alone."

She shrugs. "Doesn't matter, sweetheart. You're part of this, like it or not. Anyway, I'm not going to waste time begging, but I'll give you a fair heads-up: I *will* be telling your story. You can decide whether or not you want a chance to help me figure out how to do that."

She winks at me, nods at Jonathan, then turns on her heel and marches through the restaurant toward the lobby.

"Shit," I say.

"It's a tough industry," says Plank. "She's right about one thing: someone's going to tell your story. But don't let her fool you: she doesn't have to be the one to do it. Our paper has a good reputation, and there's enough interest in this story that a feature article about you, with an exclusive interview, would go viral pretty quickly."

I shake my head. "Not gonna happen."

"Worth a shot," he says. "Just promise me something? If you do change your mind, will you give me some serious consideration? I promise I'll respect your boundaries."

Reluctantly, I nod.

"You know, Dee," he says, "I asked for this assignment. Begged for it actually. I don't even write crime stories anymore. I'm on the sports beat. But I...I want to find out what happened to Sibby too. I've never been able to get beyond it."

"Yeah, well, join the club," I say. I stand and reach out to shake his hand. "Thanks for talking to me today."

"Anytime. Seriously."

I find a rear exit, so I don't have to walk through the parking lot and encounter Quinlee again.

It's almost dark by the time I leave the Best Western, and the wind has picked up a bit, sending a sharp chill through my coat and sweater. I pull my scarf tighter around my neck and put my head down against the cold.

As I walk home, I think about Plank's version of events. If it's true that someone from town took her, isn't there a really good chance that they're still here? But what am I supposed to do, start interviewing people one at a time? Hardly a good way to keep a low profile.

This gives me an idea. I step into a bus shelter to get out of the wind and pull my phone out of my pocket, searching quickly through my contacts.

Brianna answers on the first ring.

"Delia," she says, her voice crisp. "This is a surprise."

"Hey, Brianna. I've been thinking that you're right. I should help out more. With the school and stuff," I say, cutting right to the chase. "Do you still need someone to take care of raffle tickets at the hockey game?"

There's a pause before she speaks again, and I know I've taken her by surprise. "Actually," she says, and her voice is suddenly cheerful, even chummy. "That would be a huge help. I couldn't find anyone else to do it, and I was going to have to run double-duty myself. It's this coming Saturday though."

"Yeah," I say. "I know. I can do that."

"Perfect. Just show up at the arena an hour before the game and I'll get you set up."

I hang up and shove my phone back in my pocket.

25.

The Carmichaels live in a condo right downtown. It's a fancy building, with a doorman and a glittering lobby. Elevators with mirrored walls and brass handrails.

It's not what I expected. The Carmichaels weren't poor—at least no poorer than anyone else who lived on our street when I was growing up—but they definitely weren't rich either. I remember Sibyl's clothes being handed down to her little sister, Greta, and their parents collecting empties on the back porch to return for the deposit money.

This is not a "save your bottles for cash" kind of place. This building is rich.

The Carmichaels are expecting me. I found Mr. Carmichael's email address online, and after a day of waiting, he responded. When I give the doorman my name, he runs his fingers down a list on a clipboard behind his little booth and smiles.

"Yes," he says. "Here you are. Go right on up, fifteenth floor."

As I step out of the elevator, a door at the far end of the hallway clicks open, and Grant Carmichael, Sibby's father, appears.

"Delia," he says, extending both hands in a greeting as I approach. I'm not prepared for how different he looks. His hair is still thick, but his temples are gray, and in his expensive-looking gray wool slacks and thin blue sweater, he looks like a magically aged version of the man in my memory all this time. I remind myself that time has passed for him, just as it has for me. For his daughter.

"Hi," I say, suddenly awkward.

"Please, come in." He turns sideways and gestures into the apartment, and I hurry to move past him.

He closes the door behind us, and I kick off my shoes and drop my backpack onto the floor of a gleaming white marble foyer. I catch sight of myself in a gilt-framed mirror and almost laugh. I've done my best to dress in what passes as "nice" clothes, but I am still so out of place in this apartment it's almost ridiculous.

"Come on in," he says, and I'm relieved that his voice makes him sound more like the suburban dad I remember. He puts a hand lightly on my back and guides me around a corner into a large living room. I have a vague impression of expensive furniture and fresh flowers, but my attention is almost completely drawn to the woman on the other side of the room.

Astrid Carmichael, Sibby's mother, is perched on the edge of a charcoal armchair. She's attempting to stand, but even from across the room, I can see that her entire body is trembling. Her hand grabs an arm of the chair and grips, and although her mouth is half-open to say something, she can only stare at me, her eyes wide.

Until now, I've managed to stay collected, calm, working myself through this entire exercise step-by-step. Get on the bus. Follow the map on my phone to their building. Talk to the doorman. Say hello to Mr. Carmichael.

Now, it all crumbles, and the anxiety that is emanating from Mrs. Carmichael in waves surrounds me like a contagion. I have the sudden feeling that my knees are going to drop out from under me, and my head swells with rushing blood and emotion.

Like her husband, she's dressed completely differently than I would have expected, in her case, a pale yellow silk pantsuit. My best friend's mother, the pretty woman who liked to wear simple cotton sundresses and bake German treats like her mother had, who plastered Band-Aids on my knee when the situation arose, now looks like a society woman.

She recovers herself, I assume because she knows that one of us has to, and comes across the room to me. I have not recovered, and I stand still, wishing myself somewhere else entirely, as she walks to me and wraps me in a hug.

We stand like this for at least a minute, neither of us saying anything.

Finally, Mrs. Carmichael pulls back, leaving her hands on my shoulders. I manage to pull myself together, and when she smiles into my face, I return the expression.

"Delia," she says. "I'm sorry. I thought I'd be as cool as a cucumber. I guess that's just not possible."

"It's okay. I feel the same way," I tell her.

She gestures toward a low-slung sofa of soft, caramel-colored leather, and I sit. She returns to her chair, and Mr. Carmichael drags an ottoman next to her and perches on it.

Greetings over, we sit in awkward silence. I know I am supposed to be saying something, explain to them why I'm here, but I can't collect my thoughts.

"How's Greta?" I finally ask.

They both smile, and I know I've asked the right question.

"She's wonderful," says Mr. Carmichael. "She's in her third year at Sisters of Supreme Sacrifice, has lots of friends. She's actually there this afternoon, practicing for a debate tournament next month."

Mrs. Carmichael gets up from the sofa and takes a framed photograph from a shelf in the corner of the room, crosses over, and passes it to me.

I have to force myself not to gasp. The girl in the picture looks exactly like an older version of the Sibby I remember, right down to the confident, amused expression. I think about how it must have felt to the Carmichaels as Greta passed Sibby's age when she was abducted and kept going. A daily reminder of the girl they lost.

"Wow," I say, managing to keep my emotions subdued. "She's all grown up."

I hand the photo back to her, and she smiles down at it. "This was actually taken a couple of years ago, when she was thirteen. She's a far cry from the little girl who used to tag along behind you and Sibyl. I remember the two of you going out of your way to leave her behind."

I don't correct her, tell her that it was Sibby who did her best to leave Greta out of our plans.

"I suppose I should be thankful for that," she says. "When I think about what could have happened if she'd gone with you girls that day…" She trails off, and her posture slackens. As she drops back into her chair, Mr. Carmichael smoothly reaches out to take the photo from her, and places it on a side table.

"We don't need to think about that, Astrid," he says. He turns back to me and slaps his hands onto his knees. He clearly wants to wrap things up, and I know it's time to get to the point.

"I know it must have been a surprise to hear from me," I say. "But I'm sure the two of you have heard about Layla Gerrard."

They exchange a glance that tells me they've been expecting this.

"Yes," says Mr. Carmichael. "We had a visit from the police."

"For a moment, we thought maybe this would lead to information about Sibyl," says Astrid. "It seemed as if the two cases might be connected."

"You heard about the note?"

They both nod. "We'd be lying if we said it hadn't given us some hope," says Sibby's dad. "But it appears as if the two cases weren't connected after all."

"It's dragged up a lot of memories for me too," I say. "That's why I'm here. I wanted—needed to ask if you ever had any theories about what happened to Sibby."

There's an electric pause as they stare at me. Finally, Grant speaks up.

"We honestly had no idea," he says. "Still don't. It was so random, so out of the blue. There was no ransom note…nothing. Our heads were spinning."

"I suspected no one and everyone," says Astrid. "I suspected Sibyl's teachers. I suspected the mailman. I suspected neighbors. For months afterward, I walked around staring at people, wondering if they'd done it."

"Eventually," says her husband, "we had to leave Redfields. You know better than anyone, Delia, that it doesn't matter who we suspected or what we thought. None of it brought Sibby back to us. At a certain point, we had to decide to let go and move on with our lives."

I look at Mrs. Carmichael. She seems to have aged a dozen years since I came into the room. "I'm quite tired," she says. "I think I'll go lie down for a while. It was very nice to see you again. Please give my regards to your parents."

Mr. Carmichael puts his arm protectively around her shoulder. "Just give us a moment, Delia," he says, as he walks her out of the room and down a corridor. I hear a door open and then softly close.

Quickly, I pull out my phone and lean in to take a couple of shots of the photograph of Greta. If the anonymous emailer did see Sibby five years ago, she would have been about the same age as Greta in this picture.

I hear the door open again and slip my phone back into my pocket just as Mr. Carmichael returns. It's clear from the expression on his face that he expects me to leave, so I stand to make my exit.

"Believe me, Delia," he says when we reach the foyer. "I

know this is hard on you too, and I understand why you feel like asking questions. But you need to take my advice and move on, like we did."

I step out of the apartment, and when I turn to look at him, something passes between us—a shared understanding that we'll never really move on. Then he closes the door.

26.

Greta's school is only a few blocks away, a stately stone building on a tree-lined street. A high iron fence surrounds the
campus, a reminder to passersby that these students are being
kept apart from the world. A simple, classically lettered sign
bolted to the fence near the opened gate reads *Sisters of the
Supreme Sacrifice Girls Academy*, a reminder to passersby who is
really in charge here.

While I'm waiting to spot Greta, I pull out my phone. It's
the perfect way to disappear into a crowd. If you have your
phone out, staring intently, occasionally moving your thumb
toward the screen so that it looks like you're engaging with
it, people ignore you. I've perfected the angle of eyesight
required to give the illusion of distraction while watching the
scene around me unfold. I'm not a voyeur, because I don't usually care what other people are doing or talking about, but

experience—if that's what you want to call it—has taught me that I should be as aware as possible of my surroundings.

As the girls stream out of the wide, arched gate, I lean back against the fence, pretending to watch my phone, and let them pass me like a wave. Only a few of them give me curious looks, since most are engrossed in their own little dramas, but I feel like a sore thumb nonetheless. Even more so than I did in the Carmichaels' apartment. There, at least, I felt like it was a fair matchup. Here, all these prim girls with their plaid skirts and expensive winter jackets look like an army marching to prove how out of place I am.

The majority of girls pass, and although they're moving quickly, trying to get away from the school, I'm pretty sure I've gotten a good look at most of them, and Greta is nowhere to be seen.

Then the door to the school opens, and two girls in the middle of a serious discussion come out. One of them looks up, and it's her. She and her friend stop at the top of the steps and hover over a binder that one of them is holding out. There is an exchange of papers, notes, or homework assignments shoved into backpacks, and then they continue down the steps and toward the gate.

"Greta," I say, stepping forward. The girls start, and Greta takes an instinctive step backward.

"Yeah?" she asks. "Can I help you?"

I can tell by the way she talks that she is a serious person. Wary, which doesn't surprise me at all, but not flighty. Cautious in a way Sibby never was. I wonder how much of this is a result of what happened to her sister and how much is just the way she is, the way she would have been either way.

"I was wondering if we could talk for a minute," I say.

She hesitates, and although she doesn't step closer, her head moves forward just a little bit, her eyes narrowed, taking me in. "Do I know you?" she asks warily.

"Yeah," I say. "I mean, you used to know me. I'm Delia Skinner. Dee."

I don't know what I expected exactly, but I didn't expect such a calm response. She nods as if someone has just explained a particularly complicated theory to her and everything makes sense to her now.

"What's going on?" asks the friend.

"It's cool," says Greta. "Why don't you go on ahead, Paulette. I'll text you later."

"You sure?" asks Paulette.

Greta just nods, her eyes still on me.

"Okay," says the other girl. "Just text me if you need anything." Still, she hovers for a moment before deciding that Greta is serious, then continues on down the sidewalk, turning once to glance back before disappearing around the corner.

"You want to get a coffee or something?" I ask her.

"Yeah," she says, "okay. There's a place a couple of blocks away."

As we walk, she unslings her bag from her shoulder and digs around in an interior pocket, coming out with a thin metal case. She opens it and, to my surprise, pulls out a cigarette. She stops to light it, eyeing me sideways.

"You want one?" she asks after a deep breath and release of smoke.

I shake my head. "I wouldn't have pictured you as a smoker."

She shrugs. "You haven't seen me since I was five," she says. "Most people don't picture five-year-olds growing up to be smokers. Anyway, I only do it because I know it would upset them if they found out. My parents."

"But they don't know?" I ask. "Kind of defeats the purpose, doesn't it?"

She laughs. "Yeah, it does. I'm not rebellious. I don't get into trouble. My grades are excellent. I have good friends. I'm not interested in being messed up. It's just…"

I wait, giving her space to explain on her own.

"It's just, they want *so badly* for me to turn out okay, that they don't even realize that they've gotten their wish. They're waiting for something awful to happen, like what happened to—" She breaks off abruptly, gives me a nervous sideways glance as she sucks on her cigarette.

"What happened to Sibby," I say.

"Yeah," she says. "Of course." We've reached the coffee shop, and we step around to the side, away from the door, so she can finish her cigarette.

"I'm their only remaining hope," she says. "Their second chance to hang on to a daughter, make sure she grows up happy and healthy and…and safe. I'm not going to be the asshole who ruins that for them, not after what happened. These"— she holds the end of her cigarette up, then drops it onto the sidewalk and crushes it into a snowbank with her boot—"are my one self-destructive habit."

"Gross habit," I say.

She nods, lets out a little laugh. "The truth is, I hate smoking."

Inside, we sit across from each other at tiny, almost useless, wooden tables. Our hands are cupped around our drinks, a chai latte for Greta, an Americano, black, for me.

"I saw your parents today," I say. "I visited them at home, at your condo."

She rolls her eyes. "God, isn't it tacky?"

"It's all right," I say.

"Try growing up there. *Keep your feet off the coffee table! Don't drink juice around the good furniture!* Do you remember our old house?"

"Yeah," I say. "I remember it really, really well."

"Well, I don't. I was too young. I only remember it from pictures. It looked comfortable."

"It was," I tell her. "It was like most houses in the neighborhood: old furniture, toys all over the floor, ugly lamps. It was a bit of a surprise to see the new place."

"Well, people might not change," she says, "but the things around them sure do."

"Do you remember Sibby?" I ask.

"Vaguely," she says. "I remember her voice and how she was bossy to me when we were playing with dolls. Not mean bossy, just in-charge bossy. Mostly though, she's like that house we used to live in: she exists in a bunch of pictures that remind me that things used to be more relaxed. Better. I remember that things were one way for as long as I remembered, and then, suddenly, they were very different."

I feel a twinge of guilt, realizing that I have much clearer memories of Sibby than her own sister does.

"You're here because of that girl, aren't you?" she asks. "The one who went missing."

"It's dragged up a lot of shit," I say. "And it's made me realize just how much I don't know about what happened back then."

"You know," she says, staring down into her drink, absent-mindedly stirring with the little silver spoon, "things were never the same after. I mean, obviously, right? But they were really not the same. I mean, a complete change. The thing that bothers me the most about it is that I was too young to even realize. I only have little snippets of memory. But at Christmastime, my mother always makes us sit and watch these old home videos. It's so awful, everyone sitting, blank-faced around my mother as she cries. My dad used to sit and hold her hand and they'd both cry, but even he hates it now. He wants her to move on, but there's no good way to tell her that."

I nod. I hate home videos, and in my house there's no tragedy woven into them; they're just embarrassing.

"The worst part is that it seems like we're watching completely different people," she says. "The people in those videos are my parents, but they aren't."

"I think I kind of know what you mean," I say. "I felt that way when I visited them."

"My mother blamed everyone," she says. "My father was more realistic. I remember him saying that she was being ridiculous, that she couldn't just point around, looking for someone to blame."

"Was there anyone in particular?" I ask.

She thinks about this. "It was a long time ago, but I remember she was fixated on that family across the street. Their little boy used to play with you guys."

"The O'Donnells?" I ask, shocked. "You know their uncle Terry was arrested in connection to Layla Gerrard, right?"

"I haven't paid that much attention," she admits. "I try to maintain boundaries for the sake of my mental health. But it wasn't him. It was his girlfriend. The blond."

Now I'm really surprised. "Sandy?"

"Yeah, that was her. Apparently Mom caught her playing with me and Sibby in the backyard one afternoon. Like, she let herself in through the side gate and was just hanging out with us. A bit weird, I guess, but the police looked into it, and she had a tight alibi. Mom was just looking for someone to fixate on. She was out of her head at the time, obviously."

She drains her chai and then flips her phone over to check the time.

"I've gotta go," she says, starting to gather her things. "I'm meeting with my study group in a little while."

I pull on my coat, and together we leave and walk out onto the street, where she pulls out her cigarettes and lights up again.

"It was good to see you, Dee," she says. "I hope you find whatever it is that you're looking for." She doesn't lean in for a hug or anything, just hikes her bag higher on her shoulder and turns away, walking down the sidewalk, lifting a hand into the air as she goes, without a look back.

27.

I've gone to plenty of my brothers' hockey games, but only the away games, where I can climb out of my dad's car and not know everyone in the parking lot. Where I blend in a bit better, and nobody stops to stare across the arena at me.

The home rink is just the same as all the others; it's clad in corrugated aluminum and has a large painted, plywood sign bolted to the front above the doors, announcing that you've reached *Redfields Arena*.

I meet Brianna at the front doors, where she's standing by a folding table with a clipboard and a roll of tickets. She's wearing her royal blue Redfields Girls Volleyball Team windbreaker, and her hair is pulled up into a perfect high ponytail.

"I was surprised you changed your mind," she says. She purses her lips and gives me an obligatory smile. "It helps, so thank you."

"No problem," I say. "What do I do?"

"It's easy," she says. She's beginning to show me how the tickets work when a woman approaches the table.

"Just watch me," Brianna murmurs.

The woman stops in front of us and peers down at the sign.

"We're having a 50/50 draw!" says Brianna brightly, the sarcasm completely absent from her voice. "To fund the annual Winter Carnival Dance!"

"I thought you might be raising money to find that girl," says the old lady with a frown.

Brianna doesn't skip a beat, and a perfectly pretty little frown of her own pops out to indicate how seriously she's taking the entire thing too.

"I know," she says. "Isn't it just terrible? The student council and the entire student body, for that matter, are putting forward every effort to find that poor girl. But it's important for us to keep doing the things we've always done." Her voice takes on a pious tone. "It's what Layla would want."

I doubt Layla gave a shit about the Winter Carnival Dance, but the old lady doesn't even seem to hear her. "I think the father did it," she says with a stubborn grimace.

Brianna politely ignores this, reaching past me instead for the roll of tickets and holding them out. "Can I interest you in a 50/50 ticket? Two dollars each, or three for five."

"Why do you think that?" I ask the woman. "That the father did it?"

Brianna coughs lightly, disapprovingly, and her foot begins to tap next to me.

"He looks like a real piece of work," she says. "Probably looking for the insurance money. Wouldn't surprise me."

A few other people have stepped up behind the old woman. Brianna cranes her neck performatively to look past the woman at the growing line behind her.

"I haven't heard anything about insurance money," I say to the woman.

"Quinlee Ellacott thinks it's something to do with a gambling debt," says the woman. "I watch her religiously. She's a smart cookie, that one."

"I'm sorry to rush you along," says Brianna, "but there are a lot of people waiting to buy tickets." She gives me a pointed look as the woman rummages in her purse to pull out a couple of bills. I make the exchange and then smile up at the next person in line.

"I've got it from here, Brianna," I say. "You go do whatever else it is that you're supposed to be doing."

"Are you sure?" she asks dubiously. "You don't need me to help you figure it out?"

"Like you said, it isn't rocket science. I've got it under control."

"Okay then," she says. "I'll come back after the game has started and we'll sort out the float."

She leaves and walks into the arena with an uncertain backward glance at me.

The raffle table is busy but not crazily so. It goes in fits and starts, so I have time to watch people coming into the arena. I know most of the faces from around town.

My biggest fear, that people will recognize me as the girl from the woods, doesn't come to pass. For the people who do know me—friends of my parents, teachers, neighbors—it isn't a novelty. For everyone else, I don't think they recognize me. I remember that it's been almost ten years, and I'm not the little girl from the newspapers anymore.

On the other hand, I can tell that there are a lot of hushed conversations going on. I keep overhearing snippets of conversations, people throwing around theories and speculating on what actually happened, but I can't focus on any of them long enough to catch what people are saying. But I do pick up a lot of talk about Layla and the O'Donnells.

I freeze in the act of ripping off tickets as Sarah Cash and her parents stomp their feet as they come into the arena foyer. She's laughing, and as she pushes back her hood and shakes out her hair, her eyes meet mine and her smile freezes, goes flat.

"Hello?" asks the woman in front of me, waving a twenty-dollar bill at me.

"Sorry," I say, turning back to my customer. By the time I've pulled off the tickets and made change, Sarah and her parents have moved on, and I just catch a last glimpse of her coat as they disappear into the arena.

Through the heavy doors to the arena, I hear an announcement come over the loudspeaker, followed by some cheesy '90s dance music, and I know that the game is about to start. There's a flurry of activity in the foyer as people hurry to make it inside and grab seats, and the line disappears entirely.

I'm so deep into the act of counting money, writing down amounts on a piece of scrap paper, and organizing it into the proper slots in a small metal lockbox, that I don't notice that the inner door has opened and closed again until a deep voice startles me out of my daze.

"Hello, Delia." It's Detective Avery, standing next in line, wearing a parka and stocking cap with jeans. He looks so different out of his typical detective's outfit that it takes me a second to place him.

"Oh," I say. "Hey there."

"Everything going well with you?"

I nod. "Sure. Yeah, everything's fine. Just helping out the student council."

"I saw you when I came in earlier," he says. "I wanted to talk to you, but I could tell you were busy." His face is so serious that I worry he's going to drop some new bomb.

"Is everything okay?" I ask.

"Yes," he says. "Certainly. I just wanted to see how you were doing. I'm sure that this whole episode has dragged up some bad memories for you."

"They didn't really need dragging up, if I'm being honest," I tell him.

He nods and drops his gaze. He picks up the construction paper sign and examines it carefully, as if he's deeply interested in the details of our 50/50 draw.

"I thought I should tell you, before the media finds out tomorrow, we're going to change from a search to a recovery."

It takes me a moment to catch his meaning.

"You mean you're going to be looking for a body?"

He puts the sign back on the table and meets my gaze. He nods, his face grim.

"Yes. We don't think that O'Donnell is keeping her alive anywhere. We're pretty sure that if he'd hidden her, he'd have fessed up by now. Unfortunately, with the weather we've had, it's going to be hard to know where to start. The snow has covered a lot of possible evidence."

"So you still think he did it?" I ask.

He nods. "It's clear at this point that he was responsible. He's not talking, but his fingerprints are all over that room in the abandoned house, along with paper clippings that match the cutout letters on the kidnapper's note. And…" He trails off, and I find myself gripping the edge of the table.

"And what?" I demand.

"We found hair that has been proven through DNA to match Layla's."

I feel sick and weak, like I might faint.

"I'm sorry, Delia," says Avery. "I know this is all quite awful news to hear, but I wanted you to hear it from me before it goes public tomorrow. Of course it goes without saying that I'd appreciate it if you keep this under wraps. It'll be common knowledge soon enough."

"Thank you for telling me," I manage to say, even though my throat is dry. "I won't tell anyone."

"At this point, our goal is to bring closure to the family," he says. "It might not be the outcome we've all hoped for, but hopefully we'll at least be able to give them that. It's something that we weren't able to give the Carmichaels." He reaches across the table and puts a hand on my shoulder, giving it a light squeeze. "Or you, Delia. That isn't lost on me."

He turns to leave, letting in a blast of icy January air when he opens the door. I watch him through the window as he walks away through the blowing snow.

Brianna comes to find me as I'm finishing the count.

"You don't have to stick around for the draw," she says. She casts me a sideways look. "Unless, you want to? You're welcome to come out onto the ice with us between periods."

"No," I say. "It's okay. Thanks."

"Suit yourself," she says. I detect a tiny whiff of something surprising. Could it be disappointment?

"I'm not really a big fan of attention," I explain.

"Fair enough." She looks like she's struggling with herself, deciding whether or not to say something, then something happens to her face, a guard coming down.

"I'm sure this whole thing has brought up a lot of bad memories," she says. "The little girl who went missing."

I'm so surprised that I don't know how to respond, and when I don't say anything, she gets defensive.

"I mean, I'm shaken up, and I wasn't there when Sibyl went missing, but maybe I read it wrong. Maybe you don't care."

"Of course I care, Brianna," I say. "I'm just a bit surprised that you do."

"Why?" she asks, sounding pissed off. "Sibyl and I were friends too, you know. Good friends."

"I know that," I say. "I remember. But I've never spoken to you about her, never heard you talk about it at all."

She rolls her eyes. "Come *on*, Delia. We were kids when it happened, and anyway, you were basically off-limits afterward. We were all told to leave you alone, and then it's not like you grew up into a warm, approachable person. When the hell would we have talked about it?"

I nod. She's not wrong.

Something occurs to me. "What do you think happened?" I ask her.

She looks taken aback. "What do you mean?" she asks.

"With Sibby," I say. "You must have thought about it."

"God yes," she says. "I thought about it forever. We were so young. Do you know, I overheard my parents refer to the kidnappers as monsters, and I took it literally. I had nightmares for months."

I just look at her, trying to absorb this new person I didn't know existed.

She shrugs. "Maybe it was monsters. We'll never know. Do you know what did strike me though, was when Burke's uncle was first arrested, I remembered him right away. I remembered him from back then, when we were kids. He and his girlfriend, that pretty blond, they spent a lot of time with us for being a bunch of kids. When the Gerrard girl went missing, and they arrested Terry O'Donnell, I thought to myself, *Well, obviously.* I don't know why. Isn't that strange? I know he had nothing to do with Sibyl's disappearance, but there's just something about the way he was around back then, building that tree fort, always encouraging us to go play in the woods, that made him, like, the perfect suspect."

"He had an airtight alibi," I say. "They were with the O'Donnell kids at a movie."

She nods. "Yeah, I know. I obviously extrapolated too much. But still… You know, I really feel bad for Burke." My face must reveal skepticism because she goes on. "Seriously, I do. It must be awful to have everyone sticking their nose in his family's business. How's he doing anyway?"

This way of looking at things takes me by surprised, and it occurs to me for the first time that the thing I was most worried about—being exposed and presented to the world by Quinlee Ellacott—has actually ended up happening to Burke and his family instead. I'm so surprised at her perceptive take on the situation that I tell her the truth. "I don't really know to be honest. He's not really in touch."

She sniffs, and her condescending poise returns as quickly as it disappeared. "He's going to screw himself over if he doesn't get past himself and start coming back to school."

I shrug. "Not much I can do about that."

"Anyway, I should get back in there," she says. "Thanks again for helping out. I'll see you at school."

With a flounce of her ponytail, she turns and pushes through the heavy doors into the arena.

I walk over to look through the thick glass at the game going on. It seems like the entire town is in there, sitting together in the cold, rooting for the same thing.

Something Brianna said is clawing at the inside of my mind, trying to escape. I'm trying to put my finger on it when the door opens again, and Sarah steps out of the arena and into the lobby. She smiles uncertainly as she approaches.

"Hey," she says. "How are you doing?"

"I'm okay," I say. "Although I've somehow been hypnotized into selling tickets."

She laughs. "Well, I'm glad you're here. I've been meaning to talk to you, and there are always so many people around at school."

"Listen," I say. "I owe you an apology. I was—"

She holds up a hand to silence me. "Dee. Just let me finish, okay?"

"I'm sorry," I say. I mime zipping my lip.

"I just wanted to tell you that I totally understand how tough all this must be for you. After everything you've gone through, it must be like reliving it all over again. I know you need your space, and I respect that, but please remember that I'm here for you whenever you need someone to talk to."

I smile at her. "Thank you. That means a lot to me. I promise I *will* want that. I just need a bit of time to work a few things out."

"Take all the time you need," she says. "I'll be here." She smiles again and slips back inside the arena.

28.

Transcript of **RADIO SILENT**
Episode 44 (Excerpt)

HOST (intro): I am *the Seeker*, and this is *Radio Silent*. I've been receiving emails from all over North America, asking me to inform our listeners about one case after another. I do my best, listeners. I try to keep on top of things, but as much as I'd like to, I can't do every case.

I wish I could.

I'm going to return today to Houston, where Nia Williams and Vanessa Rodriguez are still missing.

There've been a few developments in the case since I last spoke to you. For one thing, the meetup that Carla and Danetta organized was extremely successful. I've been in touch with Carla, who tells me that almost three dozen people showed up, and they came with information.

RECORDING: *(voice of Carla Garcia)* There was a huge turnout, and we learned from a few regulars at Impact Café, along with a couple of other servers that worked with Vanessa, that Vanessa and Nia had struck up a friendship over the past few years. As far as we know, they didn't socialize outside of the diner, but Nia always sat in Vanessa's section, and during quieter late shifts, the two of them would often end up chatting for long stretches, with each other as well as with the other regulars around the place. It was kind of amazing, because we started to hear stories about how Vanessa and Nia were really friendly. I guess you'd call them friends. Then this guy got up and told us that he works at Impact Café, and he told us a story.

RECORDING: *(voice of Bradley Plum)* I'm a server at Impact and I worked a lot of the same shifts as Vanessa, and every once in a while, she'd have to deal with guys getting fresh with her or whatever. You work in enough restaurants and you start to see the kind of shit women put up with when they're waiting tables. Anyway, there was this one man in particular who started coming in every few nights, and he liked to bug Vanessa. Sometimes she'd ask me to take his table so she wouldn't have to deal with him. But one night, Nia happened to be in the restaurant, sitting at her normal booth, nursing a beer, and the guy started to harass Vanessa.

I was caught up with a really big table on the other side of the restaurant, a bachelor party or something like that, and I didn't have time to intervene, but by the time I had the chance, Nia was already on the case. *(Laughter)* She was being pretty funny, ridiculing the guy, and people at other tables were even getting involved, turning around and laughing. You could tell that the guy was pissed. He eventually got up, dropped his money on the table, and stormed out. We never saw the guy again.

RECORDING: *(voice of Danetta Bryce)* Bradley told this story, and it wasn't anything too crazy. I mean, it's not a really bizarre thing to learn that a waitress was harassed by a man she's serving. We all live in the world, right? But the fact that both of them had this kind of encounter with some creep—it was unsettling to say the least. And then...well, we asked Bradley when all of this had happened.

HOST: As it happens, the encounter Bradley describes happened less than a week before Nia went missing.

RECORDING: *(voice of Carla Garcia)* It was like a bomb had been dropped into the middle of the room. Nobody spoke for a very, very long time. But we knew we had something.

HOST: What follows is a recording from a public press conference held yesterday by the Houston Police Department.

RECORDING: *(voice of Detective Britta Wilkinson)* Due to recent information that has been brought to our attention, the Houston Police Department has begun to investigate the possibility that the unsolved disappearances of Nia Williams and Vanessa Rodriguez could be connected. We want to be clear that, at this point, this is solely a theory, but we would like to bring to the public's attention a composite sketch of a man believed to be a person of interest.

HOST: On our show page and social accounts, you'll find a link to the sketch that a police sketch artist provided based on the description Bradley Plum provided and other details of the renewed investigation.

As always, we appeal to anyone in the *Radio Silent* community in and around Houston to pay close attention to this case, and please let us or the authorities know if you have any relevant information.

Is there something *we* can do to help?

Listen up.

Let's try.

29.

After I've posted the episode, I sit back in my chair and crane my neck to look back at the window. It's late, but I'm wide awake. There's something about shifting attention onto this case that reminds me of why I wanted to do this in the first place. Maybe I can still do some good. Maybe I don't have to do it all alone.

I stretch my arms over my head, then lean back to the computer and open my browser. There are already a few new emails, and as I watch, the app refreshes and a new one pops into my inbox.

I think I know who you are, the subject line reads.

My first instinct is to jerk back and slam the laptop shut. Has Quinlee Ellacott found me? Is this the end of my anonymity forever? Reluctantly, I reach forward and snap the computer open again, clicking on the link. It isn't Quinlee

Ellacott's address; it's from what appears to be a burner Gmail account. I roll my chair forward and read the message.

> I think I know who you are, but I'm not sure. I also think you know who I am, but I'm not sure. If you get this, turn off your light, wait ten seconds, and then turn it on again.

My hands are trembling, and my palms go dry, but I lean forward and reach out, fumbling for the chain on the light, catching it and dragging my fingers lightly down the tiny metal beads before pulling it down, turning the light off.

My heart is pounding as I pull back from my desk, sliding the chair back far enough that I can just see past the lower edge of my window down to the house across the street.

Ten, nine, eight…

I don't want to give up my secret.

Seven, six, five…

But if this is what I think it is, it's too much for me to handle alone. I need the help.

Four, three, two…

Even as I reach for the light, I'm standing up from my chair. I pull the dangling metal cord and the light turns back on. Then I walk to the window.

For a long moment I just stand there, exposed, visible and vulnerable, staring at the darkened house across the street. If she's there, she can see me clearly, and for now, that's all I want: for her to look up at me; I want her to see me in my tower. I want someone to know who I really am, and to watch me with that knowledge. I want it to be *her*.

When the light in her room comes on, my breath catches

in my throat. Sarah stands across the street, her hand against her window, looking across at me.

For a moment that stretches out forever, we stay like that, watching one another. So much closer than I ever thought I'd get to Sarah, to *anyone*, but still divided by a gulf of ice, air, and darkness. Then Sarah smiles and turns away from the window. A moment later, her light goes off again.

Shaking, I sit back at my computer, skimming my thumb across the trackpad, and the screen pops back into life. I notice right away that there's a new message in my inbox, freshly arrived.

Meet me at my car, says the subject line.

My path through the house is enchanted, every step on every floorboard light enough to keep the creaks from calling out, every shadow melting onto me, helping me escape in darkness and unbothered peace. In the main hallway, I stop and slip into my boots, then slide into my coat, wincing at the rustling slide of polyester, although there's no way that anyone upstairs will hear me at this point. Before I let myself out onto the front porch, I glance back down the dark hallway, to where the kitchen is basking in the soft blue glow of moonlight.

I let myself out, locking the door behind me, and then skimming down the veranda steps, running across the front yard, across the sidewalk, across the street, and then, without stopping, into Sarah's car.

It's snowing, thick, feathery flakes drifting around me as I open the door and slide inside. She's sitting there, staring across at me as I get in. Her face is blank, expressionless, and I wonder if somehow there's been a misunderstanding, but then she's hurling across at me, and before I know how this has happened, our faces connect.

I've kissed only one girl before. At camp when I was thirteen. A dare, really. Her dare. A moment late at night when everyone seemed to think it made the utmost sense to send the girl toward me, the girl most likely to be queer. It was short, uncomfortable, and I felt awkward and exposed afterward.

This is different. There's no confusion or self-doubt. The awkward wondering that characterized my previous attempt is gone. The flush of wanting spreads over me and wipes away all my feelings of anxiety.

She's smaller than I am, a tightly wound package of muscle and limbs. Our mouths probe at one another, softly chewing and sucking at bottom lips, breathing past one another's tongues. A rush of blood shuttles past my ears. One of her hands clasps the back of my head, and I feel my hat come off, the cold air rushing over my head, making me feel like I'm sinking.

She pulls away, and we stare at each other wide-eyed, breathless. I press my hands into my lap, willing them to stop shaking.

"I wish we could sneak inside, into your room," she says.

I smile and reach over to tuck a wisp of hair behind her ear, underneath her beanie. "We'd never make it to the attic," I say. "I can navigate the creaky steps, but you'd never make it. We'd end up waking up the whole house."

She turns and looks at her own house. "We'll have to go into mine, then," she says.

"What about your parents?"

She smiles, her eyes bright. "It'll be fine. They sleep like the dead."

I smile back. It all seems so obvious now, unquestionable. How could I have ever thought I wanted space from her?

"Yeah," I say. "Let's do it."

She opens the driver's side door and steps out, and I slide across the bench seat, following her. She shuts the door, a dull metallic *crunch*, but the sound is absorbed and muffled by the falling snow. We both stifle laughter as we tiptoe through the snow to her back door.

As she digs inside her slippery nylon coat for her key, I turn and scan the silence of the street before settling on my house, the tower, my bedroom window. For so many years, I've been sitting up there, staring down at the street, wondering who might come into sight, the things I might see if I put my face up to the glass at the right moment. Now I'm the one out here, in full sight of the half-moon eye at the top of the house.

Nobody watching me.

Inside the house, we step out of our boots, slide out of our coats, move through the mudroom into the dark main space of the house. We're in a kitchen, dimly lit by a light in the vent hood. Sarah takes me by the hand and pulls me through the dining room, into a hallway lined with soft, plush carpet, and we tiptoe up the stairs and across an upper landing. At the door to her bedroom, she stops and points across the landing at a door, partially ajar, the red glow of an alarm clock telling me that it's 3:03 in the morning.

My parents, she mouths, and I nod to let her know that I understand.

With a soft *click*, she opens the door and we slip inside.

The room is small and warm. Posters neatly line the walls.

The Misfits, The Runaways, My Chemical Romance, vintage punk, colorful gig posters.

Like a detail in a dream that tells you things aren't really happening the way you think they are, the bed is covered with an old-fashioned quilt, the kind you'd find in your grand-mother's linen closet.

Sarah lets go my hand and turns to face me, dropping back to sit on the bed as she does.

"Come sit with me," she says.

I don't need to be asked twice. I take a seat next to her, and she leans forward, pressing her forehead against mine.

"I've been wondering if something like this would happen," she whispers, and then she pulls me down onto the bed.

The part that makes me the happiest is lying there, not thinking about the things that usually fill my mind, make me tight with anxiety.

"So tell me about the podcast," she says, turning sideways to face me, the back of her hand brushing absently along the outer edge of my hip.

"What do you want to know?" I ask.

"How did it all happen?" she asks.

I close my eyes, thinking about how to answer. It's a simple question, but none of this is a simple thing.

"Basically, I needed somewhere to talk things over," I said. "To feel like I'd done something, after years of feeling like I'd done nothing. Accomplished nothing. Or no, not nothing, but the wrong thing. I'd made everything worse when I could have made it better."

"You didn't—" she begins, but I smile and hold a finger up

to her lips.

"It's okay," I say. "I know I wasn't responsible, but that doesn't keep me from feeling guilty. You know?"

She nods. "Sure."

"I was having trouble sleeping back then," I say. "So I woke up one night and decided to try doing something. I couldn't save Sibby, but I could do my best to maybe save someone else. Or at least get other people to help."

"So you started a podcast."

I laugh. "It sounds so crazy, but yeah, basically I did. It was small for like two months, and then it took off."

"The babysitter who took those kids?" she asks.

"Yeah. It was kind of crazy. It happened super quickly, and then all of a sudden, I'd actually done something, just like I wanted to."

"That's when I heard about you," she says. "People on my Twitter were all going nuts about it."

I nod. "It got big quick," I say. "A lot bigger than I ever expected it too."

She smiles and reaches over to run her hands through my hair. "It should have gone big," she says. "It's amazing. You're really talented, Dee."

The compliment makes me feel both thrilled and uncomfortable at the same time. "I do my best," I say. "Sometimes it works. Sometimes it doesn't. The hard part is figuring out what cases to cover. There are so many of them, more than you'd ever expect, and I want to make sure I pick cases that are worth the effort, that are worth the time people put into them."

"Not like Danny Lurlee," she says.

"You listened to those?" I ask.

She nods. "What a dick."

Danny Lurlee is a guy in Kansas who staged a violent abduction in his trailer, complete with his own blood, and faked his own disappearance, all so he could get away from his family and some debt and start fresh. I covered it on the show for three episodes before the LDA came up with evidence that led to his arrest as he tried to cross the border into Mexico.

"Guys like him are the exact opposite of why I started the podcast," I say. "I was furious, felt like I'd been taken advantage of. But I learned my lesson. I make sure to focus on people who deserve the attention."

"Like those women in Texas," she says.

"Yeah. It makes me feel good to know that I'm helping people who need it, especially since I wasn't able to help when Sibby was taken." I turn away, avoiding her eyes. "But now something's happened."

I feel her shift on the bed, sitting up to rest back on her elbows. "What happened?"

"I got an email," I tell her. "From someone who thinks they saw Sibby."

"What?" She sits up the rest of the way, and I turn to see her staring down at me, her face wide and surprised.

I nod, and a warm rush of relief works its way through me as I realize how happy I am to have someone to talk to about this.

I pull up the email on my phone and read it to her. When I'm done, she flips over onto her back and stares up at the ceiling, thinking.

"So what do you think?" she asks.

"It's got to be some crank," I say. "Some weirdo who thinks

they're helping by putting a random, useless theory into the world."

"Why would anyone think that was helpful?" she asks me.

"I can't figure it out," I tell her.

"What do your instincts tell you?" she asks.

"I'm not sure my instincts are much use," I tell her.

"Bullshit. You've been doing so much good work, all because your gut told you to. Do you think this is the real deal?"

I hesitate. Sarah sits patiently, waiting for a response. Absentmindedly, I reach out and stroke the back of her hand. "I think there's something to this," I say. "I think that this person knows something."

She grips my fingers and holds my hand in place. "Well, then, you have to do something," she says. "If something is telling you that Sibby is still alive, you have to do something."

"Like what?" I ask. "There's no way to trace the email, and it's not like I'm going to go and reveal everything to the cops. I mean, if there was something there that they could act on, maybe I'd have to, or at least I could just send them an anonymous note the way I always do, but there isn't anything. I need something more concrete."

"Well," says Sarah, "maybe it's time we started digging a bit deeper."

"How?" I ask.

"You're the one with the world famous true crime podcast," she says. "You tell me."

I think about it for a minute. "I spoke to Sibby's family," I say. "Her sister told me that her mom was really suspicious of someone in particular."

"Really? Who?"

"Burke's uncle Terry had a girlfriend with him that summer," I say. "Sandy. She was young and pretty, and I think we all kind of had crushes on her. And then Brianna…"

"Brianna?" asks Sarah, surprised. "I thought you hated her."

"I don't hate her," I say. "It's more complicated than that. She was one of Sibby's best friends when we were younger. She mentioned that she remembered being around that summer, and that Terry and his girlfriend were there too much. It all reminded me of something Terry said when he and I and Burke were in the woods together during the search party. He sounded guilty about Sibby's disappearance. He said that if he hadn't built the treehouse, it never would have happened."

"You think he might have had something to do with it after all?" she asks.

I shake my head. "There's no way he could have been involved. They weren't around that day. There's proof of that. And the two cases are a bit similar on the surface, but when you start to examine them, they're actually really different. Besides, the guy's a bit of a loser, but I can't picture him kidnapping a kid and killing her."

"So why bother tracking down his ex-girlfriend?" asks Sarah.

I think about it. "I'm just not convinced. Something in my gut is saying that I'm missing something. That there are pieces missing."

"Well, in that case," she says, "I think you should follow your instincts. You're closer to that case than anyone. Go find this woman and see what she has to say."

I think about this. "How?"

Sarah gives me an incredulous look. "Come on, Dee, hasn't the Laptop Detective Agency taught you anything?"

30.

Sure enough, Sandy, or Sandra as she's now known, isn't that hard to track down. After just a few minutes on Burke's mom's Facebook account, we're able to find an old photo of Terry and Sandy. Sandy's name is grayed out, indicating she's deleted her account, but her last name is still there—Willis. A bit of surfing later and we've found her.

Two days later, we're in the city, standing in front of a row of suburban townhouses that curves around a cul-de-sac, the kind that look like they were built in the eighties and never changed since. Every single one looks the same: like a shoebox standing on end, with a triangle sliced off the upper edge, dark smoky windows, a covered entryway notched into the side.

"You should go first," says Sarah as we stand uncertainly at the end of the little walkway. "You've got the connection."

It was Sarah's idea to hunt down Terry O'Donnell's ex-girlfriend Sandy, to see if she believes that he kidnapped Layla, and whether she might have some insight into what happened to turn him into a kidnapper. To find out more about what she remembers from the time that Sibby was taken.

I reluctantly cross the front yard, stepping on the round concrete pads that are set into it like lily pads, and walk up two steps to the front doorway. There's a Christmas wreath on the door, even though it's almost February. It's one of the overtly religious ones, with a cross attached to the ribbon.

As I press the doorbell, it occurs to me that I've never been in front of a mystery like this one. I've always been hidden behind the shadow of my microphone, orchestrating other people as they make inquiries. My heart beats extremely fast as I wait for someone to answer, telling me that I'm not cut out for this.

"There doesn't seem to be anyone home," I say, turning to leave.

"You only just rang it," says Sarah. She reaches around me and raps loudly on the glass window in the upper edge of the door, then steps back behind me again, shoving her mittens into her pockets.

A few seconds go by and nothing happens.

"Seriously, Sarah," I say. "I don't think this—"

The door opens inward all of a sudden, and I jump slightly.

"You look surprised," says the woman behind the door. "Didn't you just knock?"

I nod. "Yes, sorry," I say. "I just didn't think there was anyone home."

"Well, here I am," she says. "Can I help you?"

The woman is nothing like the Sandy I remember, who was trim and pretty, dressed in form-fitting T-shirts and cool jeans, occasionally dresses. Her hair was cut just above the shoulder with a slight wave in it.

This woman is much more conservatively dressed, with a thick cable-knit sweater over a long, floor-length skirt. Her hair is cut into a sensible bob, and she's not wearing any makeup. Around her neck is a thin gold chain with a cross on it. But I can tell right away that it's her. The big blue eyes staring at me as she waits for me to speak, bring me back a decade, to when I was just a little girl, and she was the most glamorous person I'd ever met.

"You probably don't remember me," I say. "I'm Dee—Delia Skinner. I was—am—friends with Burke O'Donnell. You used to go out with his uncle Terry."

Her face goes pale, and she puts a hand to her throat. Her mouth opens slightly, and she stares at me, blinking slowly.

"My goodness," she says finally. "You've grown up, Delia."

"Yeah. I guess that's true," I say. I turn to Sarah. "Um, this is my friend Sarah."

Sarah holds up a hand and gives a little wave, and Sandy nods slightly, acknowledging. We stand there for a moment, and I don't know what to say next, when Sandy manages to choke out a little laugh.

"Come in, girls," she says. "It's cold outside."

"Okay," I say. "Thanks."

We follow her into a small entryway, beige tiles and a boot mat underneath a small round mirror that's hung between two religious cross-stitches.

"Let me take your coats," she says, and we dutifully pull them off and hand them to her so she can hang them over the back of a chair. We kick off our boots and follow her into her house. The tile in the threshold makes way for a thick beige carpet that seems to run throughout the house, up the stairs, into the dining area, and beyond, to the small living room, divided from the little kitchenette by a shelf full of knickknacks.

"Come in," she says, leading us to the living room. "Have a seat. Can I offer you anything? I have herbal tea. No coffee, I'm afraid. I avoid anything caffeinated."

"I'd take a glass of water, please," I say.

She glances at Sarah, who nods. "That'd be great, thanks."

She moves off into the kitchen, and we perch on the edge of the sofa. It's deep, with a feminine curve of carved wood along the back, and a pattern of pale blue stripes and yellow roses.

As we hear the cupboard opening and water running, I look around the room. A bookcase in the corner is mostly stocked with small ceramic angels, but one shelf is lined with neatly arranged books. A Bible, some religious self-help texts. No novels or anything really interesting to be seen. There doesn't seem to be a TV of any kind.

A wooden cross is hung prominently on one of the soft pink walls, surrounded by a small collection of neatly framed prints, mostly religious scenes and Bible quotes written in calligraphy.

Super religious, mouths Sarah.

"No kidding," I whisper back as Sandy returns to the living room with two tumblers of ice water.

"Thanks," we echo, as she hands them to us and sits, smiling and once again unruffled, in a prim armchair on the other side of the room.

"So," she says. "What brings you here today?"

I take a sip of water and clear my throat. I don't know what to say, and I realize now that I should have planned it out better.

"I'm not sure if you've heard about Terry," I say.

She nods gravely. "Yes. I did read about it in the newspaper."

"You still read the paper?" asks Sarah, genuinely surprised. "Not the internet?"

Sandy smiles and points toward a table in the corner of the room, where there is indeed a newspaper folded crisply underneath a flowered china lamp.

"I prefer to read my news the old-fashioned way," she says. "As a matter of fact, I don't have access to the internet. I don't even own a computer, to tell you the truth."

Sarah's mouth drops open. "You've got to be kidding me."

Sandy laughs lightly, then her face hardens and she stares across at us with a fresh intensity that makes me feel deeply uncomfortable. "The internet is a Godless place. A modern-day Tower of Babel. There are many young people being led astray by the notions they find online. I won't be part of it."

"Notions," echoes Sarah.

Sandy nods once, then casts a judgmental gaze back and forth between us. "It isn't my place to make assumptions, but there are many ways for a soul to be led astray."

It's obvious what *assumption* she's talking about. Neither of us say anything, and I'm keenly aware of Sarah's hand on the sofa just a few inches from mine. I want to grab it, to pull her closer to me, but I know that it would only serve to have us kicked out of this strange woman's house, and I need to hear what she might have to say.

"But you have read about Terry O'Donnell in the paper?" I ask, bringing the subject back around.

"Yes," she says. "Yesterday was the first I heard about any of it: the kidnapping, the charges against Terrance. A terrible business."

She sounds like an old lady, although she can't be older than thirty-five, thirty-six.

"It's a strange coincidence, don't you think?" I ask. "That the girl was taken from my old house? Almost exactly ten years after Sibby disappeared?"

"Is that why you're here?" she asks. "To ask if Terrance had anything to do with the disappearance of Sibyl Carmichael?"

"You knew him better than anyone," I say.

She laughs. "Terry and I weren't together long," she says. "He was a road bump. One of many, I regret to say." She leans forward and clasps her hands together, her elbows on her lap. Her voice takes on a pious quality. "Girls, I don't want to sound judgmental, because I was there. I was an impressionable young woman, easily caught up in a life of cheap promises. I've since learned that there *is* an easy path to happiness, but it isn't the one I thought I was on. The only true way is to follow the Lord and trust in his goodness."

"You still haven't answered our question," I say. "Do you think Terry could have had anything to do with this girl's disappearance?"

She sighs, throws her hands up. "I honestly don't know. Like I said, I barely knew him when we were together. I haven't spoken to him since we split up, shortly after that awful situation. We went our separate ways. But I will tell you that he had nothing to do with the disappearance of Sibyl Carmichael. Nothing at all. I was with him that day, along with Burke and Mara and Alicia. We'd gone to a movie. As far as this new girl, I know nothing about it."

She stops talking and bows her head to stare at her hands, as if squeezing in a quick prayer.

"I don't know what happened to Terry after that summer, girls," she says. "When you're my age, you'll better understand the paradox of time. A decade goes by in the blink of an eye, but when you look back across it, it feels like a million years. Somehow, both things are true." She turns back to look at us. "I always knew Terry needed guidance. He was a gambler, into drugs and bad characters and unsavory places. I was naive enough to think I was the one to guide him, but of course that never works out like you hope. It turns out I needed as much guidance as he did, and I'm happy to say that I found it in my savior, the Lord Jesus Christ. I can only assume that Terrance allowed his soul to be led down the wrong path until he reached the point of no return. I can't judge him for sinning, as I'm a sinner myself. There but for the grace of God go I."

"Do you remember anything from that summer?" I ask her. "Anything weird that might stand out?"

"Not really," she says. "I've obviously thought about it a lot over the years, racked my brain to see if there was anything I might have missed that could have helped. I'm sure everyone in that neighborhood did the same thing. But nothing ever comes up. I barely knew Terry's family, let alone you neighbor kids."

"So what do you think happened?" I ask.

She gives me an astonished look. "How on earth would I ever know what happened?"

"Everyone has a theory," I counter.

She turns away and stares at the wall again, her lips pursed, as she thinks it over.

"I can't for the life of me imagine why someone would take a child," she says. "I suppose if I had to guess, I'd say some hunters just came across you and Sibyl, and the devil took control of them."

Sarah lets out a burst of incredulous laughter. "Are you serious? You think the devil was responsible?"

Sandy gives her an agitated look. "I don't know what to believe," she snaps. "I wasn't there." She gets up from her chair and walks to the cross on the wall. Clasping her hands in front her, she stands and gazes at it.

"Maybe it was the exact opposite," she says without turning to look at us. "Maybe she was taken into a home of faith. Maybe God decided she deserved a chance at blessed salvation."

I exchange a look with Sarah. Her eyes are wide as she mouths, *What the fuck?* I know we're both thinking the same thing. We stand at the same time.

"We should leave," I say. "We have to get back to Redfields before dark."

Sandy turns to us, her religious reverie broken. "I have to ask: Why are you digging this up again now?"

I'm ready with an answer. "It's been ten years," I say. "It's been on my mind lately, and I need to ask questions now, so I can stop thinking about it as much in the future."

She nods as if my answer makes perfect sense. "I'll be praying that the poor girl is found," she says. "Just as I pray for Sibyl Carmichael, every single day."

We're at the door when she reaches out and grabs me. I look down at her hand, clasped tight around my wrist, and I freeze. I allow my gaze to lift to her face and find her staring intently at me, almost furiously.

"I hope you know I'll be praying for you too," she says.

* * *

Back in the car, I lean forward and put my face in my hands.

"Are you okay?" Sarah asks, reaching over to put her hand on my back.

I sit up and exhale sharply. "I don't want to do this anymore."

She leans across the seat and kisses me on the cheek. "It's okay," she says. "You don't have to explain anything to me."

"I do though," I say. I reach down and take her hand. "Sibby has been gone for ten years, and everything I've ever learned about missing people is that the longer they're gone, the greater the chance that they never come back, and when it's been this long, the percentage is even steeper. I have to ask myself, what's the point? Why am I doing this?"

She nods sympathetically, and I slap my hand on the dash and let out a small scream of frustration.

"It's just too much," I say. "I get crank emails all the time.

It comes with the territory. It makes sense that memories of Sibby are bubbling up, and people are looking for ways to stay involved, especially now that it looks as if Layla's gone forever. If it hadn't been for my own connection, I wouldn't have given this email another thought."

"You have to cut yourself some slack, Dee," she says. "This would be too much for anyone to deal with."

"I just want to be free of it," I say. "I need to just accept that I'm never going to find out what happened to Sibby. It's time to move past it and focus on what I *can* do."

"Like the podcast," she says.

I nod. "This Houston case we've been profiling is turning into something. I can feel it. That's something I can work on."

"Then you should do that," she says. She reaches over and runs her hand through my hair. "You should be proud. You've done amazing things."

"I helped make amazing things happen," I correct her. "And that's enough for now. I don't need to do more. I want to live my life like a normal person, without this huge tragedy hanging over me for the rest of my life." I turn to look at her. "I want the podcast to move forward because it's helping, not because I need it to help me. I want to go to the winter dance with my girlfriend, and be normal for a change."

"Don't be *too* normal," she says.

I smile at her. "I promise. I'll be just as normal as I need to be, and we'll leave it at that."

"That sounds perfect," she says.

31.

Here's the thing: I don't *do* formal wear.

I like the way I dress, but when it comes to anything even close to formal, I'm out of my element. I haven't even worn a skirt since I was forced to for a family wedding when I was, like, eleven. Since finding out that Sarah and I were planning on going to the Winter Carnival Dance, my mom has offered several times to take me shopping, but the thought of making my way through the mall with her, trying on clothes in awful women's boutiques, worried about maybe running into one of the girls from school, *Brianna* even, put the kibosh on that idea.

Now that I only have a couple of hours to get ready, I'm beginning to regret my reluctance. The only thing remotely resembling a dress in my entire closet is this long sweatery thing that my grandmother gave me for Christmas a couple of years ago. It goes down to my knees and is sort of a greenish-blue wool, with giant wooden buttons down the front. It looks like a cross between an old man's cardigan and a housecoat.

I lay the sweater thing on the bed and consider it. Could I wear it ironically? Maybe with a belt and high boots? I sigh out loud and glance longingly at my laptop. I wish I could ask the *Radio Silent* army what they think. Maybe there's an laptop detective out there who's just dying to give the Seeker a makeover.

There's a knock on the door at the bottom of the stairs.

"Dee?" my mother yells. "Can I come up?"

"Yeah," I call down.

A moment later, she appears at the top of the steps and walks over to stand next to me, where I'm staring at the clothes I've pulled out and laid out on my bed. She reaches down and pulls up the sweater thing. She holds it in front of me, tilts her head to consider.

"It's the closest thing I have to a dress," I say, and she nods. She catches my eye, and we both burst out laughing.

"Over my dead body will you wear that to a formal dance," she says. "Actually, you aren't allowed to wear that anywhere. Good grief. Come on." She turns and gestures to the stairs. "Let's check my closet."

Reluctantly, I follow her downstairs.

My parents' room sits at the front of the house, big and cluttered. The bed is made, just barely, and on both sides are stacks of books.

She opens her closet and reaches up for the cord that turns on the light. She begins flipping quickly through racks, pulling things out and pushing them back in again, with repeated glances back at where I'm standing with my hands shoved into my pockets.

"Don't worry about it," I say. "I don't think this is going to work. Clothes don't look good on me."

"Hush," she says. "I'm thinking." She throws a pair of black pants on the bed and moves to my father's side of the closet.

She begins pulling out button-down shirts, one after the other in rapid succession, holding them out in front of her for a quick, squinting look, before shoving them back onto the rack.

When she gets to one shirt she stops, holding it in front of her and chewing on her bottom lip. She turns and holds it in the air in front of me, squinting. Then she nods and shoves it toward me.

"I don't think this is something I want to wear," I say.

"Please, Dee," she says. "I'm good at this. Will you just try it on?"

I sigh and step past her toward their bathroom.

"With these," she says, handing me the black pants.

I pull the clothes on in the bathroom, tucking the shirt into the waistband of the chinos and trying not to roll my eyes when I look in the mirror.

When I come back out, my father is flopped on the bed. He whistles. "Great shirt!"

"You're only saying that because it's yours," I say. "I look like a backup dancer at the Grand Ole Opry."

But my mother is already back into her side of the closet, moving quickly through the rack. She stops abruptly and smiles, pulling out a wool blazer. The fabric is woven into a bold black-and-white pattern, almost dizzying.

"I love this jacket," she says. "I spent too much money on it, but it never really suited me. I think it will look great on you."

"I'm not sure that's my style," I protest.

"It's houndstooth," she says. "Classic. Just trust me."

She holds open the arms, and I reluctantly turn around and spread my arms behind me to slide into it. She spins me around to face her, smiling as her eyes track up and down the outfit.

Dad whistles. "Looking fine as fuck," he says.

"Jake," my mother warns.

"Well, she does!"

I turn and step in front of the full-length mirror in the corner of their room.

The coat has made such a difference that I can hardly believe it. Alone, the shirt made me look like a country bumpkin, but with the crisp, tailored jacket above it, it has the opposite effect, geometric and bold, the shirt popping out with the perfect splash of dramatic color.

"It looks good?" I say.

"It looks great," says Mom, coming up behind me and putting her hands on my shoulders. I let her mess around with my hair a little bit, but eventually she has to admit that there isn't a lot she can do to it, other than add a bit of pomade and slick it over to the side. Still, the effect works, and by the time she's done, I *am* feeling fine as fuck, if I do say so myself.

"Group hug!" yells Dad, and he jumps up from the bed and envelopes us.

"Delia," says my mother once I've managed to pull away. "Your father and I are really proud of you. Things can't be easy for you lately, with that girl missing, and all the stuff about Sibby dredged up like this…"

"It's cool," I say, desperate for the conversation to end. "I'm fine. Thanks."

"We just think you're great," says Dad. "And we're allowed to tell you that, because we're your parents."

"We really like Sarah too," says Mom. "We know you guys are going to have fantastic night."

"Okay, guys, thank you for all that, but I feel like this conversation was written by a bot. We should go downstairs. Sarah's going to be here soon."

When she does show up, my parents insist that she comes inside for a couple of photos. She looks like a million bucks. Her hair is done up into soft waves, and she's wearing a vintage black cocktail dress with a little fringe around the bottom.

"Wow," I say. "You sure clean up nice."

"The feeling is mutual," she says, giving me a smile that makes my stomach flip as she reaches to take my hand. "You look amazing."

We spend the first hour sitting on the bleachers at the back of the gym, making fun of people for dancing like fools. Brianna is marching around the gym making sure everything is running smoothly. She reminds me of a school governess from a vintage children's book.

Finally Sarah stands and reaches down to grab my hand.

"Come on," she says. "It's a dance after all."

I'm a bit nervous, but after a few minutes on the gym floor, I loosen up and it feels good, like this is how I'm supposed to behave. We dance and joke around, and near the end of the night, when the lights go down and the music slows, we end up swaying around in circles, breathing each other in, and everything is perfect. Settled.

* * *

When we leave the dance, laughing and kind of giddy, stepping out of the hot, sticky gym into a chilly night, it's snowing. The sky is full of the perfect kinds of snowflakes: tiny, glittering, like diamond shavings in the air.

We stand with everyone else, looking up at the night, oohing and ahhing at the sight of the snow. I feel like a normal person for a change, and when Sarah reaches over and slips a hand into the crook of my arm, drops her head onto my shoulder, I think for a moment that if I had the choice, I might actually freeze into the moment forever and stay like this, a perfect glistening statue of ice.

"Remember to drive carefully!" yells Mrs. Bellamy. "This weather is supposed to keep up, so the roads won't be clear for too much longer!"

"What do you think?" asks Sarah. "You feel safe with me driving?"

"Of course I do," I say, and when I turn to grin at her, she steps up on her tiptoes and kisses me sweetly on the lips.

"We can always stop and park somewhere if the weather gets too bad," she says. "We can probably keep each other warm."

I'm saved from having to respond, which is great, since I don't know what the hell I'd say, because I spot Burke for the first time, sitting on the stone wall across the street. He's bundled up in his parka, an oversize green stocking cap pulled down low. When he sees me notice him, he raises a hand in greeting.

"Can you hang on a minute?" I ask Sarah.

"Sure," she says, noticing Burke. "I'll get the car warmed up."

I cross the street behind a group of giggling girls a couple of years younger than me, obviously heading home to recap their first night out at an actual high school dance. They chatter off into the night as I walk up to where Burke is sitting.

As I approach, I become aware of the stale funk of weed hanging around him like a thin fog. I wonder if he's spent the whole night wandering around and smoking.

"You look sharp," he says, taking me in.

"Thanks," I say.

"I was kind of surprised to find out that you bothered to come to this," he says.

I shrug. "I guess it was worth checking out."

"Yeah," he says. "Not really my scene, but I guess people change when they start hooking up with someone."

I pull my head back, regarding him curiously. "Are you jealous?" I ask.

He snorts derisively. "Jealous? Of who?"

"I don't know, Burke," I say. "Just wondering."

He ignores me, reaches inside his jacket instead. He pulls out a piece of notebook paper and hands it to me.

"What's this?" I ask, but I'm already opening it, reading it before he answers. "An address?"

"It's a library in the city," he says. "A smaller branch."

I look at him, confused. "I don't understand."

He rolls his eyes and sighs at me. "I did a search on the Gmail address you gave me," he explains. "It wasn't tied to any social media accounts I could find, but it did pop up on a couple of message boards. Nothing interesting, just some local music fan pages, stuff like that. Anyway they were public, and the security wasn't great, so I was able to pinpoint the IP address for a few of them. That wouldn't have been much use if they'd been attached to private residences, but as it turns out, they were associated with this library."

"So what am I supposed to do with this?" I ask.

He shrugs. "How am I supposed to know?" he asks. "Listen, this is the best I could do. So do what you want with it." He hops down from the wall, done with the conversation.

"Thanks," I say. "Seriously. I appreciate it."

He stares at me for a minute, shakes his head slowly. "You know, you weren't the only person who was screwed up by Sibby's disappearance."

I take a half step back, surprised.

"What? No, of course—"

"I know you've spent your whole life feeling guilty because you were there and couldn't do anything, but I don't think you've ever stopped to consider what it was like to *not* be there. Does it ever cross your mind that I wish I'd been there to help you both?"

I stare at him, unable to process what he's trying to tell me.

"Burke," I say weakly. "You wouldn't have been able to do anything even if you were there. They were fully grown adults. We were kids."

He gives me a half smile, and I realize what he's thinking.

How is that any different from me?

"I know that, Dee," he says. "The same way you know it. But I think you forget sometimes, it wasn't just you and Sibby; it was you and Sibby and me. We were together all the time. And you got tied together with her because of that. I was just the lucky kid who wasn't hanging around that day. I lost one of my best friends too, you know, but nobody ever seemed to worry about how I was doing. They were too concerned with poor Dee."

I open my mouth to protest, but he holds up a hand to stop me. "I know how awful it sounds, Dee. Why do you think this is the first time I'm saying this to anyone?"

Before I have a chance to respond, he turns and begins to walk away, pulling his stocking cap down low and shoving his hands into his pockets before leaning into the driving snow.

It isn't long before he's disappeared into the shifting white sheet of it.

32.

I don't want to tell Sarah about the direction Burke's pointed me in. It might be nothing. It might be a mistake or the wrong clue. It might—and I doubt this, but it might—bring me right to Sibby's new doorstep. But I can't know that now, and until I know more, I want to go on my own.

The bus makes two round trips into the city every day. If I catch the 9:00 a.m. bus, I can be in the city by the time the library opens and have a few hours before I have to get back to the station at 2:00 p.m. to catch the last bus back to Redfields.

I leave for "school" early and wait around the side of the house until I'm sure everyone is gone; then I use my key to sneak in the back door, so none of the neighbors will see me, and flip open my dad's laptop.

As always, Dad's browser is open, and his Gmail account

is logged in. I quickly open a new message, type in the school's address, and type a quick message saying that Dee has an appointment and won't be in school today. I send it and wait, refreshing the browser a dozen times a minute until a reply appears from the school receptionist. "Thanks for letting us know, Mr. Skinner. We'll pass that on to her teachers."

I quickly delete the message and go into the sent folder to delete the outgoing message. Covering my tracks feels almost as bad as doing this in the first place, but I never skip school, and this time I have a good excuse. I check my time—less than fifteen minutes until the bus leaves. I'll have to run.

The bus pulls into the city depot at about 9:40 a.m., and I step off and after a quick check of the map on my phone, I walk fifteen minutes to the library. It's a newish building, and I'm happy to step out of the cold into a large, bright reception area, warm from the sun streaming through huge floor-to-ceiling windows that run along the back of the building. I walk up to an information desk and a woman looks up from her computer.

"Hi there," I say. "I'm wondering if you can point me to the public computers?"

"Sure," she says. "It's on the second floor. Do you have a card? You'll need one to log in."

I hadn't banked on this, but after I fill out a form, she hands me a fresh new library card and points me toward a stairwell behind a door on the other side of the room.

The lab is dingy, not as well maintained as the rest of the library, and the computers are definitely a few years old. I guess that's because most people use smartphones or laptops these days. There's just one woman in the room, sitting at a corner computer, typing, but the rest of the consoles are empty.

I drop into the seat closest to the door and realize I haven't thought too far ahead, and I'm not sure what to do next. I think for a moment, then turn to my screen and shake the mouse to wake the computer. I log in using my card, then open the browser history and search for "Radio Silent."

A box pops up, telling me there have been zero results.

I try "Sibby Carmichael" and "Sibyl Carmichael" and "Layla Gerrard" and "Redfields," but nothing comes up.

I log out, then shift one seat down to the next computer, log in again, and do the same searches. The woman in the corner gives me a funny look, but it's not like I'm doing anything wrong, and so she soon turns back to her work.

There are a total of fourteen computers in the room, and by the time I've made my way around all of them except for the one the woman is using, I've found nothing except a couple of news articles about the Layla case still sitting in the browser history. That's not really all that surprising considering it's the biggest news to hit the area in a while.

I glance surreptitiously at the woman. There's probably nothing on her computer either, but I can't very well leave one unchecked.

I stand, thinking that I might walk around and come back in a while, hope that her computer is empty, but when I glance at her again, she's looking right at me, and I surprise myself by walking right up to her.

"Excuse me, are you Pretty in Ink 31?"

The woman looks totally bewildered, not that I can blame her. "Excuse me?"

"I'm looking for someone," I explain. "I think it's a woman, but I'm not sure. Their email address starts with Pretty in Ink 31. That's not you?"

The woman shakes her head slowly and deliberately, and I wonder if she's trying not to unsettle me. "No," she says. "Not me." She reaches down and grabs for her purse, then stands and hurries out of the room, leaving me alone.

I'm sure she thinks I'm nuts, but there's not much I can do about that now. I sit down at the freshly vacated computer, a fresh tingle of anticipation running down my spine as I carefully enter my log-in details. For a brief, exciting moment, I'm convinced that I'm going to find something that points me in the right direction.

A quick search pops my balloon. Nothing.

I sit back into my chair, defeated, and I wish I could somehow channel the Laptop Detective Agency for this gig. Sleuthing is a lot easier when you have twenty thousand people sifting for clues. At this point, my only option is to sit here for a week and ask everyone who comes into the room if they're Pretty in Ink 31, which doesn't seem very practical.

Some moms push strollers into the room and set up at computers right next to each other, chatting loudly over the sound of their fussy babies, and I decide it's as good a time as any to leave.

I stand on the street outside the library, frustrated. There's someone out there who can help, and I just don't know how to find them. I have a few hours to kill before the next bus heads back to Redfields, and I realize that I haven't made any kind of plan for this occasion. I guess I was expecting that I'd spend the day following a trail of clues and…and what? Did I think I'd end up finding Sibby just in time to take her on the next bus with me?

Shaking my head at my stupidity, I cross to a coffee shop across the street.

The place is small and quiet, with just a few college students set up at little round tables, working on whatever it is that college students work on.

The woman behind the counter is distracted by something and takes my order without really looking at me. I grab a table in the window, and she brings my cappuccino over a few minutes later.

I sip on my coffee and open the browser on my phone, looking to see if there's some way I can kill a few hours, since I'm going to be here anyway.

I look up at a loud bang from behind the counter. Through a pass-through window behind the counter, I can see the woman who served me arguing with a man in a chef's hat.

"Archie," she's saying. "I told you I couldn't work this weekend."

The man turns away from her dismissively. "That doesn't help me," he says. "I need you here Saturday."

"I can't do Saturday," she says. "I can do Friday and Sunday, but that's all I've got for you right now."

"Sorry, kid," he says. "The schedule's been out for days. Sheree has to take her kid to the dentist on Saturday, and I can't leave Jimmy to do a full Saturday shift by himself."

She turns away and sighs, annoyed, then comes back out from the kitchen to the space behind the counter.

Something about their conversation has snagged a corner in my mind, but I can't figure out what exactly. I run back through their exchanges in my head.

Across the counter, the woman calls into the kitchen. "Archie, can you cover me for a few? I'm going out for a smoke."

A reply comes back, inaudible from where we're sitting, and the woman comes out from behind the counter, grabbing a coat from the rack. As she steps past me and pushes out the door, I glance up at her and see a tattoo creeping up from her back to cover her shoulders and neck, and suddenly I realize what grabbed my attention.

Don't bother writing me back. That's all I've got for you right now.

This woman just used the exact same phrase that was in the second email. Not exactly an unusual expression, but particular enough that I can't think of another time I've heard it used recently. The tattoo gives me another possible clue; is this what *Pretty in Ink* is referring to?

My cappuccino is still half-full, but I get up from my chair, pulling on my coat and hat.

The waitress is standing half in an alley beside the building, huddled over her phone, texting and smoking.

"Excuse me," I say, walking up to her. She glances up, curious and confused. "Are you Pretty in Ink 31?"

Her expression changes, goes darker, and she seems to shrink back from me a bit.

"What is this about?" she asks, suspicious.

"Did you write an email to *Radio Silent*, the podcast?" I ask.

Her eyes go wide. "Wait, what? How would you know that?"

I take a deep breath. I realize again that I haven't thought this out properly, but I'm in too deep to stop now.

"I am the Seeker," I say.

33.

At first she doesn't believe me, but when I recite back the gist of the email she sent to the *Radio Silent* account, her skepticism dissolves and is replaced by pure astonishment.

"You can't be more than, like, sixteen!" she says.

"I'm seventeen," I tell her.

She takes a drag of her smoke, shaking her head as she considers everything. "How did you know it was me, anyway?" she asks.

I explain to her how I traced the email address to the library and ended up at the café.

She looks at me curiously. "And you're willing to reveal yourself to me, on account of a girl who went missing ten years ago?"

I breathe out slowly, trying to decide how much to tell her. "There's a lot more to it than that."

She turns to glance back at the café. "Listen, I have to

finish my shift, but I'm off in about an hour. Do you want to hang out here until I sign out, and then we can go to my apartment to talk? I live around the corner."

"Sure," I say. "If it isn't too much trouble."

"No," she says. "It'll be good to get this stuff off my chest. I'm Alice, by the way."

"Dee," I say, shaking her hand. If she makes the connection to Delia Skinner, she doesn't let on, and we head back into the coffee shop.

I kill the next hour surfing on my phone, keeping up with developments in the Houston case. There's a new email from Carla, who has been working hard, looking for anyone who might have some info about the guy who harassed Vanessa at the Impact. There are no solid leads yet, but Carla is hard on the case. I almost wish I could ask her to take over the podcast entirely.

Finally Alice hangs up her apron and walks over to meet me, pulling her winter coat on. "I'm wiped," she says. "Can't wait to kick up my feet."

I follow her around the corner to a narrow brick building, and she pulls a key out and unlocks a heavy front door. Her apartment is up two flights of stairs and at the end of a dark, narrow hallway. Inside, however, there's lots of natural light from some big wide windows at the back of the room. A fat, cheerful-looking cat appears from a doorway, walking over to greet us.

"Hello, Barley," says Alice, bending down to scoop him up. I follow her into the apartment, stepping around a pile of cardboard boxes near the door and kicking off my boots. "Ignore the boxes. They belong to my ex. He's supposed to pick them up and keeps trying to arrange it for when I'm home. I have no interest in that bullshit, pardon my French. Grab a seat. I'll make us some tea."

The apartment is small but really cool. There are plants dangling from corners and in the windows, and the walls are hung with prints and paintings and random objects: a twisting length of driftwood, a beautiful piece of painted silk. The furniture is mismatched, probably thrifted or inherited, but it all works together.

"I love your place," I tell her as I sit on a low-slung sofa under the window. It's old, upholstered in teal-blue fabric, well-worn and nubbly, but stylish. Behind me, the wide windowsill comes down almost perfectly to the back of the couch and is lined with books.

"Thanks," says Alice. She's puttering about in the small kitchenette, pouring boiling water into a teapot, pulling pottery mugs from a cupboard. "I've been here for a few years. It feels like home."

On the coffee table, a couple of textbooks are stacked on top of some loose paper. I pick one up. *Design Fundamentals*, it says.

Alice, bringing the tea into the living room on a tray, notices me looking at the book. "It's one of my books this semester," she says. "I've gone back to school, hoping to get into graphic design."

"You've got the eye for it," I say, putting the book back on the table. Alice just smiles, handing me a mug. She sits across from me, and a slightly awkward silence follows.

"So you're the Seeker," she says finally, shaking her head

slowly, almost as if she doesn't believe it. "And I suppose you're here because you want to find Sibyl Carmichael."

"That's part of it," I say. "Why did you write that email?"

Alice frowns, takes a sip of her tea. "I asked myself that a lot after I sent it," she says. "But before I sent it, I asked myself a million times why I hadn't done it earlier. I mean, not just contact a podcast, but contact anyone. Police, reporters, someone." She shrugs. "It was when I first heard the story about that new girl, gone missing in the same town. The same street! I couldn't ignore it anymore."

"You didn't really say anything though," I say. "The email is totally vague."

"Yeah," she says. "I know. It was the best I could do at the time. Under the circumstances. Still is, if you want the truth."

"Why?" I ask. "Why couldn't you tell me something more specific?"

She closes her eyes and doesn't say anything, and after a moment, I realize that her hands are shaking slightly.

"Are you okay?" I ask.

She nods. "Yes. Just…just give me a moment."

She carefully places her mug back on the table and takes a deep breath, reaching out her arms to stretch high above her head.

"I've been afraid," she says slowly, choosing her words carefully. "For a long time. There are people who I used to know, who I worked hard to put in my past. I don't want them to know where I am or anything about me, really."

I lean forward in my seat, eager to hear what she has to say next.

"Do these people have Sibby?" I ask.

She closes her eyes and shakes her head, not as if she's denying it, but to get rid of a bad thought. She goes on.

"I just…I think that I saw her several years ago, like five or six years ago."

"Sibby would have been eleven or twelve," I say. "Are you sure it was her?"

She shakes her head. "It was a few years ago, but I was pretty sure at the time."

"Where was this?" I ask, and she sits back and runs her hand over her face. She's obviously unsettled, and I worry that she's going to clam up.

"I already told you I really don't want anyone to find out who I am either," I say. "But I didn't tell you my reasons." I take a deep breath. "I was the girl in the woods with Sibby."

Her mouth drops open, and I keep talking, hurrying to explain to her before I run out of nerve.

"I always blamed myself," I say. "That's why I started the podcast in the first place. To do something. But I could never bring myself to do a podcast about her, until…"

"Until that other girl went missing," she says.

I nod.

"Please," I say quietly. "Please tell me what you know."

She sighs and puts her hands on her knees, bracing herself.

"When I was in my early twenties," she says, "I was involved in a lot of bad stuff. Drugs, stealing, you name it. I left home. Eventually, I ended up in a bad place. A very bad place."

I wait for her to continue, but the silence seems to stretch out in front of us. A feeling of dread floats down to sit on my shoulders.

"What do you mean by that?" I ask finally. "A bad place."

She grimaces. "I met a guy," she says. "He was really charismatic. Told me I was one of the more interesting people he'd ever met." She laughs bitterly. "At that point, it was important to me, to hear that I was interesting, because I felt about as opposite of that as you can imagine."

"Where did you meet him?"

"At the park," she says. "Can you believe that? I'd been messed up, so messed up, for days. I woke up on a dirty mattress on some floor in some half-unknown apartment, and there were people all around me, tripping out quietly in the corner, sleeping some sleep that seemed deeper than death, and I sat up and realized I couldn't do it anymore. I pulled a T-shirt on, somehow stood up, got myself into my boots, a coat—wasn't even mine—and I left.

"It was late spring, but one of those really cold days that pop up when you don't expect it. I wasn't warm enough, and I just started walking. I had no job, no place to go, no roommates or friends, other than the people I'd left behind, the people I used to call friends. But I couldn't go back to them. So I stopped at this park.

"I found an empty bench, dropped onto it, tried to lie down and sleep, but I was past that. It wasn't happening. I sat back up and just watched people. It must have been around seven thirty or eight o'clock in the morning. There were so many normal everyday people walking to work. Just doing their thing, sipping coffee, looking at their phones. Shaking themselves awake into the day. And I wished...I wished I was one of them, that I was walking somewhere where I was supposed to be, you know? Have you ever had that feeling where everyone else in the world has a purpose except for you?"

She looks at me, desperate for an answer, and I nod. "Yeah," I say. "I have definitely had that feeling." And it's true.

"Then this guy just showed up," she says. She makes a gesture to indicate a magical appearance, someone emerging into a space. "He was tall, and…not exactly good-looking, but he had serious presence, like he was used to being the most important person in a room. The most dynamic. And he appeared out of nowhere, and he smiled at me—a soft, kind smile—and then he reached toward me with his hand."

I realize that I'm breathless, waiting to hear what happened. Although I think I know exactly what happened.

"And…I took it," she says. "I didn't even hesitate. I just reached up and took his hand, and he pulled me up and off of the bench. And that was how I met Barnabas."

My heart begins to pound. A name. Barnabas.

"Who was he?" I ask, not wanting to jump ahead.

"He was just…some guy. But so charismatic. He told me that he knew of a place where I could stay awhile, get my head straight. He said they were always looking for people to help. To get right with things. He told me I should come with him."

"A place?" I ask.

"A farm," she says. "Or, more like a commune."

"A cult?" I ask.

She laughs. "I didn't think it was a cult at the time, but now." She shrugs. "I don't know. Barnabas was really charismatic. He told me it was a farm with a bunch of people working on it, and that's what it was. There was a big farmhouse, and a pretty simple wooden bunkhouse, and there were barns and outbuildings, of course. I don't know a lot about cults, and I never felt like I was being brainwashed, but Barnabas had some really big ideas, and people really fell head over heels for what he had to say. I guess I kind of became that way too. Does that make sense?"

"I think so," I say.

"Anyway, they put me to work and fed me, and I made friends and fit in. Soon a week had turned into a month, and then a month had turned into a year and I was still there. Everything would have been normal, except for the girl…"

"Sibby?" I ask. I realize that I'm leaning forward anxiously, expectantly, and I will myself to relax, pull back in my seat. "Did she live on the farm?"

She shakes her head. "No. We had a weekly market during the summers. The markets would bring in the occasional drifter who'd heard about the farm and wanted to check it out. Some would end up staying for a while, but mostly it was people from the surrounding area who were curious about us. I'd see a lot of the same faces every week. There were always some kids around, and there was nothing special about this girl. I don't even know who she came with, but she was there once in a while. One day I found myself looking at her playing with some of the other kids, and suddenly it was like a clue being revealed on *Wheel of Fortune*. The thought just came into my mind: *That's Sibby Carmichael.*"

She looks up at me, and she must see the skepticism on my face. "I know it sounds weird," she says. "It's not like I'd been obsessed with that case or anything. I mean, I'd paid attention to the news when it happened, like everyone else, but I didn't think much about it afterward. And then, there she was. Or at least, I thought it was her. It was a few years after she'd gone missing."

"What did you do?" I ask.

She shakes her head ruefully. "There wasn't a lot I could do. That day after the market, I told Barnabas about my suspicions. He sounded surprised, or at least he acted that way. He said he was sure I'd been mistaken. The girl never showed up again, and I assumed she'd been with one of the families who would come to the farm to try out the services. It happened all the time, people drifting in and out. It's amazing what people will do to find some peace of mind. I figured they were all like me: they'd heard big things and ended up disappointed. The services weren't much to write home about. I think even Barnabas had moved past believing by the time I got there. He just needed the money."

"Money?"

"The farm was always in danger of falling apart," she says. "Money was tight. We ate what we could grow and raise ourselves, and the rest was from what we could sell at the market."

"You never saw her again?" I ask.

She shakes her head. "No, but that wasn't so weird. Eventually, I forgot about it, and about two months later, I left."

"And you just let it drop," I say. It comes out a lot more aggressively than I intend, but she doesn't seem to notice.

"More or less," she says with a shrug. "But then I heard about this missing girl, and I started reading about the connection to the Sibyl—Sibby—case. I couldn't stop thinking about it, that I might have seen Sibby. Finally I called the police."

"What did they say?" I ask.

"They took me seriously," she says. "They said they'd look into it and let me know what they found out. A week later, I got a call from the detective I'd spoken to. She said they'd gone to the farm and spoken to anyone who'd been there when I was, but there was no evidence that Sibby had ever been there."

Alice smiles sadly. "I told myself that maybe I'd imagined the entire thing. Like I told you, I hadn't been in the right state of mind at the time. But I couldn't drop it. I was googling her, trying to learn more, to see if there was some kind of clue that would prove to me that I hadn't imagined it all. That's how I found the podcast. I stumbled across it one night and started listening to all of your old episodes, and it seemed like the Seeker…like *you* really cared about the people you talked about. So I emailed you."

I remember something, pull my phone from my pocket, and scroll through my photos. I find what I'm looking for and hold it out to her to look.

"Did the girl look anything like this?" I ask.

She takes my phone and peers at it, then looks up at me.

"Who is this?"

"It's Greta Carmichael, Sibby's little sister. She's about twelve or thirteen in this picture."

She stares at the picture again, shaking her head. "The girl at the farm," she says finally, "looked exactly like this girl."

I'm holding my breath.

"It was her," Alice whispers, more to herself than to me. "It was really her."

"How do I get to the farm?" I ask.

34.

Sarah insists on coming with me. After I filled her in on Alice and her revelation, she was pissed that I hadn't told her about my visit to the city: "It could have been dangerous!" But she put her foot down when I told her I wanted to visit the farm myself.

"You need someone to drive you," she'd argued, "and to know where you've been the whole time."

Eventually, because she's probably right that some backup—and a chauffeur—would come in handy, I agree to let her come with me. It takes some convincing to get my parents to let me spend the night away from home, but I tell them that Sarah and I are going to be in the city with some friends because we need to get away from the media circus, and they eventually buy it. I feel really bad about lying to them, but there's not a lot I can do about it. I need to get in there, and if I have to lie to make that happen, so be it.

It isn't as easy to find the farm as I would have liked. They don't have a website or any kind of social media presence. Any mention of them that comes up from a Google search is usually some kind of disgruntled ex-member, but those are few and far between.

Alice's only real memory of the place is that it was in the countryside outside of Finley, a small town about forty miles north of us. It's not ideal, but it's enough to point us in the right direction.

We wake up really early and pack the car. It's easy to tell Mom and Dad that we'll be shopping in the city, might stay late to have dinner and catch a movie. To be honest, I think they're just happy that we're not going to be in town for a little while. *The distraction will do her good*, I can imagine them saying to one another.

It's still dark out when we leave, that kind of dim, crisp morning that's lit from the distant ambient glow of a sun that's still far, far away. I step quietly out the front door and crunch down the stairs onto the walkway, then cross the street to Sarah's house. She's already in her car, warming it up, and when I get in, she leans over and kisses me.

"Are you sure you want to do this?" she asks. "I really don't know if it's the best idea."

"If we don't at least go up there and ask some questions, we'll never know," I say. "At the very least, we can just ask around and see if anyone's seen anyone who looks like Sibby. I doubt I'd be able to get in, no matter how hard I try."

She looks relieved, and I turn away to look out the passenger window as she pulls out of her driveway. I don't want her to see my expression, to be able to tell that there's no way I'm leaving without getting a look at that farm.

By the time we reach the highway and turn west, the sky is lightening, and the fields and forests we pass are bathed in the light of a beautiful, lingering sunrise.

"You get to deejay," says Sarah, pointing to a shoebox in the backseat full of old tapes.

Soon we're spinning along the road, singing along to oldies and laughing. At certain moments, I'm able to forget where we're going, what our mission is, and it's so nice to have this sensation of being with someone, just out on the road. Someone I like, who likes me back. I reach out and put a hand on hers, squeeze it, and she glances over and smiles at me, surprised.

"Feeling romantic?" she asks with a grin. "I could always pull off somewhere."

I laugh. "Not yet," I say. "Maybe when we're celebrating finding Sibby."

"Yeah right," she says. "As if you're going to want to make out with me when your long-lost best friend is hanging out in the back seat. I mean, awkward, right?"

We're joking, obviously. Alice's story left no room to imagine that she's still at the farm, but I fall silent, imagining. If I do find Sibby at the end of this wild-goose chase, how will that feel? For me…more importantly, for her?

It takes us until almost lunchtime to get to Finley, which is even smaller than Redfields. Really, just a street with a few businesses along it, and a few dirt roads lined with trailers and old bungalows.

"Yowza," says Sarah as we creep along. "This place is creepy."

I murmur in agreement, staring out at the dilapidated buildings. I spot an old woman staring blankly out from between some lace curtains, but other than that, there's nobody else in sight.

"That place could be a good place to ask," I say, pointing at a small, low building. Tacked to the side is a large, hand-painted sign that reads *Groceries, Feed and Dry Goods*. "Feed means they probably supply most of the local farms."

There are only a couple of vehicles in the gravel parking lot: an old beige van and a little KIA hatchback. Sarah puts her signal on, preparing to turn in, but I point to the other side of the street, to an abandoned service station.

"Park over there instead," I tell her. "We can pull in beside it and stay kind of hidden. This car isn't exactly inconspicuous."

She follows my suggestion, doing a quick turn in the parking lot so she can back into the space beside the old cinder block building. From here, we have a clear view of the grocery and feed store, but someone would have to look carefully to see us.

"Better safe than sorry," I say, "right?"

I undo my seat belt, but when Sarah moves to follow my lead, I reach over and put my hand on hers to stop her.

"I'm here to help you," she says. "I don't want you going in there by yourself, asking strangers questions. What if you piss the wrong person off?"

I try to smile reassuringly. "Who am I going to piss off?" I ask. "I'm just asking where the farm is. If anyone asks why, I'll come up with something. If we want this to work, I have to seem like I'm here on my own."

She looks like she wants to argue, but I give her hand a light squeeze. "Seriously," I say. "Don't worry about me. What could happen?"

She flips my hand over and weaves her fingers between mine, looking down at them as she rubs her thumb carefully over mine.

"Okay," she says. "But be careful. Don't do anything stupid."

"I won't. I'm just asking some questions." I lean across the seat and kiss her, then reach into the back and grab my backpack, pull my hat down low, and get out of the car.

On the sidewalk, I look both ways to see if anyone is around, but there's nobody in sight. The sidewalks are empty, the buildings look dark and unoccupied, and there isn't even so much as a car on the street. I run to the other side and take the three steps up to the store. Bells jingle on the back of the door as I pull it open and step inside. The counter is just a few steps from the door, and an old guy sitting on a stool and the middle-aged woman he's counting out change to both look over at me with a mild expectation that they'll know who I am and a short-lived curiosity when they don't. They go back to their exchange, and I take in the rest of the shop.

It's dimly lit, just a few heavy, old florescent fixtures hanging between the aisles to reveal the sparse goods lined up on white plywood shelving units. A door at the back of the shop appears to lead into a fenced-in back area, and I guess that's where the animal feed is kept.

"Thanks, Frankie," the woman says, and I turn back as she scoops up her bags.

"Later," says the guy, turning back to his laptop before she's even pushed her way, after one last quick look at me, outside. "Can I do something for you?"

He's still looking straight at his laptop, and it takes me a moment before I realize he's talking to me.

"Maybe," I say, walking over to the counter. "I was wondering if you've ever heard about a communal farm around here?"

"Hey, Barney," says the man, looking behind me. "This girl's asking about that damn hippie farm of yours."

I turn around and realize that there's been someone in the place with us all along. A tall, bearded man wearing a flannel shirt is standing in the corner of the shop, next to a shopping cart that's piled with clear plastic bags filled with dried beans and rice. Canned vegetables. The man called him Barney. Could this be Barnabas?

"Is that right?" asks the man. He walks around from behind a shelf and saunters up to me, and my heart goes still with fright. He's good-looking in an angular, underfed kind of way, and he's smiling, with a mouth full of big white teeth. It's his eyes that make the biggest impression on me though. His eyes are insane. Intense and black and piercing.

He stops in front of me and looks me up and down.

"What's your name?" he asks. His voice isn't aggressive at all, but it's firm, matter-of-fact, as if he's used to getting answers when he asks for them.

I hesitate. His deep, dark eyes keep staring hard at me.

"Bridget," I say, reaching for my middle name. Then, because it's hard to think this quickly, I grab at Sarah's last name. "Bridget Cash."

"Bridget Cash," he repeats. "And how old are you, Bridget?"

"Eighteen," I say without hesitating. If I'm going to get into this place, he needs to think that I'm at least eighteen.

He nods, very slightly, then smiles. "Well, it was nice to meet you, Bridget Cash," he says. "I'm Barnabas." He moves past me to the counter and begins laying his items out for the cashier to ring up.

I follow him to the cash register, surprised. "Wait," I say.

He turns and looks at me, raises an eyebrow. "Yes?" he asks.

"What about your farm?" I ask.

"What about it?"

"I want to know about it," I say. I sound desperate and try to hold myself back a bit.

He turns back to the cashier, who rings him up. I don't feel like I've been dismissed exactly—more like he expects me to wait patiently, so I do. He pulls out a wad of dirty bills from his back pocket, counts them out, and slips a few across the counter. He takes his change and pockets it, then grabs his bags of groceries and walks to the door.

I turn to the cashier, who gives me a cryptic look.

"You coming?" Barnabas asks. I follow him out onto the covered porch.

Across the street, half a block away, Sarah is sitting in her car, the engine turned off. I force myself not to look at her, since Barnabas is staring straight at me, and I don't want him to read anything into it.

"So," he says, "what's the deal? What do you want to know about the farm?" He sets his bags down on the wooden bench and shoves his hands in his pockets, as if he's preparing to have a real conversation.

"I heard about it," I say. "From a friend. Back in the city."

"What city?" he asks, rocking slightly on his feet, back and forth in his big leather boots.

I tell him, and he nods. "We've had some guests from there. Word spreads, I suppose."

"Guests?" I ask.

He holds his hands out, palms up.

"Everyone at the farm is a guest," he says, "whether they stay a day or much longer. We've been there almost fifteen years, and a lot of the guests have stayed the whole time. Some people come and stay for a year or two, a month, even a couple of days. Just enough to learn about the farm, decide whether it's the right place for them."

"Oh," I say. I'm unsure how to continue, whether I should be pushing the conversation forward or not.

"How did you get here?" he asks.

"I took the bus," I tell him. At least this much I've figured out ahead of time.

"You came all this way to find out about the farm?" he asks. "Does that mean you want to be a guest?"

I open my mouth, but nothing comes out. I don't know how this is supposed to go. Will it be as simple as entering the farm and finding Sibby? Alice told me that she's probably not even there anymore. But she also said that she just left when she was done. And this man has said the same thing. There's nothing holding me here. I can go to the farm for a little while. A few hours, even, and figure out if there's anything else to figure out. Then I can take it from there.

"I don't know," I say. "I think I do?"

"Well, I guess there's only one way to find out," he says. He leans down and picks up his shopping bags, then steps down off the porch into the small dirt parking lot. He heaves the bags into the back of the van and then walks around to the driver's side door.

I haven't moved from the porch. "We don't try to convince people to come," he says. "People have to convince themselves. Find their way to us. You've made it this far on your own, and now here's a ride just waiting to drive you the rest of the way. But it's up to you."

I step down from the porch and walk over to the van. As he climbs in, I turn quickly toward where Sarah is parked. From this angle, I can only see a thin slice of her car, and I can just make out her face, craned forward over the dash so she can see what's happening.

Keeping my hands low, I give her a frantic, waving thumbs-up, trying to indicate that everything is okay. After a split second, she nods and I breathe out.

Barnabas turns on the engine, then reaches over to push open the passenger door.

"You coming?" he asks.

I turn and smile at him and then get inside and slam the door closed, obscuring Sarah from my sight line. With a shudder, he throws the van into drive and backs out of the parking lot. A couple of minutes later, Finley is gone behind us.

35.

"Tell me about your parents," says Barnabas as we drive away from Finley.

I've been searching for Sarah's car in the rearview mirror for the past ten minutes, but we're more or less alone on the road—no muscle cars stealthily following behind us. Is it possible that she didn't see what was happening, missed out on a chance to follow us?

"My parents aren't really in the picture," I say. I'm trying to steal a note from Alice's story. Trying to keep him from digging too much into my past. "I mean, they're around and everything. I've been living with them on and off, but they don't really have a lot to do with me. Vice versa, I guess."

He nods, makes a vague "hmmmm" sound. He doesn't seem interested in pressing very hard.

"So is the farm religious?" I ask.

He smiles but doesn't look at me. "Religious," he repeats. He doesn't answer, and the word just hangs in the air.

I think of my phone, sitting in my pocket, and wonder if I should just pull it out and pretend that I'm checking my email or something so I can send Sarah a quick text. But I worry it will look too conspicuous, and I don't want him to know I have a cell phone, just in case I need it down the road. I leave it hidden for now.

He slows down and turns onto a gravel road that twists over the snow-covered fields in front of us like a whip. I take note of the sign: *Brewster Road*. In the distance, a cluster of birds lifts up from a hedgerow and spins through the clear January sky.

This is the world, I think. *This is the empty space of the world. No people, no structures. As many fences as they build, it all comes back to this empty, empty space.*

I wonder, did Sibby come to this place? Did she look out the window of some vehicle, maybe even this van, ten years ago? Did she see the field, then in spring, and wonder what was on the other side of this emptiness?

I'm so hypnotized by the field, by the sense of dread in the pit of my belly, that when Barnabas finally responds to me, I have to stop and think about what it was that I asked him in the first place.

"What we do isn't religion," he says. "What we have isn't connected to an afterlife. It's connected to *this* life. The present. Every day, every day, every day, every day."

He stops, and I turn to him, mesmerized. Underneath the van, the road rumbles along, an erratic series of bumps that eventually turn into a pattern.

"Do you think about things like that, Bridget?" he asks. "Do you think about every minute when you're in it?"

I smile, thinking he's just bantering, that the stupid little rhyme is a joke. But he isn't smiling. The van clatters on, but his attention isn't on the road; it's on me, his eyes boring a hole into my mind.

"I think about time," I say uncertainly.

"Not time," he says insistently, and he gives the steering wheel a gentle whack, as if to punctuate how important it is that I listen to him, that I understand what he's trying to tell me. "I'm talking about the opposite of time. I'm talking about the space between moments. Being present in the pure empty space that is right"—he snaps his fingers—"now. Not who you used to be and not who you will be. Who you are."

I don't answer. I feel suddenly very afraid, and I have a sinking feeling deep in my stomach that tells me I might have made one of the biggest mistakes in my life.

He breathes out hard, shakes his head, lets out a little laugh. "Listen," he says, his voice suddenly soft and kind. "I'm sorry. I take it seriously. We all do at the farm. You'll understand more soon, I promise. And if you don't feel like this place is a good fit for you, that's fine. That's just fine. I'll give you a ride back to town, or someone will, and you can get back on the bus and you can leave."

He reaches out and puts a hand lightly on my shoulder, and my muscles tighten. I don't want him touching me, but his touch is gentle, and he quickly pulls it away.

In the distance, a house appears. It's a classic Victorian farmhouse, neat and well maintained, and nestled back into a large square that's been cut out of the forest. There are some outbuildings around the house, a giant woodpile under an awning. As we approach, I notice a Christmas wreath still on the door, and a nice sedan and a pickup truck in the driveway.

Barnabas begins to slow down the van as we approach.

"Is that the farm?" I ask.

He laughs. "No," he says. "That is definitely not the farm. Those are our neighbors. We've had our differences over the years, but we've learned to keep on their good side, and they try to keep on our good side, which basically means we leave each other alone."

A few minutes after we've passed the house, Barnabas slows down and makes a hard right turn into the forest, slowing to a crawl as we cross over a large bump at the foot of what turns out to be a long driveway. After a long drive, we approach a large metal gate. As he pulls up to the gate and stops the van, leaving it running, I see that the gate is part of a fence, and the fence is surrounding a massive clearing cut out of the forest: a huge square of land with buildings centered in it.

"Hang on a second," he says. He jumps out of the van and opens the gate wide. It isn't locked, which makes me feel a bit relieved, and when he gets back in and drives through, he says, almost apologetically, "We need to keep things fenced because we have animals."

We go over a slight rise and into the huge square, and I'm able to make out the collection of buildings more clearly. A few large animal barns are at the back and several other outbuildings, some of them small and specific looking, others long and narrow. In the center of all of them is a farmhouse. It's big, and in contrast to the other buildings, which look new, it looks like the kind of place that has been here forever.

As we approach the house, a door in the side of one of the smaller outbuildings opens, and a man steps out and begins to walk toward the house. He turns and gives a quick wave to the van as it approaches, and as we pull up outside the house, he stops and waits by the door.

Barnabas's door is on the side of the house, and when he gets out, he greets the man with another wave, then turns to look into the van at me.

I step out and smile across the hood of the van. The man stares, his expression unreadable. I know I can't be the only newcomer he's seen at this place, but he looks like every new person is a warning.

"This is Bridget," says Barnabas as he walks around to the back of the van to open the door and pull out his bags. Awkward, looking for something to do, I follow him, grab some bags.

The man comes to help. Closer, I can see that he's actually older and shorter than I thought. His posture is perfect, and he holds himself high and straight. He nods at me.

"Pierre," he says.

I smile at him, but it isn't returned. His expression shifts slightly, and his eyes become wary and drop away from me.

As Barnabas and I walk toward the house with the bags of groceries, Pierre shuts the door to the van. I follow

Barnabas onto the porch and through the front door, into the house. As I step across the threshold, I turn and look back at the driveway. Pierre is walking down the driveway to the gate.

He grabs onto it with both hands and, walking backward, pulls it closed as the inside door shuts behind me.

36.

A smiling woman, short and fat, with a tight-cropped haircut and thick, old-fashioned glasses, is walking down a hallway to meet us as we enter the house. She's wiping flour off her hands onto her apron, and unlike Pierre, she doesn't look wary at my arrival. Instead, she smiles broadly.

"Bridget," says Barnabas, "this is Pearl. Pearl, Bridget."

"Hi there, Bridget," says Pearl, reaching out a hand. I shake, and she holds on to my hand for a moment longer than necessary. "Welcome to the farm."

I follow them down the hallway. A staircase with a well-worn wooden banister runs along the wall to the left, and on the right, double doors open into a large living room, full of bookshelves and worn, mismatched, but comfortable-looking furniture.

At the end of the hallway, we step into a large, bright kitchen. Sunlight streams through the windows, pooling on a gigantic wooden table that dominates the center of the room. Barnabas and Pearl deposit their bags on the table, and I follow their lead.

"Pearl, would you mind taking Bridget upstairs, so she can get settled?" Barnabas says. "We'll put her in the yellow room for the night and make a more permanent arrangement in the morning."

Pearl looks at me and nods. "Come on."

I follow her upstairs and across a landing into a small, quaint bedroom with yellow wallpaper and curtains, and a patchwork quilt on the bed.

"You'll stay here tonight," she says. "But don't get too comfortable. You'll be in the bunkhouse with everyone else after this."

"Bunkhouse?"

"It's not that bad," she says. "Only the oldest of us live in the house: Barnabas; my husband, Noah and I; Pierre. Everyone else is in the bunkhouse. Women on one side, men on the other."

"That's fine," I say, knowing it won't come to that. Sarah and I have made arrangements for one night, but even if I haven't learned anything by tomorrow morning, I'm out of here.

"Bathroom is across the hall," she says, pointing.

"Can I use it?" I ask, and a flicker of hesitation crosses her face, then disappears.

"Sure," she says. "I'll wait here."

I sit in the bathroom, and finally, *finally*, I'm able to pull my phone out. I only have one bar of service, but the screen is lit up with worried messages.

Dee where are you going with that guy?

Dee wtf what is going on?

Dee I'm giving you one more hour before I call my parents.

The time on the most recent one is about half an hour ago. I breathe out and text her back.

I'm okay—I'm sorry I couldn't text, didn't have an opportunity till now.

Three dots appear almost instantly, and her message appears after a few seconds

OMG where are u??? Dee this is really messed up!

I know. I can't leave yet. I haven't found anything out.

You can't stay there! Dee that's crazy

Sarah I'm totally safe, I promise. It's fine. I need to spend the night. You have to figure out how to stay close by, so you can come get me.

??? wtf? Are you sure its safe???

There are voices on the landing. I need to hurry up.

I swear! Just hang tight until morning. Stay at the motel in Finley and I'll find out what I can. I will be ready to leave in the morning. Don't worry, Sarah. I can come and go as I please. I'm choosing to stay.

I know this is putting her on the spot, but I can't leave now. I've made it this far, now I need to take advantage of being here and find out what I can.

The dots appear, and after a moment, I get a response.

Okay. Where are you?

I send her a pin and she responds immediately.

Please please be safe. I'll see you in the morning.

I will. Gotta go c u tomorrow.

I flush and stand up, then run the water and wash my hands. I dry them on a towel and I'm about to leave when I think of Pearl's face when I asked to use the bathroom, and something tells me I should hide my phone.

There's a knock on the door.

"You okay in there?" Pearl calls.

"Yep!" I call back. "Just coming out!"

I stare around the room, trying to figure out what to do with my phone. There's a tall wicker shelf in the corner with piles of toilet paper and cleaning supplies. Underneath it is a gap of about an inch. I turn the water back on, then I quickly kneel and slide my phone underneath it.

I toss water on my face and run some through my hair, so it will look like I've been in here for a reason.

When I open the door, Barnabas and Pearl are standing outside, smiling at me.

"Sorry to rush you, hon," says Pearl kindly. "You were just taking so long. We were just hoping you were doing all right in there."

"You have to understand," says Barnabas. "There have been…troubled people here in the past. People with drug issues, mental health issues…"

"Yeah," I say, laughing nervously, my brain spinning as it looks for an excuse. "I'm sorry. I haven't washed in a few days. I feel gross."

Barnabas nods, his face serious. "We'll make sure you have the chance to take a shower after dinner," he says. "And I'm sorry about this, Dee, but we have to search you."

"Search me?" I ask. Something about it doesn't seem right. I'm happy I listened to my gut and hid my phone.

"For drugs."

"I definitely don't have drugs," I say.

"I'm sure you don't," he says, but he still gestures toward Pearl, who steps over to me and begins patting me down firmly and efficiently. I don't want this woman touching me, but I feel like I'm walking on thin ice—I need this to go as smooth as possible.

Pearl finishes quickly and steps back. "She's clear," she says. "Sorry, hon. It's necessary."

"No phone?" he asks, and Pearl shakes her head. "We don't allow phones on the farm," he explains. He smiles and tilts his head, curious. "You must be the only teenage girl in the world without one."

"My parents took it from me," I lie. I try to sound like a petulant teenager. "Joke will be on them when they realize I'm gone and there's no way to reach me."

Barnabas narrows his eyes, considering, as if he's trying to figure out whether I'm lying or not, but then he smiles. "You'll have to contact them at some point," he says. "But there's plenty of time for that. In the meantime, let's introduce you to the family."

In the kitchen, a few people are standing around the table, talking, mostly women, along with an older man and a couple of kids. Everyone stops talking when I enter the room, standing just inside the threshold of the door. The people are almost all older than me, and a couple look old enough to be my grandparents. The kids—a boy and a girl—both look a bit younger than ten.

There's no sign of Sibby at all. Of course I wasn't expecting her, but a soft hollow of disappointment emerges in my stomach.

Pearl precedes us into the kitchen. "Everyone," she says, "meet our new guest. This is Bridget."

She proceeds to introduce me to everyone else. I quickly lose track of all but a few names. A friendly looking older man turns out to be Pearl's husband, Noah, and the kids are Tansy and Al. They stare at me curiously, the way kids tend to, but there's nothing in their faces that makes me think they're in any kind of danger. If anything, they seem totally normal, poking and teasing at each other, as their parents tell them to settle down.

In fact, it seems everything about the farm is normal. As they go back to their conversations, I pick up snippets of news about chores and the work that's going into preparing for planting season.

I'm happy when Pearl gets me chopping vegetables, because I'm trying to settle in without drawing attention to myself. A few minutes later, a door in the back of the porch opens and some boots stomp in the entryway, along with the sound of men talking. It fills the space with the boom of authority and confidence, enters into the empty space of the next room.

A few moments later, Pierre comes into the back mud-room trailed by four men in their late twenties. They kick the snow off their boots and enter the room, followed by a couple of big dogs. The men notice me right away, and a couple of them exchange looks that are hard to decipher, and the dogs are equally curious. They immediately bypass everyone else in the kitchen to investigate me.

"This good old girl is Raven," says Barnabas, pointing at a sleek, black mutt who is sniffing furiously at my jeans, while an enormous white Great Pyrenees stands back and regards me suspiciously. "And this big fella here is Snowman. Meet Bridget. A guest for this evening. Perhaps longer, if she decides to stick around for a while."

The men nod at me, but nobody offers me their names. I wonder if any of them were here at the same time as Alice.

The men go off to clean up, and after allowing the dogs to satisfy themselves that I'm not a threat, I move into the kitchen and occupy myself with helping Pearl cook dinner.

Dinner is good but hippie-style. Some kind of a vegetable stew with chickpeas and raisins, along with roasted squash and brown rice.

I'm surprised when Pearl directs me to sit at the head of the table. When I demur, she insists, gently pressing on my shoulder so I sit into the large, armed chair beneath the huge window at the back of the room. "You're the guest of honor, hon," she says. "It would be an insult to refuse."

Large chipped pottery jugs filled with water are passed around, and we fill our glasses. As Pearl directs the action of spooning out the food onto the plates, she asks me unthreatening questions about myself, but nothing too personal, which leads me to believe they're used to people wanting their privacy around here.

Before we eat, a well-rehearsed silence descends on the table. Barnabas, at the opposite head, puts out his hands, and I follow suit to reach out and take hold of the people beside me, Pearl and Noah.

We clasp hands, and as Barnabas begins to pray, I glance up from beneath my lashes. Everyone has their eyes cast down or closed except for one person.

Pierre is staring at me from across the table, and when my eyes catch his, he holds my gaze until I look away.

37.

After dinner, I attempt to get up and help with dishes, but I'm pushed gently away by Pearl.

"You'll have plenty of time to help in the coming days," she says. "Go to the living room. I'm sure Barnabas will want to learn more about you."

I step out of the kitchen and through the dining room, where a couple of people are quietly clearing the table. They glance at me curiously but drop their eyes when I glance back at them. In the large living room on the other side, Barnabas is sitting by the fire, chatting with some of the young men about the construction of a root cellar. They drink tea, and the big dogs are curled by the fire. Raven opens one eye as I enter to stand in the doorway and watches me warily, but Snowman continues to sleep easily.

I watch the scene in front of me for a moment, allowing my

eyes to wander around the room. The house is old; heavy timber beams run across the living room perpendicular to the heavy, oiled floorboards that peek out from beneath a mismatch of hand-woven rugs. There's no television, just a wall full of books and an old radio in the corner, softly playing classical music. On the floor in the corner, the two kids are playing cards.

This house doesn't seem like the kind of place that would harbor a kidnapped child. It seems quiet and safe and warm and comfortable. Everyone is polite and helpful. Am I supposed to believe that Sibby is locked up in a basement somewhere? It just doesn't make sense. I wonder if it's too late to text Sarah and ask her to come get me now. It's only about six thirty, but it's entirely dark outside.

"Bridget." I turn at the sound of my middle name and realize that Barnabas has finished his conversation and is looking at me. "Come talk to me," he says.

He gestures to a small wooden stool near his chair, and I grab it and pull it over next to him.

"Is there anything you'd like to know about the farm?" he asks.

I wish more than anything that Sarah were here, even Burke, someone who would be able to come up with the right questions, who wouldn't choke in the line of fire. Even better, I wish I could send out a message to my listeners, ask them to take over for me. I've never been the investigator. I'm the person who organizes the investigations and sits back, waits for the clues and tips and solutions to come back to me.

I want to ask him *Where is Sibby? Did you even have her? Was she ever here?* Instead, I ask, "How long have you been here?"

"About fifteen years," he says. "A group of us decided that

we wanted to leave the outside world, learn to grow as much of our own food as possible. Pearl and Noah, Pierre, myself, several others, we found this house, a small field, enough wood to keep ourselves warm in the winter, and to build the shelters and buildings we needed."

"And people came to you?" I ask.

He nods. "With time. There were many years of growth." He stands and walks over to the cabinet on the other side of the room, pulls out a large book, and comes back. When he opens it on his lap, I see that it's a photo album.

"We've taken a picture every year at the end of harvest," he says. He flips through, and I see that on each page, a full-color photo fills the frame, an image of the farm and its inhabitants. The first few pictures are basic, just the house, a makeshift shed behind, and a large vegetable garden. Eight people turn into twelve, then fourteen for a couple of years, and then I turn the page and the number has more than doubled. I stop, staring, and he laughs.

"That was the year that things seemed to stick," he says. "We grew really quickly. Doubled our food production, built the barns, and began raising cattle and chickens. The first babies were born that year, and new guests seemed to show up almost every day."

I flip again, trying to keep up with the math. I'm on the sixth year, the year Sibby disappeared. In the photo, it's the fall, so it would have been about six months after she went missing. The population has grown again, and in the front of the picture are about eight kids. I quickly scan their faces, looking for Sibby, but she's not there.

She's not on the next page either, or the next, and as I make my way through the album, my heart begins to sink. Sibby isn't in this house. She was never in this house. Alice meant well, but she admitted herself that she hadn't remembered where she'd seen the girl.

But still, something nags at me. It doesn't seem right. Alice seemed *sure* that she'd seen Sibby. Not just suspicious. Confident, as if there was no question in her mind.

Around five years ago, the numbers of people begin to dwindle. Dropping bit by bit, until we get to the most recent picture. Fifteen of them, more or less the same people who are here right now.

"What happened?" I ask, looking up at Barnabas. He has a wistful look on his face.

"People left," he says. "We couldn't keep up with the demand, although we did our best. Nobody starved, but ultimately, it turned out that as much land as we have here wasn't enough for more than fifteen, maybe twenty people. "It's a good life though," he says. "If you're looking for something like this." He stops and sweeps his hand around. "It's comfortable. It keeps us fed, busy, as distanced from the outside world as we like. Over the years, many people have come to us who are trying to escape from something," he says. "The way you are, maybe. People who've had enough of their old lives, families, relationships, responsibilities, patterns. It's easy enough to disappear, if you really want to."

I wonder if that also means it's easy *to make someone* disappear. I know better than to speak that out loud. I know he's right. I've been following missing people forever, and the ones who want to disappear, the Danny Lurlees of the world, they manage to do it when they really want to.

He continues. "The reality is, farming isn't for everyone. It's been good for some people. It's been therapeutic, and that's great. But not everyone has it in them to stick around."

"I don't know," I say. "I mean, I heard about this place from someone, and I thought…"

"You thought it might be a good way to escape your life," he says.

I nod.

"If you want my honest opinion, Bridget," he says, "I'm not sure this is the right place for you. This isn't a place to come to get away from something. It's a place to come when you're looking for something."

"You're probably right," I say.

"It's okay," he says with a smile and a little shrug. "We are always interested in meeting new people. Tomorrow I'll give you a tour of the farm. You can meet the animals, learn more about the work we do here. If you don't think it's a good fit for you, I'll give you a ride back to town."

I smile at him. Alice was one of the people trying to escape their old lives. Is it so crazy that she could have imagined Sibby into existence? Created a purpose to justify the years she spent here? I realize now that this has been a wild-goose chase. Barnabas is just a guy trying to keep his vision alive, his group together.

I hang out in the living room for another hour or so, flipping through some old books on the shelves, then I call it a night. The sooner I go to bed, the sooner I can wake up and get away from here.

Upstairs, I brush my teeth with a freshly packaged toothbrush that Pearl gives me. I carefully slide my phone out from the hutch and then cross to the bedroom. When I'm under the covers, I text Sarah.

Hey.

She responds right away.

Omg Dee, this is so scary. Are you okay?

Yes, I'm totally fine. I'll be ready to get out of here first thing in the morning. There's nothing here. It was a false alarm.

Okay. That's good. Parents are pissed but we'll make it up to them. I'll fill you in tomorrow.

Lol—we've earned their trust, right? Okay, good night.

Good night, can't wait to see you and hear everything xo

Xo

The bed is comfortable, and this part of the mystery, at least, has been solved. I close my eyes, and immediately, I fall asleep.

* * *

I wake with a start, ripping myself up from a nightmare. Something is nagging at me. Something someone said or something I saw, but I can't put my finger on it.

I reach back for my dream. Something in the back of my mind is unsettled, but I can't think of what.

Suddenly, I want to get away from this house. Everything seems like it's normal, but somehow, it doesn't fit.

Around me, the house is sleeping. I slip out of bed and pull back the curtain to look out of the bedroom window. The sleeping house is dark, and the only light is the ambient glow cast on the ground from the external spotlight on the barn.

I reach under my bed and grab my phone. It's 4:00 a.m.

Are you awake? I text.

Sarah responds a few moments later.

As if I could sleep. Everything still okay?

Yeah, but I'm ready to leave. I think I'm going to slip out and walk down to the road. You think you can meet me? It's about a 20 minute drive.

Yes thank god

There's a barrier on the driveway, so just pull in at the end and wait for me there.

K. I'll see you soon.

I dress as quietly as I can without turning on the light, then I slip out of the bedroom and into the hallway, taking the steps slowly. I still think everything is safe and fine, but there's something holding me back from feeling totally safe. Something nagging at the back of my mind.

At the bottom of the stairs I stop and stand totally still, listening to the house sleeping around me. There's no noise except for the tiny creaks and shifts as the house bends with the wind. I find my boots and jacket by the front door, neatly set beside a few other pairs. I pull on my boots, drag my overcoat over me, and slip my hat on, which was in the bin next to the door. I glance at my phone and figure that Sarah will be here in about fifteen minutes. It will take about ten to walk down the driveway, so I might as well leave and walk down to wait for her.

But I don't. I stay put, thinking. Something is trying to get through to me. Some kind of hint into the mystery about what is actually going on.

I close my eyes and try to reach back for the frayed remains of my dream. What was happening?

My eyes shoot open and I feel my breath go shallow. I remember what I was dreaming, and suddenly, the hidden clues inside my memory float to the forefront of my mind, and connections begin to fall into place, and I realize with a sudden mind-wrenching certainty that these are the people who took Sibby.

Sarah will be here any moment. I should go, but I can't. Not without some kind of proof. I wrack my brain, frantic to think of some way to find evidence.

Aware of the weight of my boots, I do my best to cross the hallway silently and step into the living room. I pull down the album from the bookshelf, flipping ahead to the year of Sibby's abduction. When Barnabas first showed me the album, I was so caught up in examining the children, that I barely noticed the clusters of adults around them. Now I scan the faces, looking for something, anything that will prove my theory.

Barnabas is standing in the middle of the group, at the back, a head taller than everyone, which tells me that he's probably standing on a crate or something. Immediately surrounding him, I recognize other faces, Pearl and Noah, Pierre, and many others I don't recognize. I assume they're old guests who decided to leave.

And on the far corner, her eyes squinted against the sun, laughing and smiling, is a face I recognize. A face I spoke to recently. If I'd only met her as she exists today, I might not make the connection here, but as it happens, I knew the young woman in the photograph when she still looked just like this.

It's Sandy.

My mind is spinning, and I can't yet figure out what it all means, but I know it means something. I pull back the cellophane sheet that holds the photo in place, and I remove the shot, shoving it inside the arm of my jacket.

I pull my phone out to check the time. Sarah will be here any minute. As I fumble to put it back in my pocket, I hear a creak behind me.

"What are you doing?" asks Barnabas.

38.

I turn around, and even as I'm trying to think of what to say to tamp down his suspicions, I can see that his gaze is on the open photo album on the coffee table beside me.

"Who are you?" he asks. "Why did you come here?"

I only answer the second question. "I know that you took Sibby Carmichael. I want to know what happened to her."

He makes a show of looking confused. "Sibby Carmichael? I don't know who you're talking about."

I don't even bother to play along with him.

"I saw Sandy in the album," I say.

Barnabas shrugs. "Lots of people have come here over the years. Some stay for years, and some leave. End of story."

"Okay," I say. "I guess I was wrong. Why don't I just leave?"

I take a step to the door, but he moves to block me. I notice one of his hands clench as his face shifts into something far nastier than he's let me see up to now.

I step back, trying to keep the distance between us. I know he's trying to corner me in the back of the room, but I do have one big advantage: I'm already dressed to be outside in this winter air, and he's barefoot, in sweatpants and a T-shirt. Sarah will be here soon. If I can get out of this room, if I can get to her, I'll be okay.

He steps again and I move backward, but this time I risk a quick glance at the sofa to my side. He follows my stare, then looks back at me, and for a long, pregnant moment, we both stare at each other, aware of what is going to happen next.

He calls my bluff and fakes at me, and I bend down in one quick motion and flip the coffee table toward him, then leap to the side, jumping up and onto the ragged, beat-up sofa. I'm quick, but he's quicker, and just as I'm about to clear him and make it to the hallway, he scrambles sideways and grabs my ankle.

My ascent into the air is stopped midjump, and I fall heavily to the ground, knocking a lamp onto the floor. He's on the ground too, not letting go of my ankle, dragging me back into the room as he pulls himself up and into a crouching position, and I reach for the lamp and throw it. It careens wildly, missing him by a mile, but it's enough to make him pull back. I use the opportunity to flip around and use my free foot to kick him square in the chest.

He lets out an *oof* and staggers back into the room, and I flail, trying to find my center of gravity, trying to discover enough awareness of the space to stand. I stagger to my feet and catch myself as I run for the door to the hallway.

He's on his feet again though, and he reaches out and grabs me roughly by the shoulder as I try to get away, into the hallway, to the front door. His thumb pushes painfully into the back of my neck, and he presses down on my shoulder at the same time, forcing me to the ground. Quickly, he twists my arms behind me and presses a knee onto my back, squeezing the air out of me.

Upstairs, doors are opening, lights are coming on.

"Barnabas?" a voice yells from upstairs. "What's going on?"

I do the same thing I did when Sibby was taken. I go slack, I let the fight leave me, and I slump beneath him. He's still holding me tight, but I can tell that he registers the shift in me. He loosens his grip and sits back, and I know he thinks he's won this fight.

But he hasn't accounted for the main thing: I'm not the same person I was back then.

I'm big enough to fight back.

I let my face press to the floor. "I thought I could do something," I whisper, letting myself sound defeated.

He relaxes away from me a bit more.

I flip onto my back and whip my right leg up with as much force as I can muster, whacking it directly into his nuts.

He drops backward, screaming, and I manage to wriggle out from under him. I know I only have two or three seconds to work with, and I spin on my foot and rush for the front door. It's locked, but I grab the deadbolt and twist it, and yank the door open. I can hear him behind me, moving again, and feet are already pounding down the stairs.

"You bitch!" he yells after me, as I run into the night.

I hear the dogs barking as soon as I'm outside, and although at first it's obvious that they're inside some building somewhere, the noise soon gets louder, telling me they've been let out. I chance a glance behind me and see that the lights in the outbuilding have come on.

The floodlights in the yard are on as well, and as I race across the brightly lit expanse between the farmhouse and the top of the driveway, I hear voices calling out, but they are still back at the house, which tells me I have a decent head start.

I face a new problem once I've skittered beneath the barrier. The forest presses up against the narrow gravel lane from both sides. Do I run into the woods, hiding in the shelter of the trees as I try to make it to the road where Sarah is waiting before they do? Or do I continue on the driveway, which will be faster but leave me in full sight of my pursuers? I hear barking behind me, rapidly getting closer, and I realize I'm going to have more trouble than I expected if I don't think of some way to handle these dogs.

Raven arrives first, barking and snarling at me, and Snowman is close behind.

I know dogs well enough to know that I can't let them see me scared, and I have an advantage: they already know me. I've been a guest in their house.

"Stay," I say in as commanding a voice as I can muster. Their teeth remain bared, but to my relief, they stop.

"Look!" I say, and I point at the woods. Both dogs turn quickly, then catch on to the trick and turn back to me. If I didn't know any better, I'd think that they looked irritated.

"Sit!" I command.

The dogs hesitate, shuffling uneasily as they try to figure out if I'm really in control. Behind them, lights scan the ground, rounding the bend in the drive.

"Sit!" I say again.

This time, they both sit, and I almost laugh with relief.

"Stay," I command, and then I quickly scan the ground for a stick. When I find one big enough, I raise it into the air, and both of their heads follow its motion. With one hard, fluid movement, I whip the stick through the air toward the flashlights. It's heavy, and it goes far, and I hear someone yell in surprise as it lands. The dogs are also off, disappearing toward the stick and the people, and I take advantage of the opportunity to turn and begin running down the driveway.

My heart is in my chest and all I can hear is blood pumping and my hard, pained gasping for air. I taste blood, and behind me, I can hear the sound of footsteps.

"Stop!" someone yells.

Then, ahead of me in the predawn gloom, a light catches my eye and I realize that it's a car driving slowly up the driveway toward me. Sarah!

Somehow I pick up my speed and run faster toward her car, and as the headlights pick me up, it comes to a crunching stop on the icy gravel driveway.

I can tell from the sounds behind me that my pursuers are gaining on me, but the Nova is closer, and I race to it, reaching out to slam my hands onto the hood, stopping myself. I skid, frantic, around the side and wrench open the passenger door.

I'm only barely aware of Sarah's shocked face as I throw myself into the car and yank the door closed.

"Dee!" she says. "What's going on? Are you okay? I waited at the end of the road but—"

"Drive!" I say, cutting her off. "We have to get out of here!"

A shot echoes in the night, and we both turn to look out the windshield. In the glow of the headlights, four figures approach the car, two of them holding flashlights.

"We have to go, Sarah," I say. "Now."

She doesn't move, seemingly frozen in her seat. "Dee," she says, her voice a croaking whisper, "who are those people?"

As they get closer, the flashlights drops to the ground, and I can see that it's Barnabas, Noah, Pearl, and Pierre. They stop, brightly lit by the headlights, snow swirling erratically around them.

Noah steps to the front of the pack. He lifts the shotgun and points it at us.

"Sarah!" I say, reaching forward to slam on the dash. "You need to go now! Back up!"

She seems to snap out of her trance and reaches over to shift the car into reverse. The car lurches backward and begins to accelerate, as the sound of a gunshot fills the air.

"Hurry!" I yell, and the gun is fired again, this time pinging off the hood. We both scream, but she's picking up speed. I know that we're almost at the road, and they're sprinting after us now. I can see Noah in front, stopping to take aim, and he fires the gun again, this time hitting one of the front tires, blowing it out, just as Sarah spins us into a hard backward turn and skids onto the main road.

Sarah's face is grim, and she kicks the car into first gear and presses on the gas. I turn to see our pursuers running out from the driveway onto the open road.

Noah lifts the gun again.

"Duck!" I yell, grabbing for Sarah and pushing her head down, as he fires another shot, the rear windshield shattering.

"Not today, you bastards," says Sarah, and she pulls the car into third and we accelerate away. Barnabas and his henchmen have turned and are running back up the driveway.

"They're probably running to get into their trucks," I say. "We don't have much time."

"We can't make it far like this," says Sarah, and I listen to the sound of the busted tire dragging and scraping along the icy gravel road.

Ahead, the classy Victorian farmhouse emerges from around a corner.

"Pull in here," I say. "We can ask them for help. Barnabas said that they're neighbors, but I don't think they get along."

Sarah skids off the road and up the driveway, pulling around to the back of the house. We jump out of the car and run to the front door, knocking furiously. After a few moments, lights come on upstairs and, after another pause, downstairs. A curtain in the window draws back, and someone peers out at us, then the door opens and a tired, confused-looking elderly man appears.

"What's going on?" he asks, and I'm relieved that he looks concerned, not angry. "How can I help you girls?"

"We're being chased," I say, frantic.

"Chased?" He looks taken aback, and his grip tightens on the door. I worry that he's going to shut us out.

"The people at the farm," I say, rushing to get the story out before the trucks appear. "Barnabas."

His eyes narrow at the name, and he turns to call back into the house. "Ginette! Will you come here?"

A moment later, an old woman comes down the stairs into the room. "What's all this about, Bill?" she asks.

"Barnabas," says the man, and his face takes on a new look of grim understanding.

"Come in out of the cold, girls," says the woman.

"We need to hide the car," I say. "They'll know we're here."

The man and woman exchange a look. "We don't want any trouble from Barnabas and his crew," says the woman.

"We can't leave them to fend for themselves, Ginette," he says. "They're just girls."

"I'm not suggesting anything of the sort," she says. "We can call the police."

"We will," he says, "but we need to do something first, or a bad situation might turn into a worse one. There are guns involved. I always knew that man would end up digging himself a hole. I just don't want to end up at the bottom of it."

He looks past us into the driveway. "Is that your car?" he asks.

"Yes!" says Sarah. "They shot at us!"

"We need to hide it before they arrive," he says. "They'll be after you."

He steps into a pair of heavy boots next to the door. "Do you have the keys?" Sarah hands them to him, and we watch as he hurries out to the car and starts it, then drives around the corner of the house and up to a large shed. He gets out of the car and runs up to the doors, then opens them, gets back into the car, and slowly moves the car into the shed.

The woman moves to the woodstove in the corner of the room and opens it, begins stoking the embers. "Come in out of the cold, girls," she says, as she shoves some logs into the fire.

We kick off our boots and step gratefully into the kitchen. We stand next to the stove, waiting for it to heat up, trying to get warm. The yard outside is still dim, but brightening into early morning, and through a window above the sink, I can see the man coming back down through the yard toward the house. The car is nowhere to be seen.

I pull my phone from my pocket. No service. "Can we use your phone?" I ask, just as the back door opens and the man steps onto the porch, stomping to get the snow off his boots.

"I'll call Sheriff Taylor," says the man. "Tell him that Barnabas is up to his tricks. More runaways."

"We aren't runaways," says Sarah. "We're looking for someone."

"Did one of your friends join with those goddamned hippies?" he asks. I turn to Sarah, willing her to be quiet, but she doesn't notice my expression.

"Not exactly," she says. "We think they might have kidnapped a child. Years ago."

The woman's eyes widen and she turns to look at her husband. "Kidnapped!" she exclaims.

Her husband shakes his head again, angry, and strides into the kitchen and through a door into what I assume is their living room. A moment later, we can hear him speaking into the phone.

"Diane, it's Bill Drummond from down Brewster Road. We've got a situation here, and I'd like you to ask Taylor to come down here with a man or two as soon as possible. Barnabas and his crew are up to no good again."

There's a pause. "Yes, that'll be good. Thanks, Diane."

He returns to the kitchen. "Cops are on the way," he says. All four of us turn as we hear the sound of a vehicle on gravel. Sarah steps over to me and grabs my arm as Bill walks over to look out the window.

"It's Barnabas and Noah," he says. "We've got to hide you two. Ginette, get the girls down into the basement. I'm going out to talk to them."

"Be careful," I say. "They've got guns!"

He waves away my concern. "I know how to handle Barnabas."

Ginette hurries us from the kitchen into a long, dark hallway. She unlocks a door that's set into the back of the staircase that leads down to a half-finished basement. A workbench and tools are set up along one side, and a door along one wall leads into a small carpeted room with a shelf full of fabric and preserves and a sewing table set up along the opposite side.

"I'm sorry, girls, it's a bit cold down here," Ginette says. "Keep your coats on, and there's a space heater in the corner if you need it. I'll be back down as soon as I find out what's going on."

She leaves, closing the door behind her, and I follow Sarah to the tiny window set into the wall at the top of the room, just above eye level. We stand on tiptoes and peer through the window into the driveway, where we can see the boots of several men standing around.

"Can you hear?" asks Sarah. I shake my head; there's muffled conversation, but nothing distinguishable. After a minute, the boots start moving, away from the truck, around the house.

"Oh my god," says Sarah. "They're coming in! I hope the cops arrive soon!"

But something else has caught my attention: the sound of a bolt sliding into place on the other side of the door. I rush to the door and yank on the handle, but it does no good.

We've been locked in.

39.

"What the hell are we going to do?" asks Sarah. She's not hysterical—I don't think Sarah does hysterical—but she's definitely panicked, and I know that there's plenty to panic about.

I look around the room, trying to figure out what we're supposed to do. Along the edge of the wall, there are two small windows at ground height. There's no way in hell that I'd squeeze through one of them, and although Sarah might have a fighting chance, there are bars across them both, bolted into the cement foundation from the outside.

The door is solid, and I'm pretty sure it's metal, aluminum maybe. There are two bolts instead of one, and the handle is also locked.

"Shit," I say. "We're not getting out of here."

Sarah doesn't respond; she's moving stuff off an old kitchen chair, brown vinyl padding on the seat, and moving it across the room, underneath a tiny air vent.

"Sarah," I say, as she climbs onto the chair. "That thing is like four inches wide. You wouldn't fit up there in a million years."

She gives me a look like I'm a complete idiot, then puts a finger to her mouth and stands on tiptoe, twisting her head sideways to point her ear toward the hole.

I finally get what she's doing, and I move to stand next to her by the chair. Together, we stand as quietly as possible and strain our ears.

There's a heated conversation going on above us, somewhere in the room above. The energy of the words is obvious, but the words themselves are harder to make out.

Let them go drifts down at us, and we exchange a hopeful glance, only to be shattered by the stomp of a foot and a deep, authoritative bellow. *Absolutely not! They've seen—*

The words break off abruptly as someone, I assume inadvertently, moves and a foot blocks the air vent. The voices become completely unintelligible, a dull mutter from above the ceiling. A few moments later, the foot moves, but the voices move with it, and footsteps move across the ceiling and away from us, toward the front of the house. Soon, there are no voices within earshot, and we're left to mull over what we've heard.

"I don't know what's going on," I say, "but the cops are not on their way. He just pretended to call."

"Shit," says Sarah. She gets down from the chair and sits wearily.

"We should move that back," I say. "In case they come down and see what we've been doing."

She nods but makes no move to stand up. After a moment, I sit cross-legged on the floor in front of her. "It probably doesn't matter," I say.

At some point, the door unlocks, and Ginette pushes it open, carrying a tray. I glance at Sarah and know we're both thinking the same thing. She's old, and although she looks healthy enough, it would be easy for the two of us to overpower her.

"Don't waste your energy," says Ginette. "Bill is at the top of the stairs with his rifle. We don't want to hurt you, but we will if we have to."

There's no way to tell if she's telling the truth, and I put my hand on Sarah's arm to tell her to stay where she is. Through the open door, I can see the workbench, and a set of steps leading up to a cellar door, like the one from *The Wizard of Oz*. Another exit, if we could only get to it.

"What are you going to do with us?" Sarah asks.

"We're trying to figure that out now," she says. "Now eat something and try to get some sleep."

She puts the tray on the table and turns to leave.

"What do you know about Sibby Carmichael?" I ask. She stops, and her back stiffens.

"I don't know who you're talking about," she says after a brief pause. Then she walks back out the door and closes it, and almost instantly, we hear the soft metallic *snip* of the bolt sliding into place.

"We have to get out of here," I say. "There's no way they're going to let us go after this. They know something about Sibby, and they know that we know. There's a reason they didn't call the police."

"How?" asks Sarah. "There's no way out of here."

We spend the next couple of hours doing our best, but it turns out she's absolutely right. The tiny window is too small for either of us to crawl out of, and after a couple of attempts, feet appear, and a moment later a piece of plywood is pressed up against our only view, and we can hear it being drilled into place.

The door is even more of a barrier. It's steel framed and locked tight. It makes me wonder if anyone else has ever been locked in here.

The day disappears, and although we keep futilely bringing our phones out of our pockets, there's no signal. To make matters worse, Sarah's phone is almost dead, and mine has only about 20 percent battery left. Eventually, we agree to put them on airplane mode and put them away entirely, in case we have another opportunity to use them.

Footsteps come into the house on and off throughout the day. Although we occasionally hear voices upstairs in long conversation, they're quieter, and we can't make out what they're saying or even who is talking. Most disturbingly, Ginette doesn't reappear, even when dinnertime comes and goes. A cold chill makes its way through my body when I consider what that might mean.

Eventually, the house settles into quiet, and I imagine Bill and Ginette heading up to bed as if everything is completely normal. Sarah and I curl up next to each other in the corner, and I put my arm around her. Eventually, she falls asleep, but I stay the way I am, wide awake, although my body desperately wants me to rest. The feeling of deep fatigue combined with a steady rush of adrenaline is strange and unsettling.

I'm not sure how long I've been sitting like this when I hear light footsteps above us in the kitchen, and then someone descending the stairs. I quickly shake Sarah, who groans and then jerks awake when I lightly cover her mouth with my hand.

"Shhhh," I whisper, and the two of us get to our feet and crouch by the door. "I didn't hear the upstairs door close again," I say. "This might be our only chance. I'll jump at whoever it is, and you run for the cellar."

She looks like she wants to argue, but I shake my head. There's no time to make another plan.

I hear the bolt slide open, then the latch turn, and a moment later the door slowly opens. I'm ready to jump forward and tackle Ginette or Ron, whoever has come down here, but I stop in midjump.

It isn't Ginette or Ron or even Barnabas or one of his crew, for that matter. It's a teenage girl.

She's not dressed like any teenager I've ever hung out with. In fact, she looks like she stepped out of a time machine. Her face is young and clear and healthy looking, but she's wearing a kerchief that would better suit an old lady. It pulls back her plain dirty blond hair, which is neatly cut to land just above her shoulders. Her dress is simple, with a high, buttoned collar.

All these years, I've wanted more than anything to know what happened to Sibby, wondering what I could have done differently. Wishing I could have saved her.

In the end though, it's Sibby who shows up to save me.

40.

"Sibby," I say. It comes out only a bit louder than a whisper, her name catching in my throat now that I have someone to say it to. I'm vaguely aware of Sarah turning to look at me, her mouth dropping open at the name, but I'm more aware of this girl's reaction. She looks confused, unsure who I'm addressing or what I mean.

She steps quickly into the room, quietly nudging the door partway closed. I realize now that she's holding boots, our boots, and she puts them on the floor before standing straight again.

"My name is Rachel," she whispers. But it isn't Rachel; this is Sibby. If I've ever known anything in my life, I know this. It might have been a guess, just a guess, if I hadn't met Greta. But I have met Greta, and there is literally no denying that the girl standing in front of us is Greta's sister. They could be twins.

Her confusion looks sincere, but this isn't exactly the time to figure out what she thinks she knows.

"We need to move quickly," she says. "I heard my parents talking with the men from the farm, and they are going to do something bad to you. I know it."

"What should we do?" I ask.

She points at the boots. "You need to go. As quickly as you can."

"Can we get to my car?" asks Sarah. "Your father put it in the barn."

She shakes her head. "I don't know where the keys are," she says. "And the barn is locked, always. Your best choice is to get into the woods, and then follow the tree line along the road to the highway. It's about two miles. You can make it."

Sarah opens her mouth to protest, but I reach out and grab her arm. "We have to do this," I say. "It might be our only chance."

"Do you really believe that your parents would hurt us?" Sarah asks.

"They'll do anything to protect me," she says. "They'll do anything to keep the outside world from finding me. Now hurry."

We struggle into our boots, then follow her out of the room. I turn to the stairs, but the girl I know to be Sibby holds up a hand and points toward the cellar's storm door.

"If we all go upstairs, they'll hear us," she says. "I know this house. I can move through it without making any sound, but you can't. There's a wooden bolt across the outside. I'll sneak outside and open it from there. Wait here."

Without another word, she's gone, disappearing into the

shadows of the basement and sliding up the wooden steps, stepping carefully from spot to spot. As she claimed, she doesn't make a sound, not even a creak, as she moves.

I reach out, and Sarah and I fall into each other's arms. I can feel a deep tension in her that I know is reflected in me. This is the only chance we get.

"I'm sorry I got you into this," I whisper.

I can feel her head shake against my chest. "We got into this together."

Above us, I hear the sound of something heavy being dragged away, and then the cellar door opens. A rush of freezing, bone-dry air rushes down into the basement, and Sibby is standing above, looking down at us, her silhouette stark against the deep blue sky. She beckons us to hasten out, and we step up and out of the cellar. I help her close the door so it won't bang, and then she picks up a plastic bag and hands it to me. Inside are two knit caps and some mittens.

"My mother knits a lot," she says, smiling. She turns and points to a spot at the edge of the forest. "Go that way. You'll find a shallow stream just beyond the line of trees. You should be able to follow it without leaving tracks, and it will take you to the highway."

"Thank you," I say.

She smiles, and the face reminds me so much of the girl I used to know that I feel my heart compress inside my chest.

"Your name is Sibyl Carmichael," I say. "Your name is Sibby. You were my best friend."

This time she doesn't look confused; she looks sad. "I've wondered," she says. "I've wondered who I am."

"We'll come back for you," I say. I turn to reach for Sarah's hand, but as I do a light turns on in the window above us. Startled, the three of us turn to the window, just as the cellar door slams open behind us. With a roar, Bill emerges from the basement with a lunge.

It all happens so quickly that I don't have time to react, and then Sarah has been thrown to the ground. She screams in pain.

Sibby is standing to the side, her hand over her mouth, paralyzed.

"Rachel, what have you done?" yells Bill. He turns back to the house and yells up at the window. "Ginette! Call Barnabas!"

Underneath him, Sarah squirms, groaning with pain. Bill lets go of her and stands, advancing toward me. When she tries to stand, her leg buckles beneath her.

"Go! Dee! You have to run!"

"I'm not leaving you!" I yell, as Bill stands up and fixes his awful gaze on me.

"They'll kill us both," she pants. "Unless one of us gets away to tell them!"

I know she's right, but still I can't move. I can't leave her behind. I hesitate just long enough for Bill to make a sudden move and grab me by the front of my coat.

"You little bitch," he growls. "You should have left my family alone."

"It's not your family!" I yell into his face, and he hauls back an arm as if about to hit me. But before he has the chance, something whacks into his legs from behind. He screams and then buckles to his knees, and I catch a glimpse of Sibby holding a shovel in her hands.

"I'm sorry, Sarah," I say. "I love you!"

"I know," she says. "Now run!"

I turn and go. The woods are a dark mammoth ahead of me, a wall of not knowing. I run as fast as I've ever run in my life, but this time, I'm not running from the memories; I'm running toward them. I reach the edge, my heart churning, and turn to glance back. Bill is stumbling across the expanse of lawn, but he's far back, and I know I can get away from him. His arrogance might have told him three girls were no match for him, but he was wrong.

He stops and drops to his knees. He's done chasing me, but there are more coming. And soon.

I turn and plunge into the forest.

It takes me a minute to adjust, but once my eyes are conditioned to the dark, the forest seems to open up to swallow me. I pull my phone from my pocket, holding the screen against my mitten to keep the light obscured, then peeking carefully at the upper corner, hoping against hope that I have service, but there's nothing.

A dip in the terrain alerts me to the stream Sibby described, and I head toward it, sliding on snow down the bank to the burbling trickle of water. Heavy, wet stones stick up from the water at points, and I jump onto one, almost sliding in on my boots but catching myself at the last moment. It's a lot slower than running along the ground, but as Sibby pointed out, I won't leave tracks this way, and so I move along the stream as quickly as I can. It winds through the forest, and soon I am into a rhythm, skipping along steadily if not swiftly, making my way deeper into the forest.

The woods bring back my dream from last night, the dream that connected me back to Pierre's gravelly, low-pitched voice—a voice that has never completely left my memory in ten years, although it took me a little while to place it once I heard it again.

We've only got one chance at this. Now hurry up.

Pierre was one of the two men in the woods, but there's so much more I still don't understand. How did Sandy fit into things? Does this mean Terry was involved after all, and is Layla's disappearance connected in some way that nobody's yet figured out? Something's missing.

In the distance, from the direction of Ron and Ginette's house, I hear engines and yelling. They're far enough away that I think I have a good head start, but then I turn my head and my heart plummets when I see lights moving slowly only a few hundred yards away. The stream must have veered closer to the road. I stop, my heart pounding, and try to take in the terrain surrounding me. I'm running out of options, but one thing's for sure: if I stay on the stream bed, they'll find me for sure.

I turn away from the lights. On the riverbank across from me, a gnarled old pine tree sticks out at almost a right angle. I judge the distance and decide that if I can jump at it the right way, I might be able to catch it, and with luck, I can do it without my feet touching the ground and leaving behind footprints.

I jump, and my face is scratched by twigs and needles, but my left arm manages to hook around the tree, and I'm able to drag myself up onto the trunk. I glance back toward the road, and I realize that the lights have stopped moving. They've parked. A sharp stab of panic catches me as the light disappears. They've turned off the vehicle entirely. A moment later, the darkness is broken by a dim glow, the interior of a cab as someone climbs out. The glow disappears just as quickly with the slamming of a truck door.

Then a bright beam shines straight into the forest, landing on a tree not five feet away from me. I duck as the beam sways back and forth. When it drops to the ground and begins bobbing with someone's footsteps, I move. I scramble along the trunk and climb to the top of the bank.

Somehow I've managed to do it without leaving footprints, and when I get to the top, I can see that I'm deeper into the woods and underneath the canopy of the trees are bare spots, no snow. I don't have time to think it through, so I begin jumping from one to the next.

The noises are closing in, and I don't know what else I can do. Across the clearing, I see a huge tree, a maple, maybe. The biggest I've seen in this forest. I close my eyes and think to myself. Is this my only chance?

I have an idea. My phone won't work down here, but it might work up there.

I fling myself out from my hiding spot and run across the field to the tree. As I jump up into the lowest level of branches, my hat is snagged and flung from my head. I turn and watch helplessly as it falls down into the snow, and I can only hope it doesn't give me away.

I scramble up, moving higher into the tree, praying for purchase with each step. I wind my way up and up, and finally, when I'm about twenty feet into the air, I move around and position myself so I'm sitting comfortably in the crook of a branch.

I stop to catch my breath. It's very cold, and I wish I'd taken the time to drop back down and grab my cap, but even as I'm thinking this, I can see flashlights down below beneath the canopy, hear voices yelling my name. From this high up, I can see the roof of the farmhouse skimming the tops of the trees. I wonder what's happened to Sarah, if they've allowed Sibby to stay with her. At least I am sure they won't do anything to her until they find me. They know full well that if I do manage to escape, they're better off if Sarah is in good shape when they're finally caught.

My breath under control, I carefully work one of my mittens off, making sure to shove it carefully into my pocket. With my bare hand, I reach into my inner pocket and pull out my phone. I press the button on the side to spring it to life.

The first thing I notice is a message from Carla Garcia.

Incredible news! They've been found! They're alive! Msg me immediately!

Despite everything, my heart soars. If Vanessa and Nia were able to do it, so can I.

I'm momentarily hopeful to see that I have one bar of cell service. Almost right away it drops off to zero before springing back to one bar.

I have 8 percent battery left. I need to make this count.

I open the phone and dial 911. When I hold it to my ear, it rings once before beeping to announce that the call has dropped.

"Shit," I mutter to myself. Below in the trees, I can see beams of light moving around on the ground. At least four, maybe more of them, are circling through the woods. Occasionally a beam stops and shines around and upward, which tells me they're searching into the trees. I'm running out of time.

I dial again, and again the signal drops off almost immediately. My heart is pounding. This isn't going to work.

But I'm not ready to give up. Not yet.

I'm at 5 percent, and I need to think quick. I begin to compose a text, not even sure who to send it to—my dad? Burke? They'll be asleep, no question, and there's no guarantee that they'll get it until the morning. Acting on instinct, I open my recording app, and speaking quickly, I record a memo. Then I open the *Radio Silent* Twitter account, type a few words, attach the sound file, and press *Tweet*.

The little blue progress line at the top of the screen begins to move and then halts at the top of the screen. A message pops up: *Tweet failed.*

Shit! I almost yell, catching my voice just before it leaves me. My battery is at 3 percent, and my eyes are full of frustrated, horrified tears as I hit the *Tweet* button once again. This time, I stretch my arm up above my head as far as it will go. As the blue progress bar moves across the screen, I see the service indicator move to two bars. There's a long, excruciating pause where it stops moving, and then, with a rush, the tweet sends, and an instant later my phone's screen goes black. It's dead.

I breathe deeply and laugh with a wave of pure, unwashed relief. It lasts only a second, as a beam of light washes the clearing. I tuck in on myself as tightly as possible. I'm high in the canopy, but with the trees bare, I know I could be spotted, but only if someone shines the light directly on me.

"Delia, come on out. Hurry up," a voice calls out, soft and cajoling, like someone trying to lure a puppy. The tone is forced, unnatural, but I recognize the voice anyway. It's the voice my subconscious recognized yesterday, the voice that woke me out of a deep sleep and convinced me I was on the right track. Pierre is out here in the woods, stalking me the same way he stalked us when we were kids.

I close my eyes, waiting for him to move on. He takes a step, then another, moving directly below me, beneath the canopy of this giant maple.

"We aren't going to hurt you, Delia," he calls, and I take some comfort in the fact that he's speaking out, not up. He hasn't figured out that I'm directly above him. "We just want to talk. Fill you in on a few things."

He stands still, waiting for something. For a sign? After a few moments, he gives up and begins to walk away. I release my breath slowly. At the edge of the clearing, he stops and turns, gives it one more sweep of the flashlight.

The beam stops abruptly, and suddenly he's striding back into the clearing. I know before he reaches it what he's seen. And then the beam is shining up and up and straight at me, and I stare down into the light, squinting against the glare, aware that, behind it is a face and a hand holding the hat that I dropped.

41.

Transcript of **RADIO SILENT**
Emergency Episode 45

HOST (intro): You won't recognize my voice because I'm not using a filter, but this is the Seeker. *I am the Seeker.* My real name is Delia Skinner, and I'm seventeen years old. I have a lot to tell you all, a lot to explain, and I promise I will do that soon, but right now, I need help. I am in trouble. My girlfriend is in trouble. We have traveled to a farm outside the small town of Finley. The thing is, we received a tip from a listener that led us here in search of Sibyl Carmichael.

We found her.

We found her, and now I'm in big trouble. I need help, Laptop Detectives. I need help right now.

If anyone is listening to this, please contact the police department in Finley, please contact any law enforcement in the surrounding area. Please send them to the communal farm on Brewster Road and tell them that lives are in danger.

I am currently in the forest behind the farm, being pursued by some bad people. I have no idea if I'll get out of this alive. I'm not exaggerating.

And please, listeners, whatever happens to me, spread the word that Sibyl Carmichael is alive.

She's alive.

She's alive, and it's time for us to bring her home.

42.

Pierre is at the base of the tree now, and there's no doubt that he's seen me.

"Over here!" he yells louder. I realize he's trying to get the attention of his coconspirators.

The light drops, and begins to shake around on the ground. He's trying to jump up into the tree.

"Don't even think about it, old man," I yell.

"Hey!" he yells again. "I've got her! Over here!"

In the distance, I hear a hollered reply. They've heard him. Then he begins trying to get up into the tree again.

I've got few options left. I can hear the rest of them, Barnabas and Noah and Bill and likely some of the others, approaching through the woods, yelling. Below me, Pierre is moving quicker than I would have expected, clambering from limb to limb, making his way through the lower section of the tree.

I glance up. The tree goes a lot higher, and I've got a lot of room to go if I want to keep moving up, but there's an obvious issue. At some point, I won't be able to climb any higher. I don't know what Pierre intends to do when he gets to me, but even if he does find himself at an impasse, all he has to do is keep us both up in the tree until his backup returns.

"There's no point in hiding," he says. "There's nowhere to go." Although his voice is calm and almost agreeable, I can hear the exertion in it, a light wheezing, pauses as he catches his breath. Still, he keeps moving, higher and higher up the tree, approaching me more rapidly than I like.

My only option is to try to stall him.

"How did you do it?" I call down from my perch. "How did you figure out where she was going to be?"

"I don't know what you're talking about," he calls back.

I laugh. "Give me a break. I saw her. You realize that, right? She was my best friend. Of course I was going to recognize her."

"I don't know what you're talking about!" he yells again.

"I was the other girl in the woods!" I yell, losing my patience. "How stupid are you people?"

To my surprise, he laughs.

"You were that girl?"

"Yes!" I yell. "And now I've found you, and you're going to pay for what you did!"

He laughs again. "The only one paying for anything around here is going to be you," he yells. "You and that girlfriend of yours."

The branches have stopped creaking, and I can tell that he's stopped moving as well, as his attention is drawn away to my revelation.

"Pierre! Where are you?" It's Barnabas, calling from the woods, much closer than before.

In the instant that I register Pierre shifting his position in the branches beneath me, turning to yell back, I make my move. The moment I decide to let go, I do, and somehow I manage to slide down, through the branches, without getting caught on them, other than a few hard whacks along the way.

I slam into Pierre before he has a chance to holler back to Barnabas, and the two of us plummet the rest of the way out of the tree, slamming to the ground with a tremendous force. Lucky for me, he's broken my fall, and I'm able to quickly catch my wind and stand up.

From the low groan Pierre emits, I can tell he isn't going to be getting up anytime soon, but at this moment, he's the least of my worries. A light filters through the woods and into the small clearing, and I look up to see Barnabas stepping out of the trees. I don't wait to find out if he sees me.

I run.

This time, I don't bother trying to be quiet or to hide my footsteps. I race through the clearing and into the trees on the other side, aware of a shout from behind me and the sudden erratic bobbing of the flashlight's beam as Barnabas begins to chase me.

I fly through the trees, only vaguely aware of being slapped in the face by branches, righting myself when I stumble over roots and hidden hollows in the uneven ground.

"You can't get away, Delia!" Barnabas screams from behind me. "We're not going to let you!"

I'm gasping by this point, not sure which direction I'm

running in, but I keep going. I just need to buy myself time. Surely, someone will come for me soon?

There's a loud snap, followed by a blast of light, and a small explosion in front of me as a bullet rips a hole into the side of a birch tree. He's shooting at me, and a hot jet of fear propels me forward even faster, as another shot echoes through the night.

Then, like a miracle, I see more light, and the blare of a car horn, followed by several more, and the brightness and the noise are closer than I would have ever dared hope. I adjust and run toward them, the movements of my body disconnected from my rational mind, propelled only by the animal instinct to survive, and then I crash through the edge of the forest and leap across the frozen stream and as one last shot comes slicing through the air out of the forest and misses me by just a few inches, I clamber up an embankment.

I stop in astonishment as I see the cars and trucks that have parked along the side of the road, at least two dozen, stretching in both directions. Outside of the woods, the sky is lighter than I expected, and I blink, letting my eyes adjust as I take in the people who have gathered in small groups. Several people are on their phones, talking quickly and urgently, still others are taking photos, or reaching into their cars for food and blankets.

A middle-aged woman steps forward and hurriedly wraps a blanket around me.

"Are you Delia Skinner?" she asks me.

I can only nod, my teeth suddenly chattering, and the cold rapidly taking over now that I've stopped running.

"My name is Diane," she says. She turns and gestures at the other people. "We're all Laptop Detectives."

Someone farther down the line shouts, and I turn with the crowd as Barnabas steps out of the woods. He freezes as he glances up and sees the crowd that has inexplicably gathered along Brewster Road.

He turns back toward the woods, and for a moment, I'm sure he's going to run, but then he drops his gun to the ground, and as sirens sound in the distance, rapidly getting louder, he drops to his knees and puts his face in his hands.

43.

In the aftermath of everything, from the moment I allowed myself to climb down from the trees, to my first sight of the many, many people who had arrived on the road outside the farm, lined up against their cars, witnesses to this weird, specific rescue, to the first sharp call of sirens slicing like a blade through the cold night air, there was only one thing on my mind.

Sibby.

Sibby was coming home.

There was no armed standoff, no hostage situation. No shots fired. No burning farmhouse or spiteful orgy of self-sacrifice. In this way, we were lucky.

What there was:

Ginette, crumpled on the ground, keening and wailing as her husband was cuffed and shoved into the back of a cruiser.

Police leaning down to put the handcuffs on her as well, and her mournful whimpering cries as she was loaded into the back of another car.

A scream of relief and joy catching in my throat as I caught sight of Sarah across the crowd of people, and the open look of pure joy on her face when she saw me. The way everyone else slipped away as we hurried toward each other, falling into an embrace, the tears that I'd been holding up inside me for what seemed like years, falling so steadily that I thought they might never stop, that I might be like this forever. Sarah holding me tight, letting me know without words that she'd keep holding me as long as I needed her to.

"Where is Sibby?" I finally asked.

"I don't know," she said, shaking her head. "Everything happened so quickly. There were cops coming up the driveway, and we both started to run. But we got separated."

A tremble began in my legs, and then I was shaking violently, unable to speak. Is she really gone? Did I really let her disappear again?

And then there she was, being led from a crowd of people toward a police car. Someone had put a coat over her shoulders, and she looked scared and confused. At the police car, someone reached to open a door for her, and she stopped and scanned the crowd, desperate.

Her eyes skimmed right over me, continued past me, and I knew then that our reunion would never be what I'd hoped for. In the years since I'd lost her, every cell in each of our bodies had regenerated. The thin, delicate thread of connection that had been feeding back to me from the past, that I'd been hanging on to for so long, had already been broken, and I'd been the only one still hanging on to an end.

There was nothing left to hold us together.

But then her gaze darted back, stopped at me, and the fear on her face subsided. Replaced by something else.

Recognition.

* * *

The police station in Finley is small, and by the time we arrive, pulling into the back lot, there are already members of the press beginning to arrive. I spot the BNN van as it comes to a screeching halt on the other side of the chain-link fence, and I lean forward to the police officer in front of me.

"Someone should make sure that Sibyl is totally protected from prying eyes," I say. "That's Quinlee Ellacott in that red van back there, and I know she'll try to exploit this any way she can."

The cop glances out the back window, unsure, but then he nods and reaches for his radio.

"We've got some press outside," he reports.

A response crackles back right away. "Copy that. Someone's coming out to help."

A few moments later, Sibby, Sarah, and I are being ushered into a back door behind a blanket that's being held up by the officer and a receptionist. Then we are taken in different directions, all of us to different rooms, and although I know I'll see Sarah again in a few hours, I have a feeling that it is the last time I'll see Sibby for a while.

And it turns out, I'm right.

By the time I am in a car being shuttled back to the Finley Police Detachment, my parents already have some idea what was going on thanks to Quinlee Ellacott. She'd been up and out of her hotel within ten minutes of my plea being posted on the *Radio Silent* Twitter account, driving to my house, desperate for a comment, for something that would give her the scoop. Of course, even Quinlee Ellacott and the fast breaking news team at BNN are no match for the sheer power of virality on social media.

By the time she stumbled through a rough explanation to my bewildered parents, my plea had already gone viral, sweeping the internet, even being turned into a video, the clip of my cold, frightened voice laid down under a photo collage that someone had assembled of old newspaper clippings of the Sibby case, photos of her that had been pulled from the internet in no time at all, in the blink of an eye, the snap of a finger, as quickly as someone can snatch a small girl out of her life.

Quinlee wasn't able to get more out of my parents than bewildered looks before they shut the door in her face. She used it, of course. She used every scrap she could find to pull together a narrative. She'd missed the scoop, but she wouldn't miss the story now that it was playing out, and she was already on its doorstep.

I was in a room at the police station when they arrived, my phone charging in another room, thanks to a nice young female cop.

I explained what I could to them, their facial expressions

shifting between horrified, relieved, and proud. It was a lot to take in, but nothing they couldn't handle. They'd made it through the events of a decade ago, and now here I was safe, and Sibby had been found, and wasn't that all a miracle?

* * *

Burke comes to visit me the day I get home, running up the stairs to my room without knocking and surprising me with a tight hug. When he pulls away, I'm even more surprised to see tears in his eyes.

"I'm really glad you're okay, Dee," he says. "And I'm so happy you found her. I really am. I always knew you had it in you."

"I don't know about that," I say. "Right place at the right time."

"Bullshit," he says, dropping onto my couch. "You made this happen."

"I barely know the whole story," I say. "Detective Avery called this morning to tell us that your uncle Terry has been filling the police in on everything he knows."

"He's telling them he wasn't involved," Burke says. "Do you believe him?"

"I think maybe he suspected something afterwards," I say. "But I don't think he knew at the time. You remember how angry he was at himself about the treehouse?"

Burke scoffs. "That stupid treehouse. I mean, he built the fucking thing. How can he *not* have known?"

"He built it because Sandy suggested that he build it," I say.

"I honestly don't think he knew what he was doing. I think she played him."

Burke considers this. "Mom says she dumped Terry a few weeks after Sibby disappeared, and he was devastated."

Other facts have been more solidly established. Barnabas, along with his first followers, Pearl, Pierre, and Noah, started the farm with almost no money and only a small patch of land in the woods.

When they approached Bill and Ginette Drummond about buying a piece of their land, the couple refused. But when Barnabas approached them again, offering to find them a child, they had a change of heart. They'd had no luck during their attempts to have a child of their own, and the temptation was just too great.

Sandy, now firmly in police custody just like the rest of them, was among the first, most dedicated members of the commune, and when Barnabas tasked her with finding some-one who could lead them to a kid, she began hanging out at a local roadhouse, where she met Terry. He was unattached, unemployed, and when he mentioned his brother's big family, she floated the idea of going to spend some time with them, and he was only too happy to show up with his friendly, beau-tiful new girlfriend.

During the month they spent in Redfields, Sandy made it a point of getting to know all the kids on the block and zoned in on Sibby as the most appropriate target. She orches-trated the building of the treehouse, arranged daily playdates, and knew enough of the children's schedules that when she suggested that she and Terry take the O'Donnell kids to the movies, she assumed, rightly, that Sibby and I would end up at the treehouse.

She notified Barnabas of the plans, and he sent Pierre and Noah to wait in the forest. They were there, hiding, when we showed up. The rest is history.

"He was so relieved to hear that Sibby was alive," says Burke. "But then he completely broke down. Says he feels responsible."

"The farm was responsible," I say. "Barnabas and Sandy and the rest of them. I really don't think Terry knew what was happening."

Burke slumps in his seat. "I guess it doesn't really matter either way, since they still think he took Layla."

"He's still denying it?" I ask.

Burke nods. "He swears he had nothing to do with it, but now he's changed his story and admits that he was using that room in the empty house. He panicked when they cornered him, because he knew that the scrapbook looked incriminating, which…yeah, the evidence is pretty strong. I don't know what to believe, Dee."

"I don't blame you," I say. "A lot of shit has happened really quickly. It's hard to keep on top of things."

"Speaking of that," he says, and I can tell he's happy to change the subject, "what's going on with the podcast? Brianna told me about those women who were found in Houston. That's pretty wild. You're just nailing wins to the wall, Dee."

"I'd love to say the podcast helped," I tell him. "But those women saved themselves."

When I finally had a minute to respond to Carla's message, I learned the unbelievable story behind Nia and Vanessa's escape.

"Some asshole kidnapped them," I tell Burke now. "He'd formed some sort of grudge against the two of them and managed to keep them locked up in the basement of his house. Apparently they managed to trick him into letting his guard down, and together they overpowered him and knocked him out. They ended up breaking down the front door and walking out on their own."

"That's amazing," says Burke.

I nod. "A lot has happened over the past little while, and all of this has me thinking about what I want the podcast to be. I want to make sure it's focused on women who are fighting for their lives to get out of basements, instead of dirtbags like Danny Lurlee who fake their own disappearances or clueless teens who hide out in cabins without telling their families where—"

It's like a switch is flipped inside my brain. I stand up from the table so quickly that I almost knock over my coffee mug.

"What is going on?" asks Burke, alarmed.

I realize I'm shaking, and I grab on to the edge of the table for support before lowering myself back into my chair.

"Burke," I say. "Something just occurred to me, and if I'm right, your uncle really didn't have anything to do with Layla's disappearance.

44.

It's cold but bright, and I have my shades on, and my hood up over my hat as I approach my old street. Sibyl is home, or as close to home as she's ever going to get, but there is still a girl missing.

Although I wonder how missing a person is when someone else knows where she is.

I know where Layla is. At least, I think I know. I think I could prove it without a lot of effort, but first I have a stop to make.

Standing on the sidewalk, staring across the street at my old house, I pull my phone from my pocket and take a deep breath before making a call. It only takes a few minutes to explain myself, and by the time I hang up, I'm convinced that my story has been taken seriously. I only have a few minutes before things begin to happen, so I force myself to move past my feelings of insecurity and cross the street.

When I ring the doorbell, I hear the responding muffled chime inside the house, and it triggers a deep and distant memory. A window breaks open inside me, and voices call out from the past. My father? Maybe my mother? Both? *"Who's there?"* *"Can somebody get that?"*

But I'm on the outside now, and the things happening in these walls have nothing to do with me. Except maybe now, for a moment, they do.

Layla's mother answers the door. She looks exhausted, unhappy, beaten down.

"Hello?" she asks when she sees me. I get the sense that she's trying to place me, then her eyes widen with recognition. "You're that girl," she says. "The one from…"

She doesn't finish, but I know what she means. "Yes," I say. "It's me. Can I come in for a minute?"

She looks surprised but doesn't argue. She manages a smile and steps aside. "Sure," she says. "Would you like some tea? I just made a pot."

I nod, then follow her up the stairs into the kitchen.

I'm in a dream. It's the only way to explain the haunted feeling that moves across me as I walk up the stairs from the entryway to the kitchen. I haven't stepped into this house since I was eight years old, since we moved across town just a few months after Sibby went missing.

The walls and steps and windows are the same, but ten years of new furniture, freshly painted walls, different dishes, and unfamiliar photographs on the walls have swept in to fill the space like a disguise. I feel like I just need to close my eyes and breath myself to sleep, and when I wake, everything will have slipped away. The house will be the same as it was, and I'll be the person I was, hurrying through breakfast so I can go outside and play with Sibby.

In the kitchen, Mr. Gerrard is sitting at the table, his hands around a steaming mug of coffee, staring out the window at Mrs. Rose's house. He turns to look at me as I enter the kitchen, and his face is blank and unreadable. As Mrs. Gerrard walks past him to the counter, she reaches down and gives his shoulder a quick squeeze. Adam Gerrard doesn't react, just continues to stare at me.

"This is the girl who used to live here," his wife says as she reaches into the cupboard for another mug. "I'm sorry, I don't remember your name. It's Skinner, right?"

"Delia Skinner," I say. "Dee."

"Have a seat," she says.

I pull a chair out at the end of the table. "I lived here when my friend went missing," I say. "I'm sure you both know all about that."

Mrs. Gerrard puts a mug in front of me and then pulls out a chair next to her husband. She sits, then reaches out and puts a hand on his knee.

"Yes," she says. "An awful story. An awful coincidence."

"It isn't a coincidence, Bonnie," says Adam Gerrard. It's the first thing he's said, and from the tone of his voice and the confused look on her face when she turns to him, the last piece of the puzzle drops into place. "There was a note, remember?"

"That man left it," she says. Her voice tells me she believes this. "That O'Donnell man. It was a diversion."

Adam shakes his head and laughs bitterly. "A diversion."

He turns and looks at me. "What are you doing here? Why did you come here?"

I stare back at him for a moment before responding. "I wanted to ask you to your face," I say. "I wanted to give you a chance to tell me what happened to your daughter."

Mrs. Gerrard stands up so suddenly that her knees catch under the table, shaking my tea and spilling some over the edge. She looks at me like she's been slapped.

"What the hell are you talking about?" she asks. "What is this all about?"

Across the table, her husband has kept his composure. "What makes you think we have anything to tell?" he asks calmly. "I know about your little podcast. Do you think that gives you the right to come into my home and make accusations?"

"I didn't accuse anyone of anything," I say. "Not yet."

"Okay," says Bonnie Gerrard. "That's it. Time for you to leave." She moves toward me, and I stand before she has the chance to take me by the arm and throw me out.

At the kitchen doorway, I stop. "I just have one question," I say. "Is she free to leave when she wants?"

Bonnie Gerrard's face twists into a knot of complete confusion, but I'm not looking for her reaction. Her husband's face remains blank, and after a moment, he drops his eyes, unable to meet my gaze. It tells me all I need to know.

I turn and walk back into the entryway, pulling on my boots as the Gerrards follow me.

"I don't know what kind of bullshit this is," Bonnie says, "but if you had any idea the pain we've been through these past few weeks, you'd reconsider this cruel interrogation."

"I think your daughter is alive and healthy," I say as I pull my hat down over my head. This brings her up short, and she stops, staring at me. Outside, cars come to a screeching halt against the sidewalk. When I open the door, Officer Avery is already out of his car and striding toward me, followed by Chief Garber and a couple of additional uniformed officers.

"Delia," says Avery. "You shouldn't have come here alone."

I shrug. There's no way to change that now. Behind me, Bonnie Gerrard steps outside, still in a T-shirt, shivering and wide-eyed.

"What's going on?" she asks. "Is it true what she says? Have you found her?"

"Mrs. Gerrard, we're going to have to ask you and your husband a few questions," says Avery.

Adam Gerrard follows us out. He's pulled on a jacket and boots, and as he walks over to where Avery and I are standing, he glances at his wife, and the look he gives her is almost unbearable.

"I'm sorry, Bonnie," he says. "I didn't think it would come to this."

"What are you talking about? Adam? Tell me what's happening!"

He ignores her and steps up in front of us.

"I'll tell you what you want to know later," he says to Avery. "This has gone on long enough."

He glances at me, and the look is enough to tell me that he doesn't resent me for figuring out his secret. If anything, I know that he must be ready for it all to come to an end. An understanding passes between us, and I nod at him before we turn together and move past Avery to old Mrs. Rose's house. He follows us up onto the front porch, but it's me who rings the doorbell and Adam Gerrard who steps inside the house first, once Mrs. Rose, slightly befuddled, opens the door for us.

"Hi, Mrs. Rose," I say when we've stepped inside. "Is it okay if these nice policemen come inside with us?"

She smiles broadly and nods. "Yes, of course, dear," she says. "Come in. Come in. I'll put on a pot of tea."

She turns and heads into the kitchen, ignoring the fact that five people have just come inside her house. I glance at Avery, wondering what the proper procedure is, but Adam Gerrard is already moving toward the living room.

"Stay here with Mrs. Rose," Avery orders his companions. Kicking out of our boots, we follow Adam, vaguely aware of Mrs. Rose chatting away to the officer in the kitchen.

At the top of the basement stairs, Adam Gerrard stops and turns to look at us. His face has fallen, and the depths of sorrow in his eyes make them hard to look at.

"I can't," he says. "I can't do it."

I step past him, hurrying now as I walk down to the basement, Avery close on my heels.

The basement is similar to how I remember it. A rec room that's looked the same since the 1970s: plaid furniture and wood-paneled walls, a wet bar in the corner of the room with colorful vinyl stools and a gold-flecked mirror filling in the space behind. This room, where Sibby and I used to play as children, now smells musty, mildewy. Unused.

Boxes fill the space, and the piles of garbage and old magazines that fill the upstairs of the house are even more prominent down here. At the back of the rec room is a narrow passageway cleared between the boxes leading to a door.

"In there?" Avery asks.

"Yes," says Adam. He's emerged downstairs, and tears are now streaming down his face. He moves past us toward the door, reaching into his pocket. He pulls out a key and puts it in the lock as Avery and I step up behind him.

The room is simple. Warm enough, thanks to a radiator along the wall. In one corner is a table with a small refrigerator plugged into the wall beneath it. In the corner of the room, another door is half-ajar, revealing a small bathroom. A bed in the middle of the room and an armchair underneath the small, narrow basement window complete the furnishings.

Layla Gerrard is standing at the foot of the bed, her eyes wide.

Adam drops to his knees and opens his arms, and Layla rushes into them.

"Daddy?" she asks. "Am I allowed to leave now?"

45.

Transcript of **RADIO SILENT**
Episode 46

HOST (intro): I am *the Seeker*, and this is *Radio Silent*. This is the first episode since...*everything* happened, and I won't lie: it feels weird. It's kind of awkward and really exciting and totally new to me to be recording and releasing an episode without disguising my voice. But after the events of last week, I can't go back and pretend you don't know who I am. So let's start again, from scratch.

I am Dee Skinner. I am also *the Seeker*, and this is *Radio Silent*.

Before I say anything else, I need to say thank you. It's such a small phrase, and it will never come close to expressing how I feel about the LDA and all the people who've helped me with this podcast.

You saved my life. Literally.

I realize everyone wants to know about Sibyl Carmichael. About how I was involved and how I came to find her. My inbox has been full of questions, and to tell you the truth, it's a bit overwhelming. I never thought I'd see a day when my identity was revealed, when my connection to Sibby's disappearance was unearthed, and there's a lot to say, but this podcast isn't the place to say it.

But you will learn more soon. I promise. And as soon as I can tell you more about that, I will.

In the meantime, I will tell you about another case though. The disappearance of Layla Gerrard.

We're still learning details about how and why Adam Gerrard faked his daughter's disappearance. But we do know some things.

The family was in a bad situation financially, and Adam owed a lot of people a lot of money. He and his wife, Bonnie, decided to make a fresh start and move to a small town, and as fortune would have it, they ended up in Redfields, in the same neighborhood where a notorious kidnapping had taken place almost ten years earlier. In a house where, as it turned out, the girl who had been in the woods with Sibby that day had lived.

They'd moved into my old house.

When Adam learned from a neighbor about the circumstances of Sibby's disappearance, and his new home's connection to the case, the wheels began to turn, and he slowly concocted a plan. He decided to fake the disappearance of his own daughter and then stage an elaborate rescue. After that, he figured, the media opportunities would come rolling in. Interviews. A book deal. Maybe even a movie.

Money.

He didn't tell his wife about the plan, but he had to tell Layla, and she agreed to help him. They'd befriended an elderly neighbor, a widow who had become a hoarder, and when Adam offered to help her move some boxes into her basement, he realized that this house could be the perfect hiding spot. A basement bedroom with an en suite bathroom. Easily accessed from a back door, right next door to the Gerrard home.

Even better, another house was sitting empty right on the other side of the elderly neighbor's house, an ideal place to stage a fake kidnapper's lair.

Adam Gerrard's plan was to set up the empty house with some fake evidence, indicating that someone had used the empty house to spy on the Gerrard family, then take Layla and hide her in the basement of their other neighbor for a couple of days, then orchestrate her safe return with a wild story of a dramatic escape from her captors.

Everything was on track until Terry O'Donnell stepped into the picture. It turned out he'd also been using the abandoned house as a place to hide out, smoke cigarettes, and be alone. A terrible coincidence that meant it was a lot harder for Adam to follow through with his plan. While the cops buzzed around the O'Donnell household and the media set up in Redfields, he was forced to keep Layla hidden, sneaking in and out of the basement hiding spot to bring her food and keep her morale up.

Two days turned into two weeks, and Layla dutifully remained hidden. Her father, after all, had told her that their family was depending on her.

Adam Gerrard is in police custody, and he'll go to trial. Who knows what will happen to him after that. More important, Layla is home with her mother. She's safe.

Maybe someday she'll decide to tell her story, but for now, that's where it ends, at least as far as *Radio Silent* is concerned.

I know about being thrown into a terrible situation as a child, a life full of questions. I don't want to contribute to that.

As you all know by now, the two missing women in Houston have been found. Scared, underfed, but alive. Their resilience is an inspiration, but they too have a long recovery ahead of them, and I want to make sure they have the space to come out of their experience strong and intact, on their own terms.

But I also want to ensure something else. I want this to be the focus of *Radio Silent*. I want *Radio*

Silent to find the overlooked and undervalued, the people who need our attention and rarely get it. I want this to be a space that works hard every day to find the ones who most need finding.

Sibyl Carmichael. Layla Gerrard. Vanessa Rodriguez and Nia Williams. Three stories and three happy endings.

I have one more happy ending to tell you about. Mine.

Finding Sibby has changed something inside me. Or maybe that's not the best way to describe it. Finding Sibby has revealed something to me, as if a light has been flipped on and brightened a corner of my mind that I had never really noticed.

You see, I always thought it was my job to tell the stories, and everyone else's job to figure them out, help bring them to a satisfying conclusion.

But now I know I was wrong. We *all* have a part in telling these stories, just as we all have a part in figuring them out. This podcast has only ever worked because people have been willing to work together, to share information, to hit the streets and start looking.

It's only worked because we've all been willing to pick up the loose threads and keep the stories going until they finally find their way to the end.

It's time for me to step away from my role as the Seeker. I've decided that I need to live my life in the open for a while. The page has been turned on one of my chapters, and this podcast is an important part of that chapter. But I've realized that not every story is mine to tell, and now it's time for the Seeker to move on and create space for other voices.

Starting with the next episode, *Radio Silent* will have a new host, one of many new hosts going forward, I hope.

Carla Garcia, who did such an incredible job leading the search for Vanessa and Nia in Houston will be the new voice of *Radio Silent*. We'll wait to learn what she calls herself, but I know she'll be incredible under any name.

I'll be around, in the background. Helping out where I can, keeping the social media feeds running and the tips organized and the cases neatly filed away.

This isn't the last you've heard of me. But the next time you *do*, it will be somewhere new. Somewhere surprising. Somewhere that fits the new life I'm about to start living.

Thank you for everything, Laptop Detective Agency. You saved my life, but there are still many more lives to save.

Can we do it?

Listen up.

Let's try.

46.

The bus lets me off on a busy corner, and as I jump down from the step, I only barely manage to make it across the puddle of slush and grime that's collected in the dip at the corner of the sidewalk and the crosswalk. It takes me a minute to get my bearings, moving out of the way of pedestrians and fishing my phone from my pocket to open my map and figure out which way I need to start walking.

I point myself in the right direction and start to walk.

It's one of those rare days in early March when there's a tiny bit of warmth in the sun, and if you're not careful, you'll let yourself believe that winter is actually coming to an end. I've been around long enough not to believe it—even as I left the house today, Dad was talking about how the temperature is going to drop again tomorrow—but for today, I'm just happy that I can feel my face and that I'm not going to arrive at my destination feeling ragged and sweaty under my clothes, with dry skin and a runny nose.

I arrive at the café a bit ahead of schedule. The place is a lot busier than the last time I visited. Students on stools hunch over laptops at the long wooden work surface that runs along the length of one wall, a couple of moms with strollers squeezed in by their seats, an old man sitting in the window sipping on a mug and staring out at the street.

A bearded twentysomething with a wool cap pulled down over his shaggy hair smiles at me as I approach the counter.

"What can I get for you?" he asks.

"Actually, I'm just wondering if Alice is working today."

"No," he says. "Alice actually quit a couple of weeks ago."

"Do you know where she went?" I ask.

"No idea. Sorry."

Another customer has stepped up behind me, so I step out of the way and work my way through the cramped space to the door.

I know I could still figure out how to get to Alice's apartment from here, but I have a feeling she doesn't live there anymore. Even if she doesn't, she hasn't responded to any of my emails. Maybe that tells me everything I need to know.

The door jingles, and I turn to see a girl my own age walk through. I'm not sure what I was expecting, but this can't be Sibby. This girl is too tall, too poised, dressed in jeans and a sweater underneath an unbuttoned peacoat, her long hair pulled back into a ponytail.

But she scans the room, and when her eyes land on me, she smiles, a half twist of the corner of her mouth, the edge of an eye tooth slipping over the edge of her lower lip, and I realize that it's really her. It's the exact same person I knew better than anyone when we were seven. The girl I watched be taken away.

It *is* Sibby.

We order cappuccinos and then grab a table in the corner, both of us making a bigger deal out of taking off our coats than we need to, avoiding one another's eyes until we're actually sitting and can't avoid it any longer.

I smile, awkward.

"So how are you?" I ask.

She nods slowly, affirmatively, before answering.

"I'm good," she says. "I'll be in counselling for the rest of my life, but so far, the adjustment is okay."

"Did they—" I hesitate, worried about how to ask, but then I spit it out. "Did they hurt you at all?"

She shakes her head and looks down at her hands, where they're wrapped tightly around her mug of coffee. "No. Not in any way that you mean. They took away years of my life. My whole childhood. But they were kind to me. I know they loved me in their messed up way. And I loved them." Her head lifts and her eyes meet mine again, almost challenging. "It's complicated."

"I understand that," I say. It's only partly true. There's no way I'll ever fully understand how she feels.

We fall into silence for a moment.

"I feel bad for my real parents," she says after a minute. "This is hard on me, but I think it's even harder on them."

"How are things going?" I ask. "Being back with them, I mean."

She smiles, but there's no joy in it.

"It's okay," she says. "It's weird. It's been tough learning who we all are after all these years. My parents seem like they're walking on eggshells all the time. Greta has been great. This can't be easy for her, but she manages to act almost normal, unlike the rest of us. She jokes around. She actually *talks* about what happened—I mean, not just when there's a therapist present. Sometimes it feels like she's the only stable person under our roof."

"Greta's a good girl," I say. "I like her."

"She told me to tell you hello," she says. "My parents wanted to come with me, but I convinced them that I needed to do this on my own."

I nod. "They'll come around," I say.

"You're probably right," she says. "We're all just figuring out how I'm supposed to fit back in after ten years." She pauses, stares at me intently for a moment, as if she's looking for some kind of answer in my face. "I'm not the person I was back then."

"You were a kid," I say, stating the obvious, since I can't think of anything else to say. "Now you're almost an adult."

"It's more than that though," she says, leaning forward. "I can't stop thinking about who I would be if this hadn't happened. I would have been a totally different person, and I'll never know what that person had in them."

My breath catches in my throat.

The pain on her face drops away and she smiles at me with an expression of understanding. "I guess you've been thinking the same thing about yourself," she says.

I manage to nod.

"I guess…" I say finally. "I guess it must work both ways. If I'd been taken instead of you or if it hadn't happened at all, and we'd both come out of the woods that day, we wouldn't be the people we are now. The only difference is…" I trail off, and she finishes my sentence for me.

"We wouldn't be wondering about it." I nod, and she reaches across the table and takes my hands. "It doesn't matter either way. We can't move backward, so we just have to keep moving."

"Did you know who you were?" I blurt, finally making my way to the question I've been holding in for so long. "I mean, did you remember that you were Sibby Carmichael?"

She pulls back into her seat and stares at the ceiling, considering. "I've known forever that something was wrong with me, that I was not the person they said I was."

"How could you forget in the first place?" I ask.

She shakes her head, looks at me with a strained expression, as if she's trying to figure out how to say something in a language she doesn't understand. That neither of us understand.

"It's hard to explain," she says finally. "I remembered who I was for a while, of course I did, but the Drummonds never called me Sibby or Sibyl. I was out for a long time. I don't know how long. I must have been drugged. When I woke up, I was in a new bedroom in a new house, and there was a friendly looking couple sitting on the end of the bed smiling down at me, and a cheerful-looking man in a white doctor's coat, with a stethoscope and a clipboard.

"They told me I'd been sick, that I'd almost died. I wanted my parents, of course. I wanted my mother. My sister."

She glances across the table at me, a fleeting look, almost shy. My stomach drops, terrified of what she'll say next.

"I screamed at them, hysterical, asking what had happened to you."

I smile, about to shrug it off, when something goes off inside me like a lightbulb, and I feel myself get weak, only vaguely aware of reaching out to grab the edge of the table.

"I'm sorry," I manage to choke out. "I'm sorry I couldn't stop them. I'm sorry I couldn't keep it from happening to you."

She stares at me for a long time, and I worry that I've said the wrong thing, but when she speaks again, there are tears on the edge of her voice.

"None of this is your fault," she says. "You saved me."

She says it with such certainty that it brings me back up for air.

"You going to be okay?" she asks.

"Yeah," I say. "Sorry. I'm fine."

"I heard about the other girl," she says, releasing my hand. "They say that you saved her too. It sounds to me like you have nothing to be sorry about."

I nod. "Somehow the pieces all just fit together."

"Her father really put her through that for money?" she asks.

"Looks that way," I say. "Apparently, he thought Layla could just reappear, with some wild story of escaping from kidnappers, and then he could turn it into media gold. A book deal. TV interviews. The works."

"My parents have been getting lots of emails from Quinlee Ellacott," she says. "She wants me to tell my story on her show."

"Of course she does," I say, rolling my eyes.

She laughs. "I turned her down, of course. My parents want to find me a lawyer to help me figure out the best way to tell my story, but I told them I trusted you with this."

Now that I'm sitting across from her, I can't believe this is the same person I remember when I was little, the same bossy, confident, adventurous friend who wasn't scared of anything. This girl couldn't be more different if she tried, and then I realize that she's *not* the same person. She's totally different.

She's eighteen, and she couldn't be more different from me. In itself, that wouldn't be so weird, but she's like nobody in my school. Nobody my age that I've ever met.

I might be far enough away from this world to be completely unique, but even I have connections with the others—common ground, shared experiences. I've laughed with people in my class, rolled my eyes about teachers. I've gone to hockey games, usually against my better judgment, and ended up cheering for Redfields with everyone else.

I think about the world that Sibby has inhabited for the past ten years. A quiet, insulated space, speaking to the same two people day in, day out. No school, not the way that we know school. No dances. No boyfriends or girlfriends. No phone. No TV. No computer.

I've heard it said that everything good that happens to

you wouldn't have happened but for every bad thing that happened to you before it.

But if that's true, then doesn't it stand to reason that the opposite is true as well? Wouldn't another good thing have happened too? Another outcome skimming into more and more outcomes until infinite possibilities are scattered against the edge of time.

"The girl who was with you," says Sibby.

"Sarah?"

She nods, smiles. "Is she your...Are you guys together?"

I can't keep a grin from stretching across my face, and her smile widens in response. "Yeah," I say. "We are. I want you to meet her. I mean *really* meet her."

"I'd love that," she says.

"Not to mention that Burke has been driving me crazy, wondering when he's going to get a chance to see you again."

Sibby laughs. "I honestly can't wait to see how Burke has turned out. It's so great that you two are still good friends. I feel like I've missed out on so much."

"We'll make up for lost time," I assure her. "I'll come back with them soon. Or maybe you even want to come to Redfields? We could hang out with Burke and Sarah." I swallow, force myself to continue. "I know Brianna would really like to see you too."

"Would you make that happen?" she asks, and she looks so eager and anxious that it kind of breaks my heart.

"I will," I say. "I promise. Let's get through today and then we'll start taking things one step at a time."

The door jingles, and we both look up to see Jonathan

Plank walking into the café, pulling his hat off and unzipping his jacket. He glances around and sees us, then smiles and lifts a hand.

"That's the guy?" Sibby asks.

I nod as he begins to approach our table. "I'm glad you agreed to do this with me," I say.

"It's our story," she says. "We should tell it together."

ACKNOWLEDGMENTS

In 2017, I applied for the Lambda Literary Writer's Retreat for Emerging LGBTQ Voices and was accepted on the basis of three early chapters from this book. I owe everyone involved in the Lambda retreat a huge debt of gratitude, but in particular, I'd like to thank Malinda Lo and the entire young adult cohort for their careful, considerate, and imaginative readings of the work that ultimately became IHYL. Their creative energy stayed with me throughout the entire writing of this book, which I can honestly say would not be half of what it is without their contributions.

A big thank-you to Eric Smith for his enthusiasm toward this project and for negotiating the deal, as well as everyone at P.S. Literary. Thanks so much to Wendy McClure for taking this book on and for her amazing editorial input. Thanks to the entire Albert Whitman team for their hard work, especially Lisa White, for her great promotional ideas, and Aphee Messer, who totally nailed yet another cover!

31901066882384